NO STOPPING
TRAIN

NO STOPPING TRAIN

[A NOVEL]

LES PLESKO

SOFT SKULL PRESS / BERKELEY / AN IMPRINT OF COUNTERPOINT

Library of Congress Cataloging-in-Publication Data

Plesko, Les.
No stopping train : a novel / Les Plesko.
pages cm
Includes bibliographical references and index.
1. Triangles (Interpersonal relations)—Fiction. 2. Betrayal—Fiction.
3. Hungary—History--Revolution, 1956—Fiction. I. Title.
PS3566.L45N6 2014
813'.54—dc23

2014022424

ISBN 978-1-59376-545-3

Cover design by Matt Dorfman
Interior design by Neuwirth & Associates, Inc.

Soft Skull Press
An Imprint of Counterpoint
2560 Ninth Street, Suite 318
Berkeley, CA 94710
www.softskull.com

Printed in the United States of America
Distributed by Publishers Group West

10 9 8 7 6 5 4 3 2 1

INTRODUCTION

Has there ever been a writer so committed to the page and what went on it as Les Plesko? He believed in Art, in all its honesty and beauty. The only thing he loathed was that which affronted the Real—anything false, slick, self-serving. He was in rebellion from all that. In a time which applauds those values, he was purposefully anti-trend. You saw it in his unregenerate smoking, the mismatched socks, the wild head of straggly hair, his carlessness in vast, far-flung Los Angeles. From time to time, his students said, people dropped money into his coffee cup outside a favorite Venice Beach coffee house, thinking him homeless. It was all part of his High Beat Aesthetic, which was both a conscious embrace of his romantic ideal and an increasingly involuntary corner he'd lived himself into.

I met him in the early 1990s, in the days of the legendary Kate Braverman's writing workshop held every other

Saturday in her apartment on Palm Drive. There I saw him finish his first novel, *The Last Bongo Sunset*, and start the book that would become *No Stopping Train*. Even in those early days, his views on fiction became our mantras. "Don't have ideas," he'd say, which always made me laugh. What could that possibly mean? How could you write and not have ideas? It was only as I struggled with my own writing that the meaning—and the wisdom—became clear. It meant: *don't force the work into a shape.* It meant: *don't lead with your head. Don't know so much. Leave room to discover something.*

Writing for Les was an activity of soul, of memory, of sound and dreaming, not an intellectual exercise, not a game. He shared so much with those around him—time, friendship, passion, a subtle intelligence, a wacky humor, but most of all, the flame of his purposefulness that this was *the* noble endeavor. His presence was a reminder to treasure the deep and the true.

But now he's gone. Dead, by suicide, on a September morning in Venice Beach, at the age of fifty-nine. He had become a cult figure in Los Angeles literary circles, a writer's writer, as Mayakovsky called Khlebnikov, "Not a poet for the consumer. A poet for the producer." A brilliant teacher, he taught over 1,000 creative writing students across a twenty-year career at UCLA extension. Yet at the time of his death, he was virtually unknown outside California.

Many of his friends from the old Braverman group wondered what would be done with his papers, especially the famously unpublished Hungarian novel *No Stopping Train*. It had been born in wisps and curls of smoke, and grew denser and more layered over a period of six years—though never less mysterious. It was the finest example of the unique process of addition and especially erasure, which was the essence of Plesko at work.

The tragedy of Les, as well as his greatest virtue, lay in his absolutely uncompromising stance on art and life. Unfashionably, he recoiled from any hint of commercialism. He fought against any sort of pandering to the reader, "smoothing out the bumps," planting "helpful" directional arrows, catering to the American preference for the shout over the whisper. He instinctively moved to the edges, deserts, marginal people. Suggestion, nuance, abraded surfaces were his métier, and he had confidence in readers who could walk through the doors he had opened. He required a certain sort of skilled reader who could bring his or her own sensitivities to the task, a reader able to enter his elusive work and let it unfold on its own terms.

One cannot read quickly through a Les Plesko book— don't even try. It's not meant for speed-reading. A reader who wants to "cut to the chase" will find it vaporizing in his hands. But be patient, reader, and this book will unlock itself for you.

Les wrote for those of us who can hear a confession, who know how to hear behind halting words to the depths of a soul revealing itself. Reading Les Plesko is like listening to a broadcast late at night, an urgent communication textured by distance and static. It's a lover's reception of an intimate call in the middle of the night. You hold your breath for the cadence, wait for the meaning to unfold.

His imagination has a certain texture—like overexposed film, a Polaroid taken at noontime in a desert in the 1970s.

Light and sanded glass and desperate romance, these are Les's signatures. As a man, Les was the ultimate romantic, always in love with someone, and there seemed to be no shortage of women ready to be entranced by his rumpled, Beat self.

Love was his subject, forever complicated, not so much by the conventional external obstacles—family, money, even the dire obstacles of history—as by the contradictory personalities of the lovers themselves and the messy interlocking relationships created by desire and fate. He was alert to the strange eddies of romantic entanglement, the way lovers test one another, the way they create a private world in which desire and rebellion and privacy form the rooms they live in, and language both magnetizes and repels at the very same time.

· · ·

Then there's that *sound*. How do I describe the sound of a Les Plesko sentence? It's a very particular cadence, a certain number of beats—I hear it in my own writing sometimes, that subtle music, a certain choice of vocabulary and a characteristic stress pattern. I hear it in the writing of others who knew him, people who worked with him, who read him. That unmistakable, addictive, lyrical Les Plesko line—it always makes me smile. He had it back in those early workshop days, and he had it to the end. Read a paragraph out loud, you'll hear it:

> *Now I can't forget the good parts, even under this*
> *afternoon light that absolves what remains. The name of*

this place moving past which means small bloody earth.
The man with one arm by the blinking switchbox feeds
small nervous birds, and I think how before the war, he
might have tried cupping their tight beating hearts in
both fists.

To say he was a careful writer only begins to address his precision. Les Plesko worked like a man crawling under barbed wire, moving from word to word, feeling his way, refusing to continue until each sentence offered up its full potential of fragrance and emotion. And then in a few days or weeks, more than likely he might throw it all out. For him "less is more" wasn't just a saying, it was religion.

. . .

Once *No Stopping Train* was finished, Plesko began the search for a major publisher willing to accept it. Every year for fifteen years, he sent it out. But the consolidation of publishing houses worked against him. Consolidation meant that novels were far more likely than ever to be judged for "reader friendliness" and potential for commercial success than for invention and strangeness and beauty. A work like *No Stopping Train* had an ever-decreasing chance in such a market—and Les would have recoiled even from the use of such terms as "market" or "marketplace" when referencing literature. The repulsive necessity of reducing creative works to a unit of commerce. It was one of the great sorrows of his life that this, his best book, could not manage to hack its way through the thicket of obstacles growing ever more dense on the road to a wider reading public.

Yet at the same time, he refused to consider casual publication for this novel. His subsequent books, his desert novel *Slow Lie Detector* and the tender love story *Who I Was,* were both published by his friend Michael Deyermond in loving editions in Venice Beach (Equator Books and MDMH Books, repectively). But Les was adamant; he wanted *No Stopping Train* to reach beyond the small, appreciative literary circles of Southern California. He *knew* that a broader readership existed for this book, but it would require a more experienced literary house to connect to them.

A man is not a book, and Les Plesko was more than his work, though he shared many attributes with his fiction. Like his fiction, he was quixotic, a romantic, a gentle cynic, an intellectual and also an anti-intellectual, and a Chaplinesque little tramp cycling along on a wobbly bicycle. He was nonjudgmental, in a wry, European, pessimistic way. He didn't even curse. "Oh, brother," was the worst it got— usually said in response to some display of sentimentality or self-importance.

He was Hungarian, he lived steps from the sand in Venice Beach, he didn't have two socks that matched. He lived in a single room. Students who loved him offered swankier sublets and he'd go, but found he couldn't sleep in these more elegant digs. "Too much," he'd say. He never left his Venice Beach room very long. Once, after he'd lost it during a sublet, he rented the room next door until his own was free again. He drew a map of it for his young nephews, as if it were a kingdom. I think it was the very simplicity of his circumstances which allowed him to live completely in the life of his romantic, Beat imagination.

But he was far from impoverished. Though living in one room, the breadth and depth of all Western civilization was his. A short glance at his list of recommended books, preserved by his most devoted students, reveals just how rich that life had been. The list is viewable on their tribute website www.pleskoism.wordpress.com.

. . .

Hungary, 1956. A Soviet invasion to stifle a growing movement for independence, this moment can be viewed in many ways as the precursor to *The Unbearable Lightness of Being*'s Czechoslovakia. The collision had its roots in the Second World War, where Hungary fought on the side of the Axis and experienced great hardship in defeat. In the division of Europe, Hungary fell on the Soviet side, so scores were being settled as people tried to survive, a situation Plesko brilliantly illuminates in his novel. *No Stopping Train* starts with the war and its aftermath, the girl Margit and her embittered mother, her love affair and eventual marriage to the document forger Sandor, and their involvement with the fearsome, magnetic redheaded Erzhebet, whom he'd once saved from the camps. In the years leading to the Hungarian Revolution, love and alliances will shift repeatedly, as each character struggles with his or her own level of hope and despair.

Plesko specifically chose his homeland as the setting for his magnum opus. Born in 1954 Budapest, Laszlo Sandor was the child of a love affair between a pretty young blonde, Zsuzsa, and a man whose identity Les would not know until he returned to Hungary years later, when he discovered his father had been a famous actor. Said longtime colleague, the writer Julianne Cohen, "He brought home a head shot. The resemblance, uncanny. And a story of how the actor had leapt from a building to his death." A terrible prefiguration of Les's suicide in the fall of 2013.

In 1956, his mother fled across the border with a new husband, Gyorgy Pleszko, making her way to America and leaving two-year-old Laszlo behind with her elderly parents who struggled with the realities of the revolution. She sent for him at the age of seven. He arrived in Boston, speaking only Hungarian, to meet his mother, a glamorous near-stranger, and his new family, which now included a baby half-brother. A new name. And a new language.

His encounter with English began a love affair that continued for the rest of his life. "Immediately, he was in school, and nobody spoke Hungarian, so he listened in from the back until sounds took shape and made a kind of music," said Cohen. "He listened to the radio, watched TV and listened to his mother and stepfather, who never spoke Hungarian, fiddled with a reel-to-reel tape recorder until the music became word. At some point he lost his fluency in Hungarian, gave it up for new and interesting things, all that America had to offer a boy in the '60s. Les was in love with language and in love with love and fell in love with the music all around him."

But the '60s in America had their pitfalls: "He made friends with people who were going places. San Francisco, Santa Cruz," she recalled. "He tried college but he fell in love with heroin and dropped out. When you read *The Last Bongo Sunset* you'll come to know how he broke his own heart. But the tenacious [side of himself] quit using and thought maybe he could be an artist, a musician. He recognized he possessed a feel for word and deed and an eye for beauty. So he hit the road, taking jobs along the way, searching. Fell in love with an older married woman as a hand on her ranch in the desert. It ended badly, broken hearts and incipient violence. Made his way back to Los Angeles: flag man for crop dusters, country-western DJ. He took a sales job. He had a compelling voice; it roped you in and kept you there. Laced with smoke, sorrow, and an unbeliever's faith in resurrection, he told the truth and you could trust that."

I've seen those pictures of Les as a young man, a businessman with a phone to his ear, in '70s wide lapels. They astonished me, for I knew him only after these formational years, the years that gave the raw edge to his first novel, in new sobriety in the Braverman workshop, writing the book in which he found his unique voice, his tone as an artist, and a moment of accolades. About *The Last Bongo Sunset* (reviewed just ahead of *A Void* by Georges Perec) *The New Yorker* said, "For the narrator of such extravagant, ravaging prose, it would be impossible to commit a cliché."

But now that book is long out of print, and Les's last two novels reached only the circles already aware of his work. What would ever become of the Hungarian novel, all these years in the making?

Shortly after Les's death, as friends and students wandered in dazed disbelief, the Australian novelist David Francis—a former Plesko student and protégé—seated me next to an editor from Counterpoint at a PEN USA dinner.

David knew that the story of our colleague's death and the tragedy of *No Stopping Train* soon would arise in conversation, and so it did. The editor, Dan Smetanka, was eager to see the manuscript. Who had the book? When could he read it?

Word went out. Les, a great letter-writer, had sent various incarnations of the book to his correspondents over the years, notably to Julianne Cohen, to his former fiancée Eireene Nealand, and to his devoted student Jamie Schaffner. All of them were able to produce incarnations of the manuscript. Soon Les's younger brother, George, received an offer to publish.

So comes the end of a very long journey for one small jewel of a book. It is with a profound and bittersweet pleasure that I now hold this volume in my hands. How proud Les would have been if he had lived to see this day, how happy he would be for you to turn the first page.

I wish you good reading.

JANET FITCH
Los Angeles, California
April 21, 2014

NO STOPPING
TRAIN

You are the man who sang "God Bless the Magyar" after we lost the war. I watched you sway by a bullet-pocked door, heard you testing the national anthem's loose notes, a lost war's afterthoughts. I hadn't heard it since school, and then school was called off. All up and down Saint Matyas Street, wind chased your song among tattered banners and placards and flags. Elms cast their shadows on smashed cobblestones, windowsills lined with wash. A corpse swayed against a streetlight in accompaniment, its belt buckle clinking the pole, red-checked shirt cheery against the dull sky. Its urgent clogged smell permeated the air, the sad clothes on clotheslines.

I was twenty and blond, black hair showing through at the roots. I thought I could love you, perhaps, but I wanted to know: would it last? You wiped your nose on your sleeve as you sang. You didn't see me but, Sandor, you would have been proud: I wiped tears from my eyes as I whistled along. When you looked up I stopped, I was shy. You scanned the sills for my face but I hid in the curtain's torn lace, my feet crushing glass and mousedust. There was nobody left to accompany you but the dead; you did not seem to mind.

These haystacks bundled with twine remind me of our bed. These men playing cards on this train, they remind me of you with your hair in your face, but then everything does. Torn clouds are your tattered pant cuffs. Scarecrows by the tracks guarding dirt wear your fish-patterned shirt. My palms on the train window's glass scratched with lovers' initials like ours are the same size as yours in my hair, in my mouth.

You used to say if wishes were horses beggars would ride. I've begged, now I ride, yet I still haven't figured that out. My pale hands in this dicey Hungarian light, my finger's indent where my wedding band used to rest, I hope you understand about that. If I had tears left, if you had hands that could help, I'd let you wipe them away from my eyes. Sandor, if I found my voice, I'd sing along with you now.

She had needle and thread, they had fish. They had torn clothes, Margit knew how to mend. Erzsébet poked a raw chunk of fish in a fire of mattress guts, newspaper scraps. Remnants of older fires littered the steps down the Danube's steep bank. Sandor stoked char that smoked more than burned, there was ash on his lips. One drifty eye swam behind black-framed lenses, his other eye studied her, then they switched. Margit turned away, blushed.

Erzsébet laughed out loud. "You never know if he's looking at you or some glorified future," she said.

Margit kept her gaze on the shore where thin ice abutted the bank. Opaque as the sky, it gave the illusion of firm. "Maybe he sees the past," Margit said.

"So you're a philosopher," Erzsi said.

The river encrusted two pigeons, a stump. Waves lapped a corpse, licked its face of split teeth and raw bone. Margit swallowed against its sweetness, like ice cream left out in which the vanilla has spoiled. It seemed almost to breathe, Margit thought. She wondered how it would be if hers was the body half sunk, what if she grew gills? Her hair casually turning aquamarine, the water's chlorine in her lungs. Under the panel of ice, there'd be no thinking of food, only the hiss of her own body's fumes, its bubbles escaped into green. If she stayed underneath long enough, she'd forget there had been a war, even land.

"Where'd you find fish?" Margit asked. She made herself turn from the corpse, its burst checkered shirt, its red-white-green boutonniere.

"Swapped a kiss," Erzsi said.

Margit looked at her mouth, then Sandor's.

"Not with him, he has nothing worth trading for it," Erzsi said.

Sandor did not take offense. He offered Margit the stick with the fish. Margit burned her lips and her tongue and the roof of her mouth but she managed swallowing it.

"Blow on it first," Sandor said. His glasses were mended with tape. Margit had an urge to tamp its loose ends but she was too shy and her fingers were greasy with fish.

"What are you, DPs?" she asked.

Sandor grinned. "Who isn't?" he said. "In a philosophical sense."

"He's back from the front," Erzsi said. She patted his shoulder like this might excuse whatever came out of his mouth.

Sandor leaned into her touch. "I found her all rags and bones in a camp."

Erzsébet narrowed her eyes. "I told you, don't talk about that."

Sandor shrugged, poked the fish. Erzsébet pulled out a strand of her hair seemingly without noticing it.

"My father died at the front," Margit said. She couldn't say why but she wanted a way to get close, she felt anxious and nervous for them. "He said war was inevitable, that it couldn't be helped," Margit said.

"Nothing helps," Erzsi said.

Margit watched her to gauge if this was just typical after-war cynicism. "Some things can," she replied, though she couldn't have said what these were.

Erzsébet took a lipstick from her coat. She twisted the tube, made a pout, smeared a round O on her lips, licked the edge of her mouth, her gestures flamboyant, outsized. "You haven't fucked anyone just so you won't have to starve, I can tell," Erzsi said.

Margit tried not to show she felt slapped.

"Leave her alone," Sandor said.

Erzsébet smiled. Her lipstick gleamed reckless against her wan cheeks, her orangy hair appeared perishable in the light. "You done that lately? Fucked to eat?"

Margit hugged herself. Behind her, pigeons beat wings on the steps. Someone swept, scrubbed red stains, stacked smashed bricks. On the opposite shore, boys played soldier with limbs torn from trees. The sun almost broke through the clouds, its porous warmth miserly across her shoulders and legs. What she had done or not done: it was wartime, after all. "Fucking's not such a big deal," Margit said, nonchalant.

Erzsébet bit a mouthful of fish, wiped its grease on her sleeve. "For you it's abstract because you had a choice," Erzsi said.

Sandor flapped his cuffs. "We've all become philosophers from the war."

Margit took out her needle and thread. "I'm a seamstress," she said. "I believe in the practical use of my hands." She was making it up as she went.

Across the water, a boy raised his stick like a gun. *Bang, you're dead.* Margit shivered, tugged Sandor's crease straight, licked the thread carefully, more slow than was necessary, threaded it.

"Careful you don't stick him," Erzsi said.

Margit inhaled fish and fire, the body floating in cattails and muck, Sandor's smoky scent. She smoothed his slacks with her slick open hand. "Don't worry, I know what I'm doing," she said. She almost believed it herself.

It's been four days since you've touched my arms or my neck or my forehead or cheeks or my waist or the small of my back. A week since we lost the revolt and the borders came down, I could climb on this train, I could run while I left you behind. I can't sleep for bad dreams. I hardly dare look at myself in the blackness the train glass reflects, though it smoothes my classic moonface, soothes my eyes that in daytime just ache.

You used to call me beautiful. My almond-shaped eyes, the cupidity of my mouth was a puffy kiss-bitten surprise. I was vain of my thighs and my belly and legs, the pleasing contour of my ass and my hips.

After the war, the big one, I thought my flesh was like Hungary's meadows and hills, even with shrapnel and metal and broken plough teeth underneath. Now I don't trust metaphor, I hardly believe what I see when I look at myself. My mouth tastes like my mother's unwash, her starved breath.

I lay beside her in our bed, jolted awake fully dressed, dawn swarmy as newspaper print.

"Stay with me, don't go out," Alma said.

"I'll go anyway, then you'll be sorry you asked," I replied.

I hadn't slept with you yet. What I owned was my own, I carried my needles and spools and the war in my head.

"Everyone's come home again and you're going away," Alma said. She turned on her side, a weak smear of light on her tattered nightgown.

"Make me feel bad, it's what you do best," I replied, chewed the sleeves of my dead father's coat, its tail trailing crumbs by the bed.

"I recall pushing you in the pram," Alma said.

"Pull out all the stops," I replied.

"We paused on a bench by the lily pad pond, fed the ducks," Alma said.

"It rained, you hate ducks, you never bothered to cover my head."

"I threw myself over you when bombs fell."

"It was me who did that for you," I replied.

Alma rubbed her hand where her swapped wedding band left its naked indent. "I never wanted a child."

I didn't bother to sigh. "Tell me again how you stopped eating on purpose back then."

"I lay on my belly, my fists to my gut, wished you dead," Alma said.

My fingers drew tight figure eights on the sheetless mattress. "In school we played a game, 'put your mother on the ceiling,'" I said. "We had to imagine our mothers up there. One of us said his mother baked pies, another's saved porcelain figurines."

"Smart move during a war," Alma said.

I had a habit of narrowing my eyes against sarcasm then. "I said you collected bad thoughts."

Alma tapped her nails on her teeth. "When I was pregnant, I tried to slip on the ice, but your father kept grabbing my arm. I told him, instead of delivering a baby, I'll give birth to a bone through my leg." My mother hurt to look at. The light through her gown illuminated her belly and breasts. "Once I was sure about you, I went to the park, I clung to the Tilt-A-Whirl's bars, let it drag me around." Alma smiled.

"So you've told me," I said, but it choked me all over again.

"They had to tie me to the hospital bed so I wouldn't jump out the window," she said.

I smiled back nonetheless. "If you'd eaten better, maybe you'd have had the strength."

We both laughed. I could afford to, I thought. Because, Sandor, you waited for me in the street with fish or with soap or a silver barrette. I believed you would always be there. My belief made me think I could be cavalier yet remain generous. I touched my mother, though I was never supposed to do that, all brittle bones through her gown and her hair tangled up. She wrenched free of my hands, hugged her chest. "That's a cheap shot. Don't leave me with something I'll miss," Alma said. But I did.

At the Galamb Cafe they were serving stale water in porcelain cups, air on fine china plates. "I enjoy Budapest best in the rain after war," Margit said.

"It must suit your temperament," Sandor said.

"What do you know about it?" Margit asked.

"Sad and a little bit mean, like this city," he said. Russian soldiers stumbled across the sidewalk, watches up to their elbows, grain alcohol stunned. "They flush toilets for washing their food," Sandor said.

Margit hated sitting around when she could have been mending or washing or looking for bread. Small talk gave her nerves.

"When the food drains away, the bayonets come out," Sandor said.

Damp muggy air pasted Margit's dress to her back and her chest. A cold draft raised the hairs on her neck. "The lesson is don't eat with Russians," she said.

Sandor laughed. Shadows from his glasses etched indents on his cheeks. She patted her coat for a cigarette. Two left so she offered him one.

"I don't smoke," Sandor said.

"Ciggies cut hunger cramps," she replied. Behind him she saw the Parliament dome wrecked against the skyline, the church-tower clock frozen at noon or midnight. "It seems ridiculous not to smoke," Margit said.

Sandor cupped his hands for her match. Pale light beat over his wrists. Around them, whoever had something was bartering it, chocolate bars, liquid vials. Out in the street, drunkards were singing the national anthem and pushing a powerless tram.

"The vanquished aren't meek," Margit said.

"They're going to get that song wiped from their lips, you just watch," Sandor said.

Margit blew a ring, watched faces pass busted-out windowpanes, cheekbones gaunt yet oddly lovely, like Sandor's, she thought.

"Not you, though, with those papers you forge," Margit said.

Sandor put his hand on her mouth. "You're not supposed know about that."

Margit knocked the tip from her spent cigarette, saved the butt. His hand smelled like ink and she wondered if she'd get accustomed to it. "Your girlfriend told me. Erzsébet."

A long silence fell between them. Across the street, a lorry bumped to a halt. In the gap of its tarpaulin ribs, a man and woman were chained to a bench. The woman's hair blew in her eyes. The man tried to wipe it away from her brow but he couldn't, manacled like he was.

"I'm not going to sleep with you right away," Margit said.

Sandor took off his glasses, rubbed them on his shirt. "Who said anything about that?"

Margit tapped her nails on her cup. "Because the war's over, all the men think they can have any woman," she said. "But I'm waiting for love."

Sandor stood. Gypsies and children who roamed past the tables extended their palms. Waiters flapped napkins at them. Sandor scooped up a tip not his, tossed it at the nearest hand. They all knew the coins were worthless. A pengö before the war was worth half a quadrillion pengös now. Still, they grabbed.

"I guess we're not coming back here for a while," Margit said.

Hard to keep up, she had to hold on to his sleeve he was walking so fast. "You're already in love. Maybe not with me but the idea of it. It's caused by the end of the war," Sandor said.

Margit made him slow down. "So you're just the one who showed up."

Sandor shrugged. He glanced at their reflection in an unbroken storefront. "We look all right together, well matched."

Margit stopped, tried lighting a cigarette into the wind. "You're trying to make me believe this was all my idea," she said.

Sandor turned up his palms. "What idea is that?"

Margit had to smile. "Your secrets. Your redhead." She blew smoke in his face. "You're coy," Margit said.

Sandor took a drag off her cigarette, made sure their fingers touched. "But you like that, Margit," he replied, and she longed to believe that she might.

Letters I don't send:

Dear Sandor, I better remember for us how it was.

You weren't the first. That was a soldier for candles and bread. In the cellar by buckets of piss, I made myself ready for him. Then there was a boy who wrote slogans with chalk across walls, my name beside his, an arrow pierced through a heart. In an atlas stolen from school, we'd try to find countries the war hadn't touched.

If I'd told you about him, which I did not, I don't think you would have been unkind. It would have been hard to excuse jealousy of the dead.

That was the year they sent the first boys to the front. Everyone trying to save us from bullets and bombs with more bullets and bombs, Alma said. She said it was irony that fell from the sky, all that generously meted death. It was difficult mourning just one boy with everyone mourning along.

But you'd probably already killed by then.

Your ironical uniform, the sarcastic smile of the crease in your uniform's slacks. The sly, knowing blood on your shirt, your torn epaulet's winking eye.

Then we were suddenly half-dressed in your room with its window's iron bars. You told me about your mother who put up preserves the day she got taken away. Your father the printer who had principles so they broke both his hands. The six-story window in prison left open on purpose for him. But I wasn't listening well, swooney with your printer's ink smell, already telling myself what I'd save up for now. Hoarding how you kissed my eyes.

"Make me believe this is worth it," I said. I was very dramatic back then, with my hand to my brow, all serious, moony-eyed.

Jesus, Sandor, make me stop. Instead let me tell how rain etches the train window's glass. How it's raining again in this town, its sky's wet bruise spun from low dirty clouds. The first people here gathered fruits, hunted mammoths, reindeer. They swallowed horse flesh, drank mare's milk. Now women haul twigs tied with twine across damp plundered fields, a slow recitation of picking through hoofprint-caked mud. The washroom's tap leaks, its drip burns my cold fingertips.

I used to assume certitude. Alma in her robe, father at his desk. I was the daughter playing somewhere in the house, in the yard, sometimes too far, but the chestnut vendor brought me back. Our supper was coffee that year, lumps of sugar dissolving to brown the same shade as the city at dusk. My father's slicked hair was Budapest's color back then. The three of us stood in the street, he chewed his charcoal pills. "History's ruined my stomach," he said. I could see he was telling the truth, the proof was his tongue and black teeth. My bicycle, tipped on its side in the gutter, was red. My father kept wiping his eyes. Cold wind blew through my dress, already faded though he only brought it the previous month, its seams loose, its bow lost. "Cheap like everything else," Alma said, her hair stirred by wind, not bothering to comb it away from her face. I studied her shoes, scuffed and wet. Seeing her out of the house made me anxious and tired. Sweat stains spread under her arms though she must have been cold and embarrassed in only her robe, exposed to whoever might pass. She fingered its hem as if it might turn to ash, her bare arms goosefleshed. Rain pelted her uncovered head. Her breath came in ragged white puffs. She said, "Don't leave me here with the child," words like stones, bitten lipped. She took a step back, ankles weak, on the verge of a slip.

I looked up at our window opened out so the war might fly in. I said, "Are we going to die?"

Sandor, we did die.

What happened once? It had the look of nothing. A storm, a light rain, the war came. My father left for the front, he said *when I come back*, he meant *if*.

In the city the woman who I had become wiped marzipan glaze from her mouth. She picked her teeth with her nails while you practiced your forgeries, already inventing your fate.

My hands that touch the train's glass: I'm just like my mother now, tired of my feet and my hands, my own cheap sentiment.

So here is my hand where my wedding band also leaves its white mark. I never did feel safe wearing it. My thin shift with its cigarette burn in its lap from when we both fell asleep after love, then you woke me up, said, "You were on fire but I put you out."

I've been moving toward you or away since back then, my hands held in front of my face as if trying to hold back the wind, scraps of newspapers blowing by fast.

There was a place in Kispest where old soldiers were kept. Men with one leg lived there, men who wore hats low over their faces to cover whatever was left.

Three a.m., soft autumn rain shirred oildrum fires that hadn't gone out since war's end. Margit stepped like her heels were too brittle for puddles or leaves. Figures limped across stagey flame light past gutted tank carcasses, clothing shredded and wet in their treads. A late-night bird wheeped. A cobbler bent over a crate, resoling the shoes of the dead. She could imagine them trapped in rain's runny embrace in repose everywhere.

Hard to follow Erzsébet's clues, to find Sandor's place on a night without moonlight by shattered streetlamps. Margit didn't stop for "hey girlie," an offer of free cigarettes. Behind her, the river was useless, too distant to be any help.

Over her head, the sky held no hint it would ever be daylight again.

She had to kneel on the shell-shocked sidewalk to see in. Sandor's mattress was flush by the tipped-open window's low grate. A candle burned on a chair, obscuring her dark rained-on shape, her wet dress that clung to her thighs and her chest. The rain, queasy warm, etched tears down her cheeks.

She shouldn't have come, should have kept her willful ignorance: though she hadn't slept with him yet, she already knew her heart was about to be wrecked.

Erzsébet lay on her back, her hair fanned across the mattress a violent, articulate red. Her teeth clenched the cup Sandor tipped to her lips. He held a washcloth, wiped her face. He reached inside her shirt, wiped her breasts. Under her skirt, he cleaned what was dirty down there. Margit could tell by his flame-honeyed shadow he used his tenderest hand. If she wished, she could have extended her palm and touched Sandor's brow, the ragged collar of his shirt.

"Hey, Sandor," she called.

Then she held her breath as she passed through his door with no number on it. Sandor looked up like he'd known all along she'd be there. "I thought you were mending our clothes," Sandor said.

Margit felt struck so she lowered her head, picked leaves from her dress she'd worn just for him, washed so often its poppies were merely the idea of blooms on a sheer yellow field. "I kept thinking about you and stabbing my fingers," she said.

A porcelain bowl on the floor, a plank on stacked bricks for a desk. The candle, the chair. A wedge of cracked mirror by Saint Stephen's picture torn from a book. Sandor's shoes on the floor as if they were ready to walk down the hall.

"She wants you to kiss them and make them all better," Erzsébet told him.

Margit smoothed her dress, wiped the slight from herself. "I'm not hurt. You're the one all laid out for a cure."

Erzsébet patted the bed. "Caught a cold in the camp." She lifted her chin to Sandor who fussed with the sheet. "Don't you pity me, too, like he does? Or maybe you're jealous I suffered more than you did."

Margit studied Erzsébet's face for the proof. "Suffering's not relative," Margit said. It was what her mother once claimed.

She wanted Sandor to see she was brave enough to do this: she lay down on the bed. Margit swore she felt Erzsi's fever in waves as she lifted her hand.

"Look, my nails all fell out over there," Erzsi said.

Margit looked. "They've grown back." She had a desire to strip Erzsi bare, to see for herself if there were stigmata on her everywhere.

"Nails and hair don't stop growing on a corpse," Erzsi said.

Margit thought about running her hand along Erzsébet's long skinny arm to see if its texture was really so parchment thin. She wanted to cup Erzsi's wrist to see if her fist would unclench. She touched Erzsébet's collarbone, canted like it had been broken and carelessly set. The wet Sandor spilled in her clavicle's hollow was cool over Sandor's blue thumb bruises there.

"We carried rocks and bodies," Erzsi said. "Stiff or soft, puffed with juices and gas."

"The bodies or rocks?" Margit asked.

Erzsi laughed, more a cough. Sandor stood. He looked toward Erzsi, Margit, then his coat on the peg.

"He means to save me, raise the dead," Erzsi said.

Margit lit a damp cigarette and passed it. "Kindness hurts, doesn't it?"

Erzsébet blew out smoke. "Especially from you." She raised her legs, kneaded cigarette ash into her knees' dented caps, rubbed it in like a powdery salve. Margit could not help but see where her underpants' cloth came apart from its elastic band.

"I bet you think pity is stronger than love," Margit said.

Erzsébet turned to the wall. Where her shirt came undone, her backbone seemed too loosely fused. It reminded Margit of pig's knuckles in aspic turned pale as it jelled. If she were to lick Erzsi's spine, she thought it would taste just like that, sour and vinegarish.

"Love's just hugging bones," Erzsi said.

Sandor stalled at the foot of the bed. Margit smelled Erzsi's Emke perfume, her own nerves and his sweat. "You can't prove that to me," Margit said.

Erzsébet made a noise in her throat. She climbed from the bed. Her stride was an incautious lunge like her hips were attached to yanked strings. Jerky as if she would fall, but she didn't fall as she stepped away from them both. "He carried me five hundred kilometers on his back." Erzsébet hugged herself. "Crows waited to pick out my eyes from Katowice to right here."

"She's exaggerating," Sandor said, but Margit thought she was not.

Erzsébet stood before the bit of mirror, skew-hipped. She touched her hair and her mouth. Even after what happened to her she's still vain, Margit thought.

"You look like some soft creamy thing, your figure's a pitcher of cream," Erzsi said. She pressed her concave belly, watching Margit in the glass. Margit leaned on her elbows to better see Erzsébet's loose white smile. Erzsébet pressed her stomach hard, though her flesh there seemed pliant and slack.

"Please," Sandor said.

"All you women who live. So plush, so selfish." Erzsébet chewed the ends of her hair hanging into her face. "I watch you eating and drinking, holding your lover's hands."

"That's enough," Sandor said.

"Don't worry, it doesn't pain me, everything's already happened to me," Erzsi said.

"I don't have a lover yet," Margit said. She felt giddy, unmoored on the bed.

"Pity," Erzebet said. She dug her new nails in her wrists until Margit could tell she broke skin. "You should have left us alone, but love's not wise, either," she said.

Here, a stopped clock, factory smoke, windblown leaves. Six hundred kilometers ahead, the borders are open, or they shoot everybody on sight, or we'll hang by our necks. Last I heard they'd be starving the prisoners soon, you'd be dead. I like to think rumors are leaves, insignificant on the wind.

But Sandor, you always liked facts: the Museum of Coal Mining's here. In this place they've been rooting the earth since before the Bronze Age. A plaque on the station platform says fire burned Kisveresfold in 1836, flood drowned it the following year.

I can't tell this town from the last, the same suitcases tied with twine line the tracks like the town before this. Coats, faces, soil, all run to gradations of iron and pitch. Couples share cigarettes, I watch them through scratches from coins lovers etched in the train's rattly glass and it hurts, although you never smoked. Ink from the papers you forged has never come clean from my dress. Your fingerprint bruises are still pressed against my eyelids.

I knuckle them shut so I won't remember we always did like daytime best, its high white sad grace like today.

Inside your room, our clock was the single note tick of spent rain. A radio faint through the wall jumbled lies masquerading as news, that the peasants would keep all their land. Though I only just stepped inside, I said, "I better go, you've got work." I waited for you to say *don't*, took a step toward the bed as if without purpose, intent. You stood cavalier at my back, fingers under the straps of my dress. You turned my shoulders, pressed your thumb in the cleft of my chin.

"Before you were born, that's where an angel touched you so you'd forget heaven," you said.

I laughed, it was nerves. "Leave it to God to make us forget the good parts," I said.

You touched my temple, my jaw, the flushed side of my face. "A little bit scared and a little bit sad," you said. I wasn't cold but I shook. "What we know about each other could fit in my pockets," I said.

"You're not wearing pockets," you said.

Light from the window pooled on the barren mattress. We were mostly naked by then, you in your ink-stained blue shirt, me with my underwear trapped around my ankles, my dress to my waist. There was not enough space in my throat for my heart and for swallowing at once, so I stalled, put my mouth to the sour sooty pulse at your neck.

"You're going to hurt me," I said. One sock on, I didn't know what to do with the other one balled in my fist.

"I won't mean to," you said. The kicked-aside blanket bunched like a mute chaperone at the foot of the bed.

"Intentions don't count, only acts," I replied, then I let you push and I fell. Thin light fell across my eyelids. I helped you turn me around, crumbs and coins in my knees, elbows, wrists. I thought about gathering my wits but I couldn't even gather my breath, and then mercifully I couldn't think.

I still see us plain, like this town, its sorrow of commerce passed by. Coal, severed stumps of horseradish in carts, the broken-nosed statue of Stalin that every town has. A flurry of pigeons flutters like loose afterthoughts around its bare head. A man in a shabby brown coat sails a newspaper boat on an isthmus of mud. Where the road meets the track, a woman like me swings her purse, she tucks her ambivalent smile in her scarf as she waits. I recall how that was.

Now I can't forget the good parts, even under this afternoon light that absolves what remains. The name of this place moving past which means *small bloody earth*. The man with one arm by the blinking switch box feeds small nervous birds, and I think how before the war, he might have tried cupping their tight beating hearts in both fists.

I have to not look at him, press my brow to the glass like we touched our heads to your low windowpane in 1945. We both saw the same limp-shoed men passing by as right now but it looked different then.

How can I simply explain? It's not fair you once leaned into my back, reached around with your arms around mine, tipped the window to rain. I plucked a weed through the bars for the vase on your one yellow chair. My breasts became streaked with wet rust, but I liked it, I didn't care.

"You're my torture in bed," I had said.

"Talk like that you'll get us started again," you replied. You spoke into my hair and I can't help but bless you and curse you for this: Sandor, I think plenty now, but I'm still trying to gather my wits.

A day, three, the year passed.

Long, damp sticky hours in bed, his eyelashes teasing her brow. Sleepsweat on his shirt. They'd slept in their clothes once again among crumbs and hairpins. Her tin barrette stabbed her thighs. Curled on her side, her thumb in her mouth, feet shoved in the blanket's gone heat. Bare toes tucked under his too-short pant cuffs, giddy-kneed with herself and his scent.

Margit arched her neck toward the low basement's barred window light, her body slippery under her dress. She lit a smoke, smoothed her hair, her newest approximation of blond, rinsed in the porcelain bowl where they washed, where he shaved when he shaved.

"Is it always a little sad after?" she asked.

Sandor had the grace not to tell what he knew about that. His hand nested in the small of her back and she touched where his shirttail rode up, that flagrant exposure of skin. Damp, a man's smell, she had no defense against it. Sometimes it took counting till ten to breathe normal again. She leaned over the bowl to see how she looked, but there was no water in it, and none in the tap because of the unceasing drought.

"If we had money," she said, "I could wear pretty clothes and go out."

Sandor gathered change from the sheet, copper coins he could only subtract. He put his hand on her neck, his palm cold, Margit shivered from it. "Go where? Do what?" Sandor asked.

Margit closed the window to shut out the smell of horse droppings, wet dog, the tungsten refinery plant's yellow dust. If they had a decent-sized mirror, she thought. She craved a new dress for herself, and heat in the room so she could undress without getting into the bed. What she desired was what she could use, rouge, soap that foamed, a woman had to have these.

She raised her head, spilled cigarette ash on his chest, placed her cheek to his neck with its leftover odor of sex. "We just live in this bed, is that it?"

Sandor covered her face with the smell of sour coins that were hardly enough for the tram. His hand in her hair, his white breath. "Are you tired of this?"

Margit knelt, picked lint from her red poppy dress. She could tell it was late afternoon by how much the air from the plant burned her throat, stung her eyes. Outside, the stoplight blinked, stuck on red. Across the street, a broken bench leaned, you could not sit on it. The scabbard-shanked statue was gone from the mean little park, Russians had kidnapped it. She looked down at herself, stripes from the window grill in her lap, his knees pressed against her sore legs.

"Love only keeps you warm for so long, you can't eat it," she said. What was real was cold hands, money she didn't have for nylons. Her underwear itched, she was down to her last cigarette.

"You could pick up more sewing, you haven't been home in a week," Sandor said.

She did not look at him, kept her gaze on the street where sooty Trabants gasped through yesterday's snow turned to slush. All week long she'd been trying to forget about that. Just thinking of Alma gave her a pain in her brow, a weakness that spread to her shoulders and neck. "I thought this was home," Margit said.

Sandor climbed from the bed. "We both have things we've been ignoring," he said.

She tried not to comprehend what he meant but could not help herself: She saw Sandor kneeling by Erzsébet's cot. Candleflame guttered in shadows that begged and repulsed and capitulated. Scorched moths crisped, pliant fingernails scraped until he just had to quell her lucky suffering, slake her fever with his hips.

And how could she begrudge a smoke-rescued woman her ease? Because Margit had clambered on Sandor's taut bony flesh, buried her hot face on him, to her shame, envious, Margit did.

"You're going to see her," she said.

Sandor coughed, looked about to say more but did not. Sometimes silence was so eloquent, Margit thought. Down in the street, men and women in thin winter coats stumbled into and out of the grocery store under a broken streetlamp. Pigeons flopped on concrete, performed courtships in mud caked the color of blood. Sandor bent down, squeezed her wrist. He meant reassurance but pressed her so hard she went numb in his grip.

"You don't really want to go there, it's just an idea about how you should act," Margit said.

How many other foolish things had she spoken out loud in this room on her belly, her back? She wanted to tether them both to the window's iron bars, beat herself into him until all her perspective blurred from her face once again.

Instead she scraped Sandor's lovemaking crust from her thighs, watched bubbles rise on the side of the water glass on the chair by the bed. She drank it to rinse Sandor's taste, wiped her mouth on the back of her hand. It tasted bitter, like marzipan stuck to a plate overnight.

"At least lie to me, Sandor," she said, but she knew he would not. She pulled herself up by his sleeve, tugged her dress into orderliness. In this light it was frail, like their gestures that crowded this room, the same dress she'd put on, removed how many times she'd lost count. Sandor buttoned his coat. They stood close as they could and then slightly apart.

"I could wait for you here," Sandor said. He shouldn't have bothered to lie, a feeble attempt with its answer already in it.

Someone had to take the first step toward the door and he did. In a way, Margit thought, it was kind.

"Will it always be this way with us?" Margit asked. She shivered to think she could bear that he didn't reply. That she'd stay with him, anyway, if it was.

Trees pass by the train tracks, I guess oak or elm. A city girl, I don't know names of trees from lampposts. I know my mother's names for resilient weeds that grew up from Budapest's sidewalks, green puff, yellowtooth.

Last time I saw Alma alive was a day like today. So many days in this place are exactly the same.

Outside the Saint Matyas Street house, rain turned the corner and fell. The rain through the window frame gap on parquet was a clock in a dream you wake into again and again. My mother, myself, just like it had been in that place since 1938. We stood by the glass, our same-sized palms pressed to the pane.

"It's just like old times," I said.

In the winter-burned tree, weather-beaten birds hid their wings.

"Old times was only last week," Alma said. She wore the nightgown I'd left her in. Afternoon light struck the cloth.

"I've fallen in love since last week," I replied. Almost a whole year had passed, but I hadn't dared mention it, just in case it was my fantasy.

"Love is a bad accident," Alma said.

Accidents made me think of you, Sandor, the bruises you left on my wrist, the kisses you pressed on my cheeks. Those reflections of blooms I had touched in our mirror's cracked wedge had made me misbutton my red poppy dress. Even now my shoes fill with silence just thinking of it.

"He'll leave you with nothing to show but his smell on your breasts," Alma said.

Thank God for cigarettes. I lit one and hugged your velveteen jacket to hide our bed scent. In my mother's house, my smoke drifted up, stung my eyes like the cheap sentiment of some future regret. "That man doesn't hurt me," I said like I almost believed it myself, though I sat up nights waiting for you, peeling the soles of my shoes while next door a husband and wife slapped each other around and I touched my face from their blows, listening for footsteps.

"If he didn't hurt you, you wouldn't have come around," Alma said. She fingered her nightgown's scooped neck.

"Hurt's all right when before there was nothing," I said.

Alma's mouth tugged in a smile only I recognized. "On our wedding night, I wouldn't allow your father in our bed. I reached down to the floor where he slept, but he never once took my hand."

"That's not how it was. He reached up, you refused, he told me," I said.

She leaned on the sill, looking out at the gray scuddy muck of the sky. "We walked to the church where we wed. Your father kept saying my name as if I would forget it," she said. "We ate Dobos torte on a bench by the opera house steps. He brought lilies, three hundred forints a bunch. I wore kidskin gloves. Snow fell all over his new silk shirt, ruined it."

But what I recalled was how during the war my mother had purposely shut all the windows to blow out the glass. Death was the natural order of flesh, she had said.

I said, "Why are you telling me this?"

Alma rubbed her hand where her wedding band had once been.

"Because you're in love and you think you can do anything," Alma said.

I studied my nails so she wouldn't notice the blunt satisfaction that must have been plain on my face. "You envy me because I'm not like you," I said.

Alma laughed. The jut of her hips through her gown in failed light made me sick.

Now my shoulders are holding my coat, my hair holds its barrette. My body is winter, a dark train car lit by my white hands. My hand is a glove my mother once wore. Her glove in the snow is the color of rain. My arms are crossed over my breasts, my face crossed by cigarette smoke. My eyes wet as the day, I stuff newspaper pages into my shoes for the cold. The rain is as damp as my father's corpse left to rot at the front. As our room where my mother and I touched shoulders by accident.

"You made him run off to the war, you killed him," I said.

Neither one of us spoke while we considered this. Alma's eyes became shiny and hot. Her shoulders described a practiced weariness I felt down my back, in my arms.

"That wasn't me, love did that," Alma said.

I'm half my mother's age when she died. In the cool future I see myself in a city with awnings and atomic clocks. It is a different country. Women don't wear these cheap polka-dot scarves, men don't wear hats; if they do, they don't wear them so low on their heads.

When I arrive, I'll recognize her in the wan armature of my stance in patisserie windows I pass. I'll be admiring some fluffy confection and I'll have a sudden nostalgia for lilies that I never had. If it's a place far enough, sunlight will flail my white bed, its thin sober warmth, my hand hanging over the edge. I'll call this good, and no one shouting infamous names in the square, the newspaper carrying no five-year plans or decrees. Obituaries will reveal only natural deaths. But this will mean nothing to to me, I won't understand the language.

They stood by the swing, wary, afraid to go in. Low clouds unanchored the sky, leftover rain blew chill darts on her neck. Beyond the Angel Street park sallow lights blinked in the haze from the tungsten refinery plant.

"You forgot your sewing," he said.

She breathed Erzsébet's Emke perfume, she'd smoked several cigarettes.

"You neglected to wash off her smell," Margit said. Rain had pasted black mouths to her velveteen coat she clutched tight to herself. Cold wind on her legs, she was thinking of Erzsébet's fingernails thin as eggshells. "It makes me sad we could lose everything in a moment like this," Margit said.

"But you like being sad," Sandor said.

She looked toward a wet yellow tram. Passengers clung to the straps, their poverty tarted up for cafes and what nightlife there was. Down at the end of the block, black marketeers sold East German perfume, laudanum, girlfriends.

She watched Sandor turn up his collar, straighten his glasses, aslant. This random collection of gestures was all he could offer, she thought. "That must be why I picked you and not somebody else," Margit said.

Sandor bent, gathered leaves, a rust bouquet he let fall at her feet. "It's because you love me," he said.

Wind ruffled his shirt, Margit's hem, she would not look at him. She stood in the odor of dogwood decay, arms weather-vaned north and south. *Loves me, loves me not.* The shadows of her arms and legs were the hands of a long moonlit clock across rocks.

"That word, you can't toss it around," Margit said. She could have left him right then but her name in his mouth was the scrape of their feet over gravel and mud. Sandor's coat stank of ink and perfume, something else. Pigeons flung themselves like soot stones through the sky overhead. Then they were inside, she was ripping her buttons apart, his coat's epaulet in her teeth. "You're not even sorry," she said.

Not so long ago, at this hour, she'd call her own name from the street because no one else did, so she moved to his side in the bed. To have a purpose satisfied for the moment, she thought. She leaned into his shoulder, arms crossed on her chest, both yielding to him and defending herself.

"I wouldn't blame you if you left," Sandor said.

Hurt, she held him at arm's length. Her hands on his shirt were all knuckle and knot. "You wouldn't speak this way to Erzsébet," Margit said. All through the years she'd kept on sewing and colored her hair nonetheless, so she had earned this: her *come to my arms*, her thinking *but married, a wife*, her immodest woman's desire in the way their bones fit as she opened her body to him.

After, she sat up, ran her splayed fingertips through her hair, lit her last cigarette. In the wedge of their mirror she watched coarse iron clouds skid over the sky's faded ink. Behind her head, rain bled the window's iron bars, light from the lamp in the street creased dark stripes on his arms and her legs. She felt milky and lazy and all stubborness.

"My mother says one person always loves the other one more," Margit said. She was glad for the dark so she wouldn't see if he knew who she meant.

Sandor smoked her cigarette, coughed, he had never done this. He peeled tobacco flakes from his lips, picked a leaf stuck to her thighs near the V where they met.

"Maybe when we're husband and wife we'll find out who that is," Sandor said.

Margit touched her face. It felt hysterical, if you could feel such a thing. She said, "You could ask Erzsébet."

"She has nothing to do with you and me," Sandor said.

Margit made a sound through her teeth. He'd carried that woman with fire and ash in their mouths and stars burning over their heads. "I'd have to suffer and die to become what she is," Margit said.

Sandor laughed, he swept crumbs from the bed. "Stay with me, you might get to do that," Sandor said.

For once, she couldn't tell if Sandor was joking or not. Outside, it grew into an evening Margit might have drawn as a child, the horizon's wound a rough seam she might stitch to the hem of her dress. Even this night might outlast them, she thought, and everyone's unremarkable shoes, the procession of crows in the park. The glass on the chair, lipstick stains on its rim.

"Will you promise to stop it with her if we're wed?" Margit asked.

On the frozen sidewalk, pedestrians slipped on moonlight. Beneath it mud glared like a lamp. Sandor pressed his chin to her brow, already a husbandly gesture, she thought. As casual as leaves pasted onto their shoes by the bed, he held her life like the small of her back in his hand.

"I could do that," he said.

They lay quiet, apart, their hands side by side in the light from the lamppost outside.

"How easily you say it," Margit said.

Later the temperature dropped, soon it would snow everywhere. Only then, when the bed had grown cold, as she buttoned her coat against it, did she wonder why she'd asked him her question the way that she had. Only when the only sound left was a dog, the last tram, this man's breath, did Margit suddenly realize there was hardly a promise at all in what Sandor had said.

Where were you born?

I was born in the Szentes Infirmary on April 31, 1921. That was the year King Charles tried to retake his throne. There must have been a drought. Hardly a leaf on the trees, hardly trees.

Where's that, Sandor?

There were the plains then the plains then a field, then you came to our town. It was famous for black pottery. The lane where we lived soaked with after-shower mud. Vines crept up the wrought-iron gate. They used to burn witches there for selling the rain to the Turks.

You always lived there?

Cats ran up and down the mud streets, a buckboard brought me home. Carts brought mail, rags, and milk. We had a loosely built house by the side of the road. I wore short pants until I was ten, no shoes or shoes covered with dust. An iron gate, there were four chickens next door.

Your mother and father?

He wore a thick printer's smock, she canned what fruit there was. Outside my window, the sound of her knees, of the hoe. He ran the press for the *Hódmezővásárhelyi Hírlap*. He also printed broadsides. He helped found the first Communist party, you know.

What happened to him?

I don't speak to him.

Sandor, what happened to him?

This is his shirt, I wear the same size clothes. Later, he used a cane. The Horthy government fixed him good. He tucked a hundred forints in my shirt, put me on a train. After my mother died he was old. Always, he was already old.

Tell it again, don't leave anything out.

I was born on an evening so dark. [Sandor laughs.]

All the evenings are dark in the country, Sandor.

Streetlights came late to our town. Goats in the lane with their bells driven home in the dusk. My mother was dead and my brother had died.

Your brother had died?

I thought my mother killed him, I thought I was next.

Did your mother kill him?

He was born with a cleft lip. My mother struck him with the hoe. My father set both their obituaries in the *Hódmezővásárhelyi Hírlap.*

What happened to him after that?

I told you, he died. I hid in the woodpile.

Not your brother, your father, Sandor.

We could go see him back there, but we won't.

Because you hate him?

He gave me a hundred forints, put me on the train. He said, don't look back here. He smelled like ink and compost. My brother was older than me but he seemed the younger boy. I refused to walk him to school. I wished my mother dead even if it was an accident.

It was no accident?

She got taken away, she got sick then she died, that's the proof.

[He finishes her cigarette.]

What happened to you in the war?

I was too young, but my father printed a paper so I could join up.

What happened to you in the war?

We pulled artillery through the mud. We pulled a calf from a cow in a field. We pulled a baby from its mother's womb in some hay but the baby turned blue. We pulled artillery through mud some more. I manned the big gun. We advanced, for a while.

[The lights go out.]

Is there a God?

We tied a chain around the calf in the cow, there was blood on the snow. I said *pull*. I was the sergeant by then, the real sergeant had already died. We pulled the calf loose. We pulled the baby from the womb, it breathed once, twice. We were already losing the war. This was in Russia, 1944, almost spring, but there was still plenty of snow.

Is there a God?

I said to myself I couldn't protect him because he was older than me. My mother said his harelip was a sin. It might have been an accident, what she did. Still, I was afraid I was next. When she died I was pleased.

Then the war?

We marched through four seasons twice. We covered the German retreat. Everyone died except me and the radioman and the cook. We passed through.

Then you met Erzsébet?

We covered the Germans' fleeing backs. In Stalingrad we covered the backs of their necks with our chests. When we turned to run, it was too late to turn.

Then you met her, Sandor?

If I had other clothes, I would have burned my uniform. The cook stepped on a mine. The radioman headed south, I turned west. I didn't write home. I passed through outside of a camp. Someone had made a small fire from crates and some mostly dead coals.

That was her?

Everyone dead, and that girl in my arms.

[The lights come back on.]

So we could go visit your father then, still?

He printed the obituary of everything.

If you saw us together you'd think we were friends, Margit thought. The tall woman's hand on the smaller one's elbow, they walked past storefronts reflecting spent rain. The day white, you could make out the clouds by only their movement against the white sky.

Margit studied herself in the glass, she wished she'd worn a scarf or a hat. She'd dressed carefully just for this. Last night she'd tried on all her clothes, picked a plain lime-green skirt, Sandor's fish-patterned shirt. She'd fooled with peroxide and bleach for a semblance of blond. Now she could see in a compact she wiped with her spit by what shade she had missed.

"Where do you sleep with him?" Margit asked.

Erzsébet pulled her coat tight, Sandor's coat. In the war

it had been Margit's coat. "On wooden planks like the camp. I've strung barbed wire on my walls for nostalgia's sake," Erzsi said. Margit wasn't sure if Erzsi was joking or not. The cold was so present it burned, it leached the tang on the breeze from the meatpacking plant. A lorry rounded the corner too fast, marbled ribs swayed on hooks behind torn canvas flaps.

Margit said, "My bed smells like your Emke perfume."

"I don't care for beds. You can fuck anywhere if you want to enough," Erzsi said. A smile played at the edge of her mouth.

Margit felt herself blush. Lately, she'd been eyeing her blanket for what might have happened across it while she had been out. Checking for signs of sexual prowess on the sheets, though she didn't know what these might be, a mangled garter's sprung clips, elaborate stains. She'd got down on her knees to look underneath for fancy underpants.

"It's me he loves," Margit said.

Erzsébet shook her head. "He'll always be carrying me on his back from the camp."

Margit pushed up Sandor's jacket's sleeve. "Look, his toothmarks," she said.

Erzsébet ran her hands through her hair to purposely let Margit see her arm with the numbers on it. Her face appeared remorseless with small nervous ticks. Margit felt pity for her, she couldn't stand how it filled her up with an undesired tenderness.

"He wants me to marry him," Margit said.

Erzsébet's breath was a sudden pale cloud when she

laughed. "You don't need my permission for it."

Margit looked down at her shoes, they'd gotten wet. "I need to know why he wants to," Margit said.

Erzsébet studied her face with a weary contempt. "He thinks you're a tinsely bright carnival, a cheap little fair after what came before," Erzsi said.

Margit's ankles felt brittle and weak as she tottered on them. "Things have happened to me, that's my dead father's coat you've got on."

Erzsébet leaned on scraped brick with a careless precariousness. "If we're toting up corpses, you lose."

They lit cigarettes. Wind stirred greasy puddles and trash. Leftover snow seemed illuminated from within, glazed pink from the bloody runoff gouged by trucks from the meatpacking plant. At the tail end of winter, Budapest was the same everywhere, Margit thought. The nickel-plate sky over clattering boughs of bare trees. Men on the street, hats pulled low, nearly slipping on tracks before trams. Soldiers cradling the stocks of their guns, cobalt-blue barrels recklessly aimed anywhere.

"If we're counting the living, I win," Margit said.

After her mother died, Margit remembered this: The year before war, when the war was still mostly vague fear. Down by the boats, she pressed the heel of her hand to the small of her back, squinted against the white glare. She tugged at her hem, brushed cinders and leaves from her hair.

Alma stood beside her among ankle-high weeds. Paddleboats drifted by on the pond, knocking green-yellow ribs. Saw grass poked through lily pads. Buoys seemed to anchor the water, dotted with black and white birds. Margit wanted to touch Alma's arm, her pale exposed wrists made her ache. It had been cold and no heat, wind covered their coughs into soiled handkerchiefs. Margit twisted a tube of gold lipstick, leaned over a puddle, refreshened her lips. She knew how to do this, already almost thirteen.

"There, pretty and happy," she said.

Her mother had seen them, these practiced, perfunctory strokes.

"You could teach me," she said.

"The pretty or happy part?" Margit asked.

She watched her mother bend to her small black purse, smelled her hair as she picked out a jar, smeared red on the undersides of her eyes, pastry-thin.

"That's rouge, for your cheeks," Margit said. Impatient, she rubbed quick smooth strokes across her mother's startled white face. The light was beginning to fade. They collected leaves, there were plenty of them. Margit pressed leaves down the front of her mother's familiar sweater with holes in the sleeves. Alma blushed, she said *stop*, but Margit wouldn't quit, she wouldn't have minded if they could have stayed there forever, just kept doing this.

. . .

The day Alma's body was found, the light behind Sandor was spare. In the Angel Street house Margit wiped rain from her shoes with her hem. There were birds on the sill though it was too icy for pigeons to land. Outside, a lorry went by from the tungsten refinery plant.

Oh, she already knew, she could tell by the way Sandor stood, as if shamed, ashen-faced. If he'd worn a hat, it would have been clutched in his fists. Margit thought about Alma's fingertips splayed on the pane and their dewey rosettes. About how when the war was still young, there was lace on the arms of the chairs, decorative plates on the wall just like in any decent Magyar house. Then, Alma had a small job, earning tips from the lift. When rent became due, she stacked coins on the scarred tabletop by the light from the window that never properly shut.

Always, it seemed, it was winter outside, or just passed, almost winter again.

"What happened?" she asked.

Sandor's hair fell over his brow, his shoes, too, had gotten wet. "Alma went out in the snow, they found her frozen," he said.

He enfolded her arms. Though she didn't want to be touched, she desperately needed it. She smelled ink from the press, she wasn't crying yet. Margit looked over his shoulder, bewildered that people could simply walk by on the street while her mother was dead. "But it's not even snowing," she said.

The rails curve away from old rain. Beneath me, the river draws earth from the banks, gorges itself on mud, stones, rain-swept leaves. Every place the train passes I think, *we could have lived here*. Milked goats, sap from trees. We could have cured sausages in these curing shacks, watched the progress of fat dripped in pans, the honeycomb ooze of nectar we robbed from our fat yellow bees. We could have forsaken our gunmetal press, the tindery papers we printed that burned up your hand.

But I don't know farms from carpets, bees from nicotined nails, yellow teeth. I know Budapest. In the city I was always crossing some dead hero square, some stranger's mended clothes in a sack by my legs.

When we buried Alma the sky was like this.

I smelled you on me as they lowered her in. We'd made love while her body thawed on a slab in the morgue only two blocks away. I'd never been so reckless. Her death papers crumpled beside us in bed, you hadn't had time to remove both your shoes, your hands were still blue from the press.

You touched my shoulder at the grave but I fled. At the top of the rise, they were burying somebody else.

Should I say why she murdered herself?

Seven winters she waited for him, watching the top of the tree, down on the sidewalk, the useless affairs of the weeds. Yellowtooths lay disarrayed, dug up by the usual dogs. She didn't waltz the broom, sweep. She paced across fingernail parings, dry crusts, wrote my father's name in the dust, breathed the lack of his hands. The expectation of his steps in the hall, the icebox's drip, the faucet's wet tick were her clock.

Her sweaters had holes in the elbows where she leaned and leaned. Her feet hurt, she had to lie down in the cold lardy night, unsure where her bones pressed parquet and the hard floor began. Her palms filled with dark then with light until she forgot what all the waiting was about. Sometimes she got so small in herself she hardly dared to cough.

Was she sad?

Listen, she chopped off her hair from regret. It used to fall in her eyes, just like mine. When she ventured outside, she must have tried little slips on the ice but felt my father's absent hand grab her arm. Maybe she made that small speech I had heard: "If I'd twisted a shin, broken a wrist, we could have gone to the clinic instead of the altar," she'd said.

Sometimes I rode by on the tram, sometimes I got off. She said, "Everyone's getting married again, everyone has come back." She opened her window, looked down. "Don't joke with me, Margit, not coming home, who gave you permission for that?"

"But I'm here right now," I replied. "See? Do you need anything? Are you doing all right?"

One day there was nothing out there except what had always been there, the bakery, the milliner's shop. Nothing disgraced our Saint Matyas Street except what had always shamed it. In the war before last, she knew where the bodies were stacked for the carts. *Your father used to load them.* Right on the corner, Germans rinsed helmets, boiled soup you could sell yourself for. Blond hairs floated on top, Alma said, blood-rust flakes in a blue helmet bowl.

She must have thought it might as well be 1917, 1918 again. She must have believed the dead were twice blessed, finally blameless and they got to visit the rest of the dead. She grew tired of her nails and her hands, expecting me or her husband my father or bells, the toothachy pull of cigány violins. Maybe she thought *snow*, about how to get there.

While I tromped up the stairs through Christmas, New Year's, her birthday remembered, her name day forgot. I bore insignificant gifts, hard candies, chicken wings, spent nylons robbed from clotheslines.

"It's worse when you come," Alma said, "then you're gone and I have to remember I'm getting accustomed to it." She might have waved at my retreating back, but I wouldn't know, never turned, didn't stop.

Then nothing was out in the street but a soldier, a fountain, a blue-smoked Trabant. The air had the smell of horse droppings, wet dogs. Her hair had the odor of cigarette smoke, my hasty visit in it. Her room had her lying-down scent. She thought, *years of this, my gray hair growing out.*

She'd miss it, she thought, but not much. Perhaps she'd be missed for a while, but that wasn't for her to decide. Downstairs, the door yawned. The wind blew the door open wide, it always did that. She buttoned her nightgown, she put on her shoes, her good dress so it might be appreciated at last. She did not turn around. Her heels on the stairs made her Tilt-A-Whirl queasy, a little knee-sick, thinking, *here's how I leave*, a shallow-pressed shape on a bed, a name written in dust on the sill.

How long is too long for sadness? Margit grew tender from it. Six days without washing, she wore a man's pajama top she'd neglected to mend. In the low basement room Margit sewed, then she pulled out the threads. She picked at cabbage stew Sandor made, slipped the dish through the bars on the sill.

She knelt by the window, leaned out so the rain soaked the plate and her sleeves and her face. The slant V of birds overhead tugged her arms and her legs. The distance between her Angel Street house and the blinking stoplight made an ache in her limbs.

She let Sandor trace *S loves M* in her palm, unsure how much comforting she could allow. She studied his eyes to see in his features if she was all right, but she wasn't all right. Margit pulled back her hand.

"It's not helping," she said.

In his jacket, she stood on the corner and blinked into sudden daylight, amazed anyone was alive, simply walking around. The light, cold and white, touched her breasts. She took the next tram as if it could carry her out of the country, away from herself. Out of habit, she traced their initials in steam from her breath. It took only forty-five minutes to ride to the end of the line from Kispest.

Margit studied herself in store windows she passed. Just last week she had painted her toes the same shade as her chewed fingernails, she had colored her hair. *Suicide blonde*, Sandor said, *dyed by your very own hand.* How tired she was of her vanity, gestures, her smell.

In the Corvin Cinema, she cried herself dry through the newsreel about the last harvest, the next five-year plan. She stood in the back where the seats were torn out among bottles and cigarette butts. Couples moaned into each others' necks, used the wall as a bed.

Outside her Saint Matyas Street house she watched a van carry off Alma's table and cot. The government repossessed suicides' homes, like it was the survivors' fault, and maybe it was, Margit thought. She got down on her knees, dirt and ice burned her wrists as she searched for her mother's footprints.

She returned to Sandor because rain had soaked through her clothes, because he was all she had left.

He passed her a lit cigarette. "Invented by Magyars," he said.

She tried hard not to smile. "You say that about everything."

"Electricity, algebra, applesauce."

They sat on the edge of the bed, her hair dripping into her lap. In his jacket she shivered, she thought she would never get warm. "Keep talking so I can stop thinking," she said.

He pressed against her in her father's rough coat until they were both shivering. "When I was a boy we went to see Saint Stephen's mummified hand. After he died, sixteen kings fought for succession, then Mongols invaded and killed all the peasants," he said. The light in the room like his hair was the color of iron and ink. He plucked her damp sleeve. "My father was wearing this jacket that day," Sandor said.

Margit threw herself onto her back. "Now I've managed to make you sad, too."

He lay beside her in his shoes and his pants. "It's just the Hungarian disease. When it comes, I forge a new document."

Margit tented the blanket and sighed. "It feels as if history climbs into bed with us every time we lie down."

Sandor waved smoke from her face. "Sure, even love's a political act."

Margit shook her head. "I can't believe that."

He smoothed her collar against its wet grain. "Look at us, Margit, both wearing our dead parents' coats," Sandor said.

Margit hugged herself tight, she didn't want irony now. "It's cold here, Sandor, it's the practical thing." She laughed because what had he ever cared about that? She looked at the ceiling's flaked paint, the candle a pale unlit stub on the chair in near dark. She raised herself up on her elbows and studied the dumb gravel road where weeds pushed through the cracks. The small park's swing mute in half light. A finch pecked at the plate on the ledge. "Why do you want to get married to me?" Margit asked.

Sandor shrugged. "Because politics isn't enough." A lorry, a tram, pant cuffs passed.

"Then neither is love, if it's a political act."

Sandor lifted his hands toward the watermarked stains overhead. "It's the best thing we have."

She almost believed him, though there was a gap in the logic of it. And he had his forgeries, Erzsébet. She said, "Sandor, you're not making sense."

He touched the hair that had strayed to her brow. "That's what love does to us," he replied.

She took off his glasses, hooked them on the window's iron bars. Rainwater had pooled in the plate pocked by pin-prick raindrops. Outside, the street was the same as before Alma died. Rain fell across soldiers' shoes splashing puddles reflecting dull clouds. A couple shuffled across the wet tracks, their hands on their single umbrella seemed fragile as crepe in the dusk. Margit needed to bury her face in his shoulder, his one epaulet. She breathed Sandor's counterfeit scent, how he smelled like the whole day she'd had, the rain that fell on everyone and it couldn't be helped. "All right, then, Sandor," she said.

He held her in his grasp, rocked her in the bed. "That's your answer for me, isn't it?"

Rain swelled the wall by their heads, its cracks like the wallpaper maps in her Saint Matyas house. On the opposite side, someone swore, someone coughed. Margit let Sandor touch her cheek by her wide-open eyes where her skin was too tender from crying. Though it wasn't enough, she traced an M, then that careless nonsensical word binding it to the S in his palm. "Come on, Sandor, let's take off these coats," Margit said.

To Sandor from me, Kiskunfélegyháza, November 6, 1956.

They're burning leaves in the apple orchard outside, the smoke bitter yet sweet. The newspaper says the Russians reclaimed Budapest. We won't be going through there, the trains shuttled past that new death. I half expected this. Escape is the wind through the panes of this roadside cafe, stirring red and white checked tablecloths, my hair, soiled napkins. What remains: Winter scars on the buildings' facades, this light at the height of the day. Warmth from the sun through the glass on my dress. I've ordered a beer though I don't drink beer, I've smoked two cigarettes. My yellow valise by my ankles, my hand in my pocket, the forints you gave me, a hairpin.

When I married you, Sandor, I wore a simple white blouse and a faded blue skirt. I wore pearls, they weren't real but they had a casual, cheap elegance. Your suit was the color of mud and your pants weren't pressed. We were three stories up. Steam from the radiator smelled like burning leather, fake fur. I plucked my wet blouse from my chest. The new official red flag on the magistrate's desk didn't wave. My hands damp, I dried them on my hips. Above us a fan churned a fine bureaucratic incense. I held our unmatched pawnshop rings. The magistrate said *kiss the bride*, my lipstick gone grainy and soft in the cracks of my lips. "Now I'll start calling you Mrs.," you said, although you never did.

That night we were shiny, awake. You bent over me skinny-assed with your odors of metal and ink. Lamplight smeared its sheen on your limbs, the same as before, not the same.

After, you folded a paper airplane from a counterfeit document you had made, wafted it. Some kind of residence permit with fake embossed stamps. It circled and dipped, blundered against my bare shins. "A love letter," you said.

I laughed. "Fake," I said.

You held my cool feet in your cooler hands, blew on them. Your hands were the same size as mine, your ring in my mouth tasted sour, I opened my paper-pale legs.

But this is an old story now, isn't it? How a thousand birds flew past our window while vendors pushed carts down the street past my moany relief, your trembly naked arrogance.

In the orchard nearby, they're burning what's left of the harvest, wood crates, rotten fruit. This note's porous as thought, blurred in light on this bright windy day. Imminent refugees move past the glass, hide threadbare Hungarian flags, toss placards with wishes on them to the flames.

Did you know mail's returned from the prison stamped *DIED*? But then maybe it's also a fake.

This small town, I'm already nostalgic for it. I could nurse myself here with a man playing bocci ball in the square. Show him my calves. Make him stop playing whist on a slick tablecloth filmed with soot. Bat my eyes in a tired, city way.

A box for my needles, my thimble, a drawer for unpacking my threadbare underwear. Wednesdays, kohlrabi and beets, on alternate Thursdays, the usual queue for bad meat. I'd open a sewing shop, sure, sit with a horsehair blanket on my knees as the weather got even colder than this.

But don't worry, Sandor, I have sturdy shoes, I won't linger too long in this place. I still feel your chin in the cleft of my set shoulderblades. See me retying my scarf in the street among curled blowing leaves. The sun in my face, burnt apples and smoke in my hair. Hefting my yellow valise as if gauging my will by its weight.

Her honeymoon: marsh, chokeweed, scattered tin. Margit wore her white wedding blouse, her blue skirt. She took off her flats and stood in the water that rose to her calves. She bent, touched Lake Tisza, tasted it. The water smelled green. She stirred rotting leaves, dead insects. She sat beside Sandor, picked leaves from his shins. Wind blew bits of trash on the lake imitating dead fish. "We came here when I was thirteen. My father was going to war," Margit said.

Sandor played solitaire in the dirt. Wind picked up his cards, uncomplicated his hand. "I bet you had a boyfriend by then." Margit shivered against the cool wind in her clothes, in her hair. Her legs ached, and inside her legs. "More than one," Margit lied. He had already taught her to smoke, that boy who had written her name on the walls, her lips swollen and bruised just like now.

What she recalled of this place: She would rather have been with that boy and his mouth and his hands, winter falling toward miserly spring. The creamy sky's wide endless cloud. The harsh wind that fanned the checked tablecloth, how her mother's skin seemed mayonnaise, her lips peeled windburn pink. Groggy bees droned at the hem of her skirt. She swatted horseflies, scratched her gnat-bitten calves. Wind licked Alma's blouse, the loose button dangle a mood that could break. Margit tugged the checked cloth flapping on slices of caraway rye spread with shallots, paprika, and cheese.

Her father was watching a red-white-green sailboat veer aimless through lusterless waves. A column of dense brackish smoke rose from the unruly fire he'd made, spilling ash onto sand. Margit sat cross-legged at his feet. She'd already trailed his shoe prints, chased the shadows of birds. She rolled, unrolled his socks, rubbed the ridges elastic had striped on his shins.

"Aren't you going to eat?" Alma asked. She had expended herself on deviled eggs, cucumber salad, bloodwurst.

The boat tacked back and forth. Margit's father seemed suddenly sunk in himself. "My troop train leaves in three days. It couldn't be helped."

"You volunteered. Don't bother to lie," Alma said. Her sweater was shedding its fuzzy blue lint she picked with her quick-bitten nails. Across the water, willows dipped toward the waves, forlorn yet serene. The sailboat raised and lowered its nervous whipped flag as if signaling the season's quick turn. Alma combed and combed at her hair with both hands. "I knew this was coming, but now that it's happened, it's not the same I thought," Alma said.

Margit watched how her father's thumb pressed on the bridge of his nose where his glasses had slipped. She wanted to run down the shore, dig for worms, but she thought she was too old for this. He took off his glasses, daubed his eyes, filmy, wet.

"Where's your wedding band?" Alma asked.

He pointed toward the checked tablecloth. "It's what we're not eating," he said.

Alma's calves nudged the listing, precarious bench. "You really traded our ring just for this." She looked at the pale ringless line on her husband's right hand. Margit stared at the chuff of the sailboat's one sail, heard the rasping of late winter bees. She shivered against the cool wind in her clothes, in her hair, the open containment of air. It wasn't nearly enough to feel safe, too noisy, a whip-flap that crowded her breath, that made her feel fizzy and weak.

"It's done now, isn't it." Alma lowered her head. She scooped a forkful of peas, dribbled them into the dirt. The boat floundered and bobbed, it couldn't find the right angle for wind. Margit's father was rubbing his eyes. Maybe a speck of blown chaff was lodged under his lids. Maybe it was something else. He stared like he tried memorizing his wife, her arched back, how her shoulders looked maimed.

"Don't do that," Alma said.

Margit lay on her side and rested her head on her arm so everything swooned, on a tilt. The air stung, birds too low, tar too lumped. The day was too large yet too windblown and thin. It hollowed her chest. It was like falling asleep yet staying awake, queasy flies on the bread, gnats hovering over the cucumber salad peppered with sand. She watched the fire's black plume, bacon skewered on a whittled-down stick dripping into the flame. The smoke flat, the lake tipped. What if it spilled on the land?

"I'd have been conscripted anyway," she heard her father say.

"Whatever you claim can't mean anything now," Alma said. She'd stopped combing her hair, smoothed her blouse, placed her palm on the checked tablecloth as if trying to hold down the wind.

Margit sat up, brushed dirt from her skirt. Sleepy bees swarmed by her knees. Across Lake Tisza, sunflowers bowed under the sky's marbling shale. Her father bent over, grazing her head with the knuckles of his ringless fist. "Do you understand this?"

Margit shook her head. It meant yes; it was something she couldn't admit.

"You're scaring the girl, wipe your eyes, for God's sake," Alma said. Smoke from the bacon and paprika fire bled a thin spumy ink, black to blue, to near white, disappeared.

Her father fed bloodwurst to the birds. "We'll come back here after the war."

"Stop kidding yourself," Alma said.

Margit looked up past their heads. If you stared long enough, you couldn't tell where the lake stopped, sky began. Lulled, you might fall right to sleep, droning bees in your hair. While you were sleeping they'd have a war right here by the fire where the picnic bench leaned. If you slept long enough, you might wake after, relieved.

Alma stepped toward the lake. "I'm going to find shiny stones." She looked over her shoulder. "Don't worry, I won't drown myself." She tipped her head as if Margit could follow or not. She bent so her sweater bunched on her spine, scavenged rocks among lichen, aster, hyacinth. She gathered flat stones in the fold of her skirt held high with one hand as she went.

Margit stumbled after through torn roots, she could not help herself. She wanted to be on the shivery lake in that red-white-green tricolor boat, in its small cabin, alone. What that would be like, to be floating out there, spritzers of mist in her hair. Just her, she wouldn't want anyone else. She could bring food, plenty left, a handful of stones for good luck. Maybe she'd borrow her mother's kerchief, in case she had to signal for help.

She caught her mother's glance, watching her watching the boat. Margit flushed, unused to Alma's plain gaze on her face.

"Don't just stand there and twitch," Alma said. She reached out to touch Margit's shoulder but settled on swiping the front of her blouse. "Every girl should have a boat of her own," Alma said, surprising them both.

Suddenly shy, they both had to look away fast, toward her father scuffing his shoes through dry gorse. He rolled up his cuffs, shielded his eyes from the glare, waded into the lake.

"Jesus Christ," Alma said.

He stared at his swamped feet, at the foam. "They're wet. I forgot," he called out.

Alma pressed her hand to her throat like a hedge against cold, against flies, woozy bees. The ring that was gone or his going away, Margit couldn't tell which. Alma unfolded her pleats, counted the nestling rocks there. "They've faded," she said, shifting the stones to her palm, buffing their dull with the sleeve of her sweater pulled over her palm. "Everything's cheaper the closer you look," Alma said.

Her father dipped his hands in the lake, smoothed his charcoal-black hair, splashed his face as if trying to awake. He stepped over to them, his shoes squelched, touched his fingertips to his tongue. "It tastes sweet."

Margit put her own hand to her lips. The water was briny and tart. Alma covered her mouth, didn't say anything but leaned closer to him. The wind blew their hair all together so you couldn't tell which strands were hers or his.

Margit stood to the side, socks bunched at her ankles wet, itchy with sand. She wanted her hair also tangled in theirs but they stood face to face. Alma's blouse whipped the front of his shirt.

"Take off your glasses," she said, wiped his eyes with the back of her wrist. She looked at the stones in her hand. "I won't take them home. I'd keep them a day, then what for?" She reached down, unclenching his fist, placed a stone in his palm.

"Throw it," she said.

He looked at his hand as if unsure what it was, rock or ring, like it made little difference to him.

Margit picked up a twig, tossed it as far as she could. The wind blew it back in the rust-threaded eddy of waves, a small sailless float at her feet. She watched her mother and father fling every stone one by one in the lake, to the very last pair, then they tossed these as well, wiped their hands over each other's shirts. Her father looked at the lake, at the shore, somewhere else. He waved at the small crummy boats as if beckoning them. He wants to sail, too, Margit thought. The air smelled of mulch and dry rot, spoiling food. Thin grasses staggered down to the shore under shadows of terns, their shoe prints.

"It's a storybook picture," he said.

Alma sighed. "You've closed that book now," she replied, held the wind-flapping hem of her damp empty skirt.

· · ·

She knew she'd always hold this against him: that their honeymoon lasted one day, that Sandor repawned his ring to buy not food but ink for the press he hid someplace he'd never tell. It's safer that way, he had said, unwilling to stray from his counterfeit papers, dyes and stamps, and the real reason she thought that he wouldn't admit, Erzsébet.

Margit stood by the small city pond, she stirred rotting leaves, dead insects. Sandor kicked a pinecone, tried wiping blue ink from his hands.

She took off her flats and stood by the water that floated with newspaper scraps. She bent, touched the pond, tasted it. "I'll pretend this is still Lake Tisza," Margit said. Wind blew trash where the water lapped stone, imitating dead fish. She pressed her hand to her throat like a hedge against remembering: that boy who had taught her to smoke and to kiss. *We'll build a burlap sack lean-to, live here*, he had said. *Sure*, she'd replied, they'd drink dandelion milk to survive.

We'll meet here after the war, he had said, already conscripted by then.

Her mother had not fed the ducks in this pond. After the war, when the ducks were all gone, she'd almost touched Margit's arm here.

Sandor unwrapped the bread he had brought. Wind licked her blouse like a mood, fanned her skirt. She leaned against him, smelled Emke perfume on his shirt.

"This is tiresome by now," Margit said.

Sandor turned up his palms as if what could he do about it. He tried coaxing her down to the blunt new spring grass, touched her elbows, her face.

Margit pulled away. His cockeyed grin, his slight shrug had been terrible reasons to wed. "We can't always be throwing ourselves at each other to make things all right," Margit said.

Sandor picked a sneezy bouquet. "But nothing's wrong, Margit," he said.

She looked down at herself in her come-apart white wedding blouse and her wrinkled blue skirt. She wanted to open her purse, make him count her loose change. "Everything's fine. Pigs can fly and this is our honeymoon suite," Margit said.

Sandor touched her arm. "Sure, it's beautiful here."

Margit frowned. "Compared to what, Stalingrad?"

Sandor took his hand from her arm. "What could you know about that?"

Margit sighed. "You turned what you thought was due west. To another girl's bed."

They sat on the lawn, it was only a little bit wet. "I manned my big gun but I couldn't fire a shot," Sandor said. It was suddenly colder, he fastened her blouse's top button against the cool wind. "That's supposed to be funny," he said.

She unrolled his socks, rubbed the ridges elastic had striped on his shins. His cool shirt and its smell. "All Stalingrad's roads lead to Erzsébet." She ate the stale bread, wiped crumbs from her mouth, smoked her last cigarette.

"No, to you," Sandor said.

Margit shook her head, tossed her cigarette to the ground. "Another lie, like we had a real honeymoon." Like she could have sculpted a lean-to right here from old shirts and dead bark. Fed the ducks, if the ducks had come back.

Sandor blew fluff in her hair, touched the inside of her knee with a careful deliberateness. "Eat bad soup with a big spoon, that's what we used to say in the war," Sandor said.

Her cigarette glowed as if somebody dropped it while seized by soldiers or police. "This isn't war, it's our marriage," she said. She took out her compact, her mirror, put on her red lips. Her face felt difficult, the sky pale and white, the afternoon light hurt her skin. "I want to go home now and ruin our dinner," she said.

Sandor laughed. "It won't be the last time," he said.

Margit winced but she rested her head on the back of his neck, the sparse black hairs there. Her hand felt forlorn, though she kind of liked that. She gathered a handful of dandelion stems.

"I'll make bad soup with these, then," she said.

What should she know about Stalingrad?

That they covered the Russian retreat, the whole Second Army had perished in mud, but these were just facts.

That his coat was long. Impractical as a shroud, how snow stuck to its hem. Dead artillery strangled the road until all roads ran out. The Voldova River sucked at his heels filled with mud. Gold buckthorn and sage, light and wind burned his eyes. He climbed a small rise, then he fell to his knees and he rolled but his knees didn't hurt anymore or his legs. Splayed, exposed roots, lightning-felled trees strewed his path.

"And the three of you left," Margit says. She's with him on the bed in her underwear, blouse, Sandor's socks.

"The spoonless cook, the signalless radioman," Sandor says. "My ammunition ran out. Peasant girls slept with radiomen for their belts. Anything. Rumor was they'd leave you dead with a scythe in your side. The cook absconded with my hat."

They've bought a *szendvics* at a stand, there's grease on the sheet, crumbs in bed.

"There you were under a strange Russian sky," Margit says.

"I could have slept on the clay that ran down to the bank," Sandor says.

Could have gathered leaves for a bed among narrow thistles head high, but they kept blowing out of his hands. Wind lifted them singly, in pairs, stripped from fingers too weak to hold on. Wind raked washboard waves on the river, blew hard. The wind died. Behind him, reeds bent from his steps. Any fool could have tracked his escape through the chaff, could have made out the blundering drunk of his boots as he shielded his eyes.

"I don't want to talk about it," Sandor says.

Margit pulls off her blouse. They've pushed the bed to the wall like a couch. Her shoulders are white on the white of the wall in late afternoon light.

"Is it some soldiers' code to not talk? Some soldiery thing?" Margit asks.

The river seemed so calm where wide, pastel foliage skimmed the water's green shale, yet it tore at the shore, swept bodies along hovered over by gnats. If his hands weren't frozen, he thought, if he had a curved sturdy branch for a hook or a knife or a spark.

"All those soldiers were food for ravens. We flayed a horse for its meat," Sandor says.

Margit pulls off his socks. Pulls her knees to her chest. Sandor doesn't look there then he does. She speaks through the smoke of the cigarette hanging out of her mouth: "You don't want to talk about it but you can't help yourself."

His chapped fingers tore at split chutes, scratched raw bark. "I scooped a hummock of snow for a bed," Sandor says. "I ate clay, it stuck in my beard."

"That would be something, you with a beard," Margit says. She scratches her legs. Looks up, a half smile.

So cold he threw up green clay. Rocked himself. Hair frozen over his eyes reflecting the river's blurred wash, the bone sky.

Underwear tangles her calves. "You don't have to tell it," she says.

His shirt is undone, he brushes at smoke Margit blows on his chest. "I tamped down what leaves didn't blow from my grasp," Sandor says. "I couldn't feel them, my hands, yet they burned, had to slap them against my stiff pants."

He rocked on his heels. Forced the boots from feet blacked at the toes and he knew what this meant: soon walking was finished with him.

"You should never lie down," Margit says. "You freeze then."

Clay in his beard and mustache. The snow fell, the snow stopped. Rain came, and night, the rain cleared, a new moon sliced stars falling over the river's streaked dark. Then it happened again, snow's relief, rain, dark and light.

The waxed sandwich wrapper crimps under her wrist as she pulls on his arm, says, "You weren't supposed to lie down."

Curled in a patch of soft leaves, snow pillowed his cheek, a hood of blown snow for his head. The river so seemingly calm, benign leaves on its skim, he counted each one floating by. Snowdrifts soon three meters thick, his lips moved, wind carried his shivery scent.

"You don't have to talk about it if it hurts," Margit said.

If he lay still long enough, he thought he'd remember the entire history of old Budapest. Cave paintings in Bükk. The Romanesque churches at Velemér, Esztergom.

"I kept seeing my small house's wormy woodpile, Hungary's battlements," Sandor says.

He puts his hands in her hair, she doesn't like making a big thing of it, but he knows she likes this.

"You wanted to see some last things," Margit says.

He'd wanted to see everything: how snow fell gummy, clumped, at a slant, flung fistfuls of white and the bright masquerade of the sky, the river against its worn rocks, branches dragged into it, a bird, a small floating dead wing.

Snow dirtied his teeth. A moth tested his breath, it was almost nothing.

"Strange what the body refuses to eat, what might make you stand up," Sandor says. His brother's soft mouth, his crusted, hoed scalp.

Margit sweeps crumbs from the sheet to the ground. The light from the low basement window is hard on her breasts. Almost too scared to ask: "Does your father know you're alive?"

She never asks to be touched but he needs her wanting him holding her shoulders, her breastbone's scooped indent.

He says, "Do you know for a fact yours is dead?"

The light on her side is a swatch from her neck to her thighs. He thinks she believes in the soul, but he only believes in her body, his palms try to cover the light.

"I have a certificate," Margit says in the hair fallen over her mouth.

Sandor pulls off his shirt.

"I print those."

His shoes and his pants.

She runs her hands over his legs.

"You're cold," Margit says.

Her skin is a bare document for his fingers, his body's impress.

"I froze outside Stalingrad," Sandor says.

She turns to the wall, her back pushing hard against him. "Stop trying to prove it," she says.

She felt incoherent with want, that first year they were wed. Two governments came and went. The three-year plan died in nine months, now there was a new plan: They deported the new government.

"Sandor," she called from where she lay witless in bed, stunned by buttery light on the walls. Soon the sheets were all drenched, twisted up in their damp legs.

"What would your mother think?" Sandor said.

"She's not thinking much now," Margit said. Tangled, she kissed her own arm by mistake. She couldn't be bothered with changing the sheets; she washed all the sheets, all their clothes, scrubbed the walls and the floor and threw away things she would miss. She brought stupid new stuff, an egg timer, gauche earrings that seemed so perfect when Sandor said try them on.

She bit off her nails, she smoked up her last cigarettes. "Go get me some more without leaving," she said. It seemed possible with her indolent in her dress, then without anything, just those earrings and no underpants.

Oh, the body, she thought.

She had to smell it until it was all she could smell, until her skin hurt and she couldn't stand anything against it, not Sandor's mouth or his hands. When he touched her again, his touch was the sole mercy left.

"My torture," she called him, she'd started calling him that.

Ironic, she thought, later on.

By July, his accomplices tracked mud footprints through her house, called each other comrade with sly ironical smiles. "Comrade, your shirt's hanging out." "Boil us an egg, Comrade Margit, we're starved."

That was her, patching pants by the window at night, the bravado of cigarette smoke drifting over her lap. Men put their shoes right in her bed, told shy dirty jokes, spilled pálinka over the cloth Sandor stole her to make a new dress for herself.

Margitka, Gyuri said, Laci said, Csaba said, Pista said. Margit had not heard her name ever spoken by so many men, their hands on her sleeve while they breathed their confessions, complaints in her hair, knees pressing the mattress so she had to lean against them. *Margitka*, they sighed like she was their secret girlfriend.

But she wasn't anyone's secret, yet.

She kept a straight face, mending slacks while men paced in her robe, in their none-too-clean underpants.

"This isn't my home, it's another exiled government," Margit said.

A car passing by cast long stripes on the littered parquet. Csaba and Laci rolled beer bottles over the ledge. Sweat made the needle slip from her grasp, stab her palm.

"I want my room back," Margit said.

The men shifted their eyes everywhere but the bed.

"She wants bourgeois comforts," Pista said.

She looked over at Sandor who smiled at his forged documents. Fake as the new blue ballots that threw the election again.

"Ah, Pista, I thought we were comrades," she said.

Headlights strafed Sandor's teeth when he laughed, but Margit didn't laugh.

That summer the sky was incessant with swallows, storks came. How they stood so still on one leg made Margit sad about Alma again. When she had enough of the men, she took the tram to the cemetery, stubbed out cigarettes on the grave. Her mother's name felt motherly, round in her mouth. "What I want is to know will love last." She thought Alma's silence was finally appropriate.

Later the swallows all fell from the sky, blinded by smoke from the tungsten refinery plant. Three a.m., four, Sandor stood in the door with flowers that would wilt in a day, soot and fumes already bent their stems.

"So, you love me," she said. Margit plucked weeds through the bars, yellow-puffs used to smoke and exhaust.

"At least those will keep," Sandor said. Moonlight illuminated red hairs on his shirt that weren't hers. When he took off his clothes she found hairline welts on his flesh.

"Papercuts, I suppose," Margit said, ran her hands on his chest. It wasn't fair she'd never had anyone else except for a boy who was dead. "Don't you love me?" she asked.

"Careful, you'll wear the word out," he replied.

By autumn she'd never before practiced so many words in the dark. *Laci, Gyuri, Csaba*, she tried. She told herself she just rehearsed them to see how another man's name not her husband's might sound from her mouth.

She watched Sandor tying his shoes by the door with his glasses aslant. "Here, Pista," she took off her earrings and folded his fist around them. "Take these, they hurt me," she said. To cover her blush, she blew on the dead yellow-puffs.

Soon storks left the chimneys, flew into the season's descent. The windowbars turned her palms rust, the walls sweat a cold yellow paste. She stared at moonlight on the dead little park, its green bench, at Sandor's accomplices throwing themselves from the swing.

"They'll rip their pants out again," Margit said.

Sandor searched for loose change in her purse he'd spilled on the bed. "That's all right, you'll mend them," he said.

She looked at his hand on her money, the moon falling on his white shirt. "I guess you can say any terrible thing in a marriage," she said.

Sandor held her hair away from her face, touched the front of her dress. "Come on now, Margit. Look, we have the room to ourselves."

She studied his eyes, glanced away toward the window's iron bars. "Those men are too close, you'd think they moved in." She leaned into him in the trough ploughed by knees in her bed.

He slipped inky fingers between the gone buttons on Margit's thin shift. "Don't you still love me?" he asked.

Margit thought how the body tells lies, doesn't care about fooling the heart. "Don't torture me, Sandor," she said.

"*Margitka,*" he whispered, his breath an ironic caress.

She dug her nails into his wrist. "We can't simply fuck it away, how things are."

His mouth touched the side of her face where her earring had been. "Ah, Margit, I thought we were comrades," he said.

I never thought we'd hate each other like this.

You in the same dress you wore three years ago, when I didn't know your name yet. I smelled old rain on it then, that already faded pink cloth soaked and dried and then rained on again. Rain and bleach in your hair, I watched you light your cigarette, your small steady hands wrapped around it to keep out the wet. I remember the flare from the match on your broad pale forehead.

What did you think about me when we met?

He felt her judgment of herself.

He used to believe he could guess certain things about her, what he ought to expect. He wondered how she might sound lying down, but then she hadn't sounded like that.

When she took off her clothes, his surprise at her sudden pale candor in bed made him raise his hands toward her hips.

But see how things are.

He'd ridden the tram from Kispest to Pest to not think about that. He traded forged documents for a brisket of lamb. He took the train to his father's, the sack of meat clutched to his chest. Red juice dripped in his lap. An old war wound, he could have said.

You went there to confess.

I told my father I loved you. I did.

You told him you married me, too, I suppose. And that two years had passed.

His father had asked, so then where was his ring?

They sat on crates in the shade, sucked candies until his teeth hurt. I love two women, he said. Margit my hope, Erzsébet my helplessness. Sand blew over their shoes, flies swarmed the sack by his feet. His father looked past the half-open door but they didn't go in. You always were greedy, he said, nudged the sack. Did you bring that for me?

Say something true that you haven't told anyone else.

Sometimes I like to imagine you dead. My earned grief, then my guilt.

Practicing, I suppose. She smiled with closed lips. *It's easier loving the dead. No cost, consequence.*

His shrug seemed to hurt both of them.

Maybe you love Erzsébet.
I don't sleep with her.

That's not what I said.
Not after the war or since then, or last night in the dead switchman's shack where boxcars ploughed weeds into mud. The gap in the slats parceled light from outside on the wall, on the glass of water on the floor, on the bubbles that clung to its sides. At the end of the war he poured water over her mouth. He covered her cuts with damp ashes, his spit.

I'm not accusing you, Sandor. I'm not.
But I did see her last night.
Erzsébet let her red hair fall over his lap. Only he got to see her like this. *You'll have to stay and protect me from sleep,* she had said. *I want to,* she waited for him to say it. Branches knocked on the slats like abrupt question marks. A horse stood all night by the tracks, its head bent. Erzsébet lifted her hair, she showed him where fingers left minor sunsets on her neck. A soldier spoke Russian to me so I spoke German back, Erzsi said.

You couldn't do this to me if you cared.
He'd touched Erzsébet's arm where blunt Russian thumbs left indents. *What you allow and the reasons for it are cliches,* he had said. Erzsébet pulled the hem of her dress

past her calves. *I'm like this country, I've been occupied.* She laughed. *Aren't you going to laugh?* Shadows rode up and down her bare legs. *It's all right, I might kneel but I never lie down,* Erzsi said.

When you walked out of the war, you never walked out.

What's here is the shape of my hands. This Angel Street room that floats in this Angel Street building tonight. The light from the lamp in the street on a few passing cars.

You let me love you, that's why you're punishing me.

He'd pressed his hand to the bruise along Erzsébet's neck. *If I didn't care, you wouldn't do this,* he'd said.

She yearned because summer was short, flowers bloomed everywhere. Flower boxes in windows, flower beds in the parks, by the small city lake.

Margit swung her purse by her side, unencumbered by fare for the tram. Instead of Sandor in bed she had yellow-puff chaff on her sheets and she had cigarettes. She wore lipstick and knew how a body could feel. She strolled by the tungsten refinery plant in her blowsy-kneed summery dress with its very short sleeves. She'd washed it so much if you looked you could make out her plain underpants.

"Want half my sandwich?" Pista asked.

He seemed so inevitable, Margit thought. Even sitting down beside her he was tall, his eyes on her arms and her legs.

"Are you talking to me? Me with my bourgeois desires?" she asked.

"I was being ironic," he said.

"Not you, too," Margit said. All the crushed cigarettes at her feet she had smoked while not waiting for him made her sick.

"Really, I'm naive, it's my most useful trait," Pista said.

She unwrapped his jam sandwich, took wide yawning bites, not from hunger but nerves. "If you use that word then you're not."

Dirt under his nails from his factory job, she liked that. His plain face, his chipped tooth that he worked. His shoulders and arms stretched his shirt when he showed her the tear in his sleeve. "Look, it's ripped."

Margit felt herself smile. "Why tell me?"

"I'm only talking to keep you right here on this bench," Pista said.

She blew cigarette smoke between bites, twisted her wedding band. "Our motives are often obscure to ourselves," Margit said.

He fanned smoke from her face. "Not to me."

Margit picked at jam seeds in her teeth. Of course to him they wouldn't be. One worker's party, one state, one slate of candidates. "It was something my mother believed," Margit said.

He stared at his shoes like belief might rise up through the concrete carelessly poured by the state. "Ah, your mother," he said.

Flowers pushed through the mud, sunlight fired the dust.

"She's dead," Margit said. She thought now he'd say something profound, but he took back his sandwich instead.

"I brought a new bicycle, its color matches your eyes," Pista said.

Margit held her purse to her chest. "Please," she said, but it didn't come out like she meant. She had no idea what she meant. She took out her compact, studied her eyes in the glass. She thought of a joke that was going around, *Do I look married, or do I look all right?*

"I'd like to give you a ride over all seven bridges through rain," Pista said.

Margit glanced up and down the short block. Dirty-pantsed workers went by, a slow police car, army trucks. If Sandor came down the road now, she wouldn't yet need to explain anything, but then he didn't come.

"Too bad it's not raining," she said.

Pista brushed cigarette ash from her lap. They studied his hand, a small cloud.

"It will, soon enough," he replied.

She found Erzsébet in the railroad boxcar, damp weeds stuck to her dress. Her ankles were swollen and scratched, there were leaves in her hair, wine, she'd thrown up on herself.

"Come for advice?" Erzsi asked.

Margit did not carry her, that had already been done; anyway Erzsébet was too gangly, unwieldy for it. They rode the tram to the Angel Street house like normal people did. Erzsébet's shoulder on Margit's in stuttering light. Erzsébet in her awful green coat though it was summer, still hot, like the weather could change on a whim.

Margit placed a candle on the chair, watched Erzsébet sprawled on the bed. She smelled her hair, inhaled Erzsébet's breath as though she'd taste Sandor on it. His hands that would cover her mouth with their smell of sour coins and the press.

Margit wiped Erzsi's face with a rag.

Erzsébet tilted her head toward the window's iron bars. "Save your kindness for Sandor," she said.

He was waiting out there for some man. Lamplight ghosted his shoes by the swing in the small scruffy park. He scuffed small stones and dead grass, chestnut shells. The boughs of a tree scratched odd strangled shapes on his shoulders, across his bent back.

Erzsébet gripped the bars with both hands. "That tall guy you've been with. Watch out for Pista, Pista, Pista," Erzsi said.

Margit couldn't tell if she was warning Sandor or her, both of them. She made Erzsébet stand on the bed, pulled off her clothes, pulled an unfinished dress over Erzsébet's head. Her body helpless and white, the scissors close to hand. Quickly, she tugged down the dress. Pins in her teeth, Margit knelt, the dim light made her squint.

"You watch out for these pins," Margit said.

Sandor passed from the bench to the swing like awaiting his fate.

"Poor Margit, can't eat and can't sleep, haven't even committed adultery yet," Erzsi said.

Margit's knuckles grazed Erzsébet's white skullcapped knees. She leaned into her thighs.

"You're enjoying yourself much too much," Margit said, purposely cavalier with the pins. They watched Sandor cling to the chain, the swing's three-note scree carried into the room like a scar on the wind.

"Sounds like a lovemaking bed," Erzsi said.

Margit stared past the glass toward the park as if wind had shape and leaves spoke. They had nothing to say she could use.

"He's killing me," Margit said.

"He's killed people before," Erzsi said.

They both stood on the disheveled sheet expecting to see Sandor killing somebody out there.

Margit felt a sad helplessness. "He tries to save everyone else."

They laughed as if it was some kind of a joke between them.

"I don't want him for that," Erzsi said.

Sandor kicked at loose gravel and rocks under the yellow streetlamp. All the times he had held her in bed were no more to him, Margit thought, than the wind or a leaf or a spent chestnut shell.

"It's you he loves," Margit said.

Erzsébet shrugged. "Love is like death, it falls on us all if we want it or not."

Light from a passing car drifted across Sandor's shirt. Only last week Margit had scorched up her flammable hair, burned her eyes with strong dyes, hopeful still for a miracle blond. She'd painted her nails as though she still thought it would help. Naively, she'd thought, because some things had already happened to them, that all the bad things that could happen had already happened by then.

"Perhaps he can love you a little. Maybe we can do that with someone, sometimes," Margit said.

Erzsébet stepped around on the pin-strewn mattress.

Her bare feet trod Margit's feet. "Come off it, Margit, *with someone, sometimes,*" she blew air through her teeth. She leaned down to watch Sandor pacing from half-light to pitch.

"And he doesn't love me a little," she said, the mattress a boat, her hands holding Margit upright, steadying her to keep her from falling too far to be saved.

Of course the rains came and went, brief summer squalls she had to be under to breathe. It was only like this that she could be careless yet safe: her thighs cool across wet handlebars, Pista's tires sizzing over slick streets.

His arm brushed her hip. "Don't worry, I'm shy," Pista said. He was unscrupulous about touching her, Margit thought. When she said, *look, no hands*, when she tried to light cigarettes into the wind.

"Even the shy have to try," she replied.

She was certain he swerved on purpose so she'd have to grab onto his wrist.

"The enslaved must resort to mere trivial acts." Pista laughed.

"That's just an excuse," Margit said, gripped his fists.

He pedaled too fast, they bumped across railroad tracks. "It's your husband's notion," he said.

The rain stopped, her dress flapped. She swatted wet boughs, the corners of posters they passed. "When I married Sandor, I made absurd promises," Margit said.

"That's how it's usually done," Pista said.

Spray from the tires soaked her hem, Pista's soggy cuffs snapped.

"I love him so much it makes me do stupid things," Margit said. She took off her scarf, shook her hair, let it blow in his face.

"I like him, too. Watch the spokes," Pista said.

Margit sighed into her knees. "Pista, listen to us. Why am I doing this?"

The bicycle wobbled and slipped, pigeons flailed dirty wings. "So you can stay married to him," Pista said.

Her hand on his fingers was some kind of silent assent. "I shouldn't," she said. She didn't mean marriage or what they were saying but what she allowed: Pista's sly courtship of her, her hand upon his that gave him permission for it.

"Don't let me use you," she said, though it felt necessary as the leftover rain on her legs, her need for his breath in her hair's futile yellow attempt.

"I want you to," Pista said. He let the bike roll to a stop. Rain pasted her dress to her skin, mist rising from it. She was aware of her heat, they both were, she could tell.

"It's not fair," Margit said.

Rain dripped from the trees, an elm cast its languorous shape over them. Poles where corpses had swung in the war gleamed in sodden gray light, daubed with wet pasted leaves. A man with an empty sleeve pinned to his shoulder ran past. They both watched him.

"What's fair doesn't count for much here," Pista said. She knew what he meant, the war hero Rajk had been executed. The betrayal of Midszenti sent off to life imprisonment. Sandor would have agreed, Margit thought, or might not, but he wasn't around. She stood by the bike, she looked down the road just to check. "It's a Hungarian habit, using what's happened to us to excuse how we act," Margit said.

Pista touched her hair, she let him. She wiped the bicycle's seat with her scarf, his wet face with her hands. It was wrong. It felt good. It felt good to be wrong, like revenge.

"As if we had a choice," Pista said.

Margit thought they could talk around this until that man with no arm grew it back, the dead unhanged themselves. She touched her hand to his mouth.

"Oh, we have a choice," Margit said. She leaned over the bike, *this is mine*, kissed him full on the lips.

Pista is walking with him. The Danube is jade, the sky crushed by dull afternoon heat.

"I wooed Margit here with a fish," Sandor says. The river flowed turbulent then. Now it runs sluggish but Sandor's aware how it pulls, underneath.

"I only ride her on errands when you're not around," Pista says.

Sandor picks burrs from his cuffs, searches his pockets for change: matchsticks, loose thread, a few weightless coins, not enough for the tram.

"If you want money, there's work at the plant," Pista says.

Sandor tugs at his shirt and his pants, they stick to his back and his legs. "Sure," he says, "we're the land of iron and steel, except there's no ore, and they ship off the things that we make."

"Still, I can get you a job, I joined the Party," Pista says, waves his hands. "Oh, I know how the Party behaves. Five-year plans, they send you away if you say the wrong thing at the plant."

Breezeless, the Danube smells dead. Sandor looks at the river, the sky, the cracked concrete bank. "Don't think I'm naive," Sandor says. He studies his knuckles scraped up from moving the press. "It's just Muscovites purging Tito-ists," Sandor says.

"These things matter, Sandor, you need to care about them," Pista says.

Dirty gulls screech in the wake of a barge trailing scraps. Sandor winds Margit's thread on his wrist. He never imag-ined his wife with a man quite so tall, Margit in a sleeveless red dress, her needle-stabbed fingers on his.

"I'll be even more use to us soon, I'm joining the army," Pista says.

Sandor looks away not to see Pista blush, toward the statue of Stalin that every square has. He studies the pigeons ascending from Stalin's iron head. "During the war, I used to daydream of a woman I hadn't met yet. Then she came to me, Pista," he says.

Pista looks at his elbows, his knees. "Your wife loves you," he says.

Sandor smiles to himself. "That's what you two discuss while you're wiping the rain from her hair, between errands," he says.

Pista nods. "As a matter of fact."

Sandor squints at the pigeons that wheel into leftover puddles and sully themselves. "So much the worse for us then," Sandor says.

She thought about drowing herself. It would be such a Hungarian thing, but Pista had already taught her to swim.

Face down in the tepid Palatinus Baths, that's how she wanted to stay, but he gripped her waist, he lifted her up, those large steady hands let her paddle the air.

"Sandor knows about us, doesn't he?" Margit asked.

Water sluiced from her body to his.

"Of course, darling," he said. Since he got his new uniform, he'd started calling her that.

Annoyed, Margit wiped at her wet blurry eyes. A ridiculous old-fashioned word, yet it fell so disingenuously from his mouth, charming, really, innocent. While all these excuses she'd already made to herself:

It was just a mistake.
It happened just once.
My God, it was only a kiss.

She should have felt guilty and bad with his arms around her in the pool, on her belly, face down, sputtering as she came up for air, except there was no air, anywhere.

"Pista, what are we going to do about this?"

The echoes of women and men sounded like lovemaking cries. "We haven't done anything yet," Pista said.

She should have been angry at him but she laughed, a little hysterical from his hands. Taller than her, he could carry her over his head with one hand, and he did.

"Pista, stop, put me down!" She had never done that, shouted out, her hands shaking, her thighs. "Pista, please, that's enough," but it wasn't enough. She gave herself up to his touch as he swam her around, Margit wet in the legs, but the water would wash it away, you could smell just chlorine, feet and hair, rubberized bathing caps.

"Look, Margit, you're swimming," he said.

He was no longer holding her up.

Kick your feet, keep your head in the air, move your arms, too many motions at once, she could not get herself organized. "Jesus, I'm drowning," she cried, grabbing onto his hair, spitting water over his face, Pista laughing at her, disentangling her hands.

"Margit, just put your feet down."

Oh. Margit blushed, she would not look at him. Her eyes stung, water lapped at her breasts. "Sandor should have taught me to do this, not you," Margit said. The skylight obscured by dead leaves cast its verdigris light on their skin.

"Darling, he doesn't know how," Pista said. Water dripped from his hair, raised goose bumps where it fell on her chest. She suddenly hated them both. She thought when she married she'd no longer have to decide how to act, who to choose.

"Swimming's not so grand," Margit said.

Pista touched her arm, ran a fingernail under her bathing suit's strap. He said, "Now if things go really bad we can float to the West."

The water felt viscous, thick, it was hard to step back. "The Danube flows east," Margit said.

He touches her hair with both hands, her hair that so often looks brittle though Margit is young, it's still soft to the touch.

"I'm in no mood," Margit says.

"You're in some mood," Sandor says.

She kneels over him on the bed. "I don't hear you at all, you're just moving your mouth," Margit says. The window is open to let out the smell of stale ink, their perspiring flesh.

"I know about Pista," he says.

"You don't know a thing about Pista," she says.

He wants to touch her breasts. Already he's trying to recall her white skin in the light from the street.

She rides over him. "Now I hate this," she says.

It pains him how lovely she is, slightly flushed from the heat. "Maybe he fucks you better," he says.

She jams his fingers in her teeth, his fists bruised from the press. "Sure, he's bigger, a trooper," she says, digs her nails in his ribs, tears his shirt.

"If anything happens to me, you won't need to mend it," he says.

"That's low. That's not fair," Margit says. Fresh ink from the day's forgeries stains her lips.

He covers his eyes with her palm. Her slick heaviness makes him gasp.

"Fuck you, too, Sandor, go moan underneath Erzsébet," Margit says.

He turns her around, her face pressed to the bed.

"Good, I can't stand to look at you, either," she says, though she groans as he pulls her to him, cries out on her elbows and knees.

He covers her back with his chest, their breath stirs the dust on the sheet.

"You're not who I thought."

"I can't be what you want."

Then they stay just like that, the sun on the slow rise and fall of their hips.

Soon, more rain fell. Summer turned into fall, a season of fragile gray smoke and the streetcars' complicitous bells.

Sandor sat in the car that had pulled up for him. He inhaled the driver's cologne, alcohol. "I don't suppose you're stopping for me so I can get out of the rain," Sandor said. He kept his breath shallow against the closed space, tight and rank. He recognized the car's smell, like people had bled inside it.

"You're dripping all over the seat," the man said.

Sandor turned up his palms. The car lurched across Angel Street, traffic sparse, shambling steps, the streetcars' perspiring glass. On corners, men sold horse-fat soap, shoelaces, cigarettes. Rain beaded the windshield, warm drops in a low moany wind. Broad yellow leaves mashed under the rain-spitting tires.

"You think you can alter the future with fake documents," the man said. Behind them the long boulevard telescoped in a crosshatch of telegraph wires. The man lit a cigarette, didn't offer him one.

"Forgery's not an ideological act," Sandor said.

The man moved his eyes from the street, smiled at him. "You of all people know better," he said.

Sandor noted the irony of the red-white-green boutonniere pinned to his jacket's lapel. Five years since the Russians won, the old flag with its bold Lorraine cross, its stripes and its elegant fleur-de-lis and its Saint Stephen's crown was officially gone. Then there was no sound but the wrack of the car through potholes and puddles and trash. Clothes flapped overhead with dull snaps, flurries of pigeons rose up before the car's steady advance. They crossed, recrossed the Chain Bridge. The windshield wipers ticked the span between blinking stoplights. Sandor looked at the sidewalk spackled with ovals, the shadowy ghosts of streetlamps. In open windows overhead figures bent, setting plates across red and white checked tablecloths. He saw doilies draped across chairs under miniatures crammed on shelves. The foolish comfort of ceramic milk girls, a cigány, a hussar with tiny sword drawn, its steed's broken leg carefully glued through two wars.

The car stopped.

"If you're not taking me, then we're just wasting gas," Sandor said.

The man nodded his head like confirming a fact they'd already discussed. He lit his last cigarette, crushed the pack. Sandor studied his hands, the shape of blunt fingers accustomed to handling flesh. "We like arresting the innocent first, it makes everyone guilty," he said.

The street appeared woozy, rain blurred. "I thought the new law says only class enemies can be guilty," Sandor said. Men turned their collars under the new hammer and sickle flags, women tightened their scarves. They wiped rain from their brows, smoked too much, got drunk for relief from a present that seemed like the past.

"Your father was no laborer," the man said.

Outside, vendors stooped, shuttering chestnut carts. Trolleybuses sparked feelers against their guide wires. "What am I supposed to be, then?" Sandor asked, "A cosmopolitan traitor? A bourgeois objectivist?"

The man shrugged. "We know what you are."

"Then why are you telling me this?" Sandor asked.

The man squealed the fogged glass. "We want to see what you'll do next."

Sandor looked at the sidewalk spackled with light from streetlamps. He felt himself starting to laugh. "You communists are so clever," he said.

The man's ill-fitting suit stretched over his shoulders, shiny under the lights. He lit a fresh cigarette from the butt of the last. "Maybe you think we'll outsmart ourselves," he replied.

Sandor gazed through the gauze of smeared rain as the number-two streetcar passed. Everyone knuckled rain-damped eyes at tram stops, wrung damp hands. "Let's not get carried away with false hopes," Sandor said.

In a dark window over the street, a hand lit a candle, a drawn face leaned out, saw the AVO car, doused the light. The man leaned across Sandor, pushed open the door on the passenger side. "God help and forgive us," he said. "You better go home to your wife."

It was a bad year for people who didn't come home by the time they said they would. Margit knelt by her window, left greasy imprints on the glass. Her lips were so chewed up they bled while out in the street women sighed in their polka-dot scarves, circumspect men broke the law, hoarding bread. She felt like she had in the war between one bomb and the next.

Her shins gathered bruises and soot as she paced up and down Angel Street. She found only the absence of him. She found Pista instead where loose shutters clapped in the wind. Lamplight fell over his shoulders, his hands, he had brought cigarettes. Margit touched his sleeve, but she wasn't relieved.

"You're not him," Margit said. It was merely a fact, like the name of the street or his height, the stoplight blinking over their heads, its gauzy wounded red.

"I thought that's what you liked about me," Pista said.

She shifted her glance from his hands toward an army truck's thin curfew dust. He leaned into her but she placed her palms between them.

"What if he sees us?" she asked.

Pista pressed himself against her hands. "He won't see us," he said.

She felt his new special red Party card, that cold cardboard heart by his chest. "So you know where he is," Margit said.

A car slowed and stopped, it moved on. "You know, too," Pista said, touched the front of her blouse. Margit let out her breath. His stance, Pista's answer implied her husband was held in Erzsébet's arms, not under arms by the state. She thought of Erzsébet and Sandor in her tilted boxcar while gray pigeons burbled their guilt. Maybe Pista was thinking it, too, he put his hands on the back of her neck.

"He could come any minute," she said, then she laughed at herself.

"But you know where I am all the time," Pista said.

Margit looked toward her room, the useless protection of it. She felt suddenly sorry for him, for herself. She said, "Sure, I know just who you are."

"I thought that's what you wanted," he said.

She let her brow touch his cheek. He smelled reasonable, his skin felt unambiguous. "I wish I did," Margit said.

Soldiers guarded night, the boxcars. A wet swollen moon lay across spindly trees, epaulets, the tips of their cheap cigarettes.

He stood beside Erzsébet's cot, her nails scraped a light-slivered gap in the wall by her head.

"So they're onto you now. I told you to watch out for Pista," she said.

No candle burned, the night sky seemed to blow through the slats. He touched his face, it felt like it belonged to somebody else. He searched for something to pick up, set down, but she had nothing. She'd had things and then they were gone: A porcelain egg, a macramé hanging she didn't bother to hang. A cigarette case he saw her throwing away in the rain.

"If anything happens to me then you'll take care of Margit," he said.

She lit the candle, she laughed. "Fuck you, Sandor," she said.

He sat on the edge of her cot. He kept getting told that. "When I carried you, you didn't laugh at me then."

The moon lay on the floor, on her eyes. She turned to the slats, her dress was torn straight up the back. He pressed his hand to her spine, long and damp in half light, but she shied. "I used to make silhouette shapes on my wall as a child. Eagle. Dog. A man holding a gun." She showed him. The gun's shadow fell on his limbs. "Bang, you're dead," Erzsi said.

He touched her hair but she shook off his palm. He held his elbows to himself, knuckles torn from the press. "Sometimes people console each other," he said.

Erzsébet turned, put her hand in the flame. She said, "Only the innocent get to do that."

You said hide, I said I'd rather die in your arms. "It's not a joke, is it?" I said. You said, "We've been warned. Pack your bag," and I knew what that meant. "Darling," I said, I threw myself down on the bed. "Keep packing," you said. Our silence had wires in it.

"Better stay at my father's," you said. I hoped you were only punishing me for Pista, but I could see that wasn't it. And Sandor, for what it's worth now, I did not sleep with him.

He'd brought us that small radio, it leaked through the overcast heat: Kádár's secret trial and the resettlements, we had to glean this from fake factory quotas surpassed, grain yields met.

"All our heroes are no more than names in the telephone book or on headstones," you said.

"Your heroes, not mine. Look what happens to heroes," I said.

You wanted only the news but I said it was too hot for lies, turned the dial to Russian opera instead, held your wrist. I studied your hand bruised from moving the press. I no longer wished you were somebody else.

"Better not read my fate," you had said.

I traced from the heart of your palm to your blued fingertips. "You'll desert your wife for a redheaded woman," I said. It was my only defense.

"You'll escape to Vienna with a tall Commie soldier," you said.

I tried not to blush but you must have seen Pista and me in the street. I'd told you intentions aren't acts, so I didn't have to confess: my arms bared in thundercloud light, my casual hand against his, Pista's hip-to-thigh accidents.

"I wouldn't give Erzsi the pleasure," I said. I unbuttoned my blouse, shoved coins and rags from the bed. I tried to recall if I'd ever removed my clothes out of desperation before, or regret. A Hungarian woman, so of course I had. I climbed over you like it was our very last chance.

"You were shy when I met you," you said.

"I was naive then," I said, my modesty gone like my skirt, like my sheer underpants.

Dust rose from the sheet, that place dirty but I never swept. I knew when I touched your raised ribs, I had become more substantial than you, my knees snapping cloth-marking chalk, the radio's thin tinny opera disguising our quickening breath.

"Here comes the part where the lovers are falling all over their swords out of love," you had said.

Neither one of us laughed. Dust stuck to our bellies and thighs. "It's tragedy, Sandor, everyone dies and love doesn't save us," I said.

"No, it's a farce," you replied. We were afraid for us then, your skin flaring white, my eyes wide and corrupt and determined and sad as I pressed on your legs. Dull violent light lay over your shoulderblades sharp and yet malleable as I fell against them.

"So this way is possible also," I said. Yellow refinery smoke drifted over my cast-aside blouse, your worn pants. The window's iron grill striped its cage on my arms by your head. Salt dripped in your eyes, I had to taste it.

"Do you still hate this?" you asked. Your voice held a hard sullen pity for us, your legs held my waist while the radio lied about harvests and death. I'd made up my mind to betray you with Pista, but how could I have? How terribly lovely you looked with me almost gone from our bed.

"Sandor, let's stop now, I'm scared and I'm cold, it's not safe here," I had said, but it wasn't cold it was hot, the unsafeness excited us so I couldn't stop yet.

"It's not cold, it's still summer," you said, but summer had come to end. How that came out of your mouth frightened me more than I ever had been.

I scraped my brow in your hair astringent from chemical smoke and perfume, but I couldn't afford to make too much of that then.

"It'll stay summer forever," I tried, though I didn't even like summer at all, then I died in your arms, like I wished.

"Go to my father's," he'd said and stunned, she'd said yes, but she lied, because how could she do that? When she'd never been past where streetlamps and lampposts ran out? When she loved him but it didn't do any good because he'd been found out?

She followed him to the Chain Bridge where the river was drownably swift. She tried to pretend he was any day-dreamy Budapest man peeling bark from an elm, gouging soft exposed pulp, *S loves M*, but she couldn't pretend. No mistaking his shirt perfumed by slow drifty Trabants, handkerchief-thin in the unchurchbelled four p.m. light. She didn't whistle or call, he didn't look up, though he knew she was there with her yellow valise, hair undone, out of breath.

She was glad for the tilted green bench because she got

to lean against him, whispering, "You don't want me to go, it's just an idea about how you should act."

He stared at leaves mulched by their feet with that odor of sad they both liked. She shied against leftover rain from the elm dripping cool on her neck. She said, "Just yesterday," but he shook his head so she wouldn't mention the rest, about how yesterday they had crawled on the bed across breadcrumbs and coins while wind scattered rain across glass. How she moved next to him in the low basement's window-barred light, her body warm, slippery under her dress, then the dress in a heap.

She said, "I always thought peace would be safer than war but it's worse, there's no hope for its end."

Sandor kicked at small stones. It was hard looking at him, a man almost gone, a woman about to be left. She said, "We could hide," half in jest, touched her teeth to his palm, but he pulled it away, tucked it under himself. "It's different now, Margit," he said as if she couldn't guess.

Margit shivered and tugged on her hem but she couldn't escape from the wind. Sure, she knew what came next. Soon Sandor's touch would be merely the flap of her clothes on her thighs, her dress rain-pasted to her legs. Anyone carelessly bumped on the number-two tram would have to suffice for her husband's caress. It wouldn't be betrayal, then, if Sandor didn't know who it was.

"Where will you go?" Margit asked, then she was sorry she had.

Sandor tried on his most casual smile. "Maybe Erzsi will hide me," he said. His pale skin already seemed no more than the glare in the puddle of rain at his feet, the reflection of clouds in the windows across the far bank.

"At least Alma knew my father had gone to the war, safely dead," Margit said.

They looked at each other a while then they laughed. Margit opened her yellow valise. They'd done this before, Sandor holding her mirror while she turned his wrist. The mirror with stirred clouds in it, a bird's dart, a pylon, the Chain Bridge's blurred iron flanks. She steadied his hand, saw her bleach-ruined hair, her eyes smudged with Sandor's departure in them. She daubed red over her lips, pursed her mouth for the soft smear effect. What Budapest man could resist?

"It's called Careless Red," Margit said, "You like it?"

"Who taught you how to do that?" Sandor said.

She could tell he was sorry he asked. "All of that doesn't matter much now," she replied.

Sandor looked away toward the river where slow oily barges cleaved waves like formations of migrating birds. "My father could teach you to slaughter a pig, you'll learn to beat him at whist."

Margit pretended she didn't hear what he said. She blew fine dried blush from her eyelid-soft brush, swiped it over her cheeks. Her hand shook. She dabbed cream on her lids, short sharp fingertip stabs, as if she was mad at herself. "I'm already nostalgic for you," Margit said.

Sandor stood, his heels dug narrow grooves in the dirt. Small blue cars circled ponderously through the streets. Behind him shirts whipped on a line. You could never wash out the skin-salty smell of such shirts worn a week, shirts like his.

She pulled herself up by his sleeve. Mud-smeared leaves caked her shins. They stood close as they could and then slightly apart, hand in hand and then not. "I might not see you again," Margit said. How do you stop a thought? Her words scattered over the river, windswept. She could do nothing for him but rub face-powder dust from his brow with her spit. Her mouth left a loud scarlet O on his wind-blown lapel. Someone had to turn away first. If it had to happen, she hoped he would do this for her and he did.

"Wait, there's always a minute," she said, and he turned back to her, and he took her valise from her hand, and there was.

He carried her yellow valise, he had his ideas about what to do next.

"You couldn't leave me," she said.

"I haven't."

"You tried."

"I wouldn't."

"You might."

He took her to Erzsi's boxcar, but she'd fled. Gypsies had camped, staked chickens and goats in the weeds.

"How did you know she lives here?" Margit asked.

"She doesn't," he said.

They rode the streetcar to Margitsziget, climbed the tower like everyone else. At the small city pond, she fed the lice-ridden ducks who'd been spared. He wanted to row in a green paddleboat but there weren't enough bills between them. He bought her an ice cream they ate on the opera house steps.

"I want to be just a citizen, Sandor," she said.

The sun almost gone, the streets were the color of blood. He said, "Citizens get to cross over the border for burying a mother sometimes."

She wiped vanilla from her mouth. "I'll have to dig her up, then."

"With papers, a bribe, you might get to the Yugoslav side," Sandor said.

She buried her face in his shirt. "Yugoslavia! You go!" They looked at each other and laughed and then they didn't laugh. "You have no intention of printing papers for yourself," Margit said. She hadn't let go of his hands except to light cigarettes. They had come to a door she'd passed and passed but she'd never gone up.

"Oh no, Sandor, not here." She touched Pista's bicycle chained to the rail by the darkened stairwell.

"How did you know where he lives?" Sandor asked.

Margit blushed. "That's not fair." Lamplight glazed Pista's window overhead. She watched Sandor scraping his shoe on the curb, such an obstinate man. Who or what would be sacrificed, whose sacrifice would it really be if she climbed up the steps? She'd be out of his hair and the one who was guilty as well. "This is too easy for you," Margit said.

Sandor looked toward the dark, his shrug both dismissive and helpless at once. Pista's shadow crossed overhead. She could imagine his carpet, a bureau's fringed lace. She thought of his green uniform on the bed, a lifetime of small kindnesses. She glanced toward the window and fluffed out her hair with quick petulant hands. Squared her shoulders, tugged down her blue dress. "Talk me out of it, Sandor," she said.

He picked up her yellow valise, shifted it from hand to hand, tipped his head. "All right, you don't have to," he said.

Margit hid a wry smile in the darkness that fell from the steps. "Thanks for the favor," she said.

The valise knocked his shins. He swiped the hair from her eyes with a meticulous carelessness. "No. Thank you," he said. She took Sandor's arm. They both understood what he meant.

The city was crowded and dark but not dark or large enough to hide in. She smelled rain on the wind. "You can't save me by making me leave you," she said.

But she was a burden to him. He wanted her gone because he would not have to hurt or betray her in new ways again.

The air cracked, deep blue gave way to low clouds. In the past, of a night they would lie on the uncovered bed in their clothes and their coats. He wanted only to recall Margit in her socks and her dress and then only her socks, the strand of loose hair she constantly swiped from her brow, cold light's sharp planes on her legs.

Rain fell privately over them. Sandor held Margit's wrist as they crossed any street that came next. He would miss everything. How he'd washed her underwear, he wasn't embarrased at all when she bled, he liked watching the water turn pink. He dipped his fingers, tasted it. The water smelled red. Later, he soaked his feet in the same bowl, trailed wet footprints over the floor to the bed.

Now his shadow fell over her steps. She was glad for the rain, in the rain everyone looked the same. She let go his hand because he didn't like to be touched very much. Once, she tried cutting his nails: He had batted her fingers away. She thought it a game but she looked in his eyes and it wasn't a game.

What he'd miss: Margit always laughing at him.

Warm clouds emptied water from rivers and lakes into potholes and gutters and grates. Pedestrians crossed in front and behind the wet trams, trailing white breath, gray smoke, gray coattails. The buildings gray-brown, you couldn't tell them apart from the clouds and the coats, the cigarette smoke. Her pulse beat in his fingertips, he held tight to her wrist.

Always, when she slept, he wanted to wake her but he was afraid she might not recognize who he was, or she would. He couldn't protect her from rain, he couldn't take care of Margit. He wanted her gone because she made him owe her too much. He pictured her tragically dead, he'd bring subtle flowers to her grave, he would mourn her, relieved.

Barges skimmed the reflections of damp yellow lights from Elisabeth Bridge. The two of them teetered along the embankment on slurries of crushed gravel stones, small rocks in his near-useless shoes. Windows and doors leaned open against the soft rain, the faces they passed seemed inhabited by politics. "If only there were no people," he said. "Of course I don't mean you," but he did.

"But you'd miss me," she said. "My body in bed." She thought she saw Erzsébet pass in a cloak but did not mention it. Erzsébet who owed him, who'd grown to his shoulders and back on the long walk from camp. If she left, that pain, too, would acrue to his body like war, Margit thought.

"I'd miss your gestures the most," Sandor said. They were plain, only he could see them. He'd miss how she mimicked his broody serious face like his father's had been. Her breath sour from a molar gone bad as she bent over him. They never made noise in their bed. She liked the tense quiet straining of it, her skin flushed at the tops of her breasts when she came, then she turned or she buried her face in the pillow or sheet. It wasn't from shyness or shame.

"How private we've been," Margit said. She rested her head against him, tasted his wet ashy hair. He didn't reply. He was wary of what could be given or owned. The press and his clothes and his wife and the things he just used.

"I'm going to make you some residence papers for Szentes," he said.

"We've been through this. I won't go," Margit said.

"Yes, you will."

"No, I won't."

"It's not safe to go back to our house," Sandor said.

A bird's nest had slipped from a tree, they stepped over the broken eggshells, scattered bird-bone-like twigs. Budapest was a worn metal coin rubbed and passed. It smelled like wash water thrown from apartment house doors, sheets and clothes on clotheslines. The rain fell but they stayed under it. He didn't tell her they passed by the building where he hid the press. "Wait for me by the pond, by the boats," Sandor said.

It's futile, she thought. She tried lifting her arms to protest but her sleeves felt so suddenly heavy, too soaked. "I'll wait for an hour and then I'll be drowning myself," Margit said. She waited for Sandor to laugh, but he didn't laugh. He thought it would settle a lot, the dark pond, her dark dress, only her bleach-ruined lily-swamped hair to identify her drowned death. He'd make up a bed for himself in the room with the ink and the type. Day and night both the same he would hear the walls drip, he would start making bombs while he thought of her hands that smelled like her stale cigarettes.

Rain pasted their hair to their faces, their clothes to their skin. "If I can't come back," Sandor said.

Margit shook her head, this was not what she wanted but she wouldn't beg to be told what she needed from him. They paused at the curb but neither would take the next step. "I'm not afraid to be loved," Margit said with a candor that terrified him. He looked carefully at her features to see what Margit might accept. "I haven't loved anyone else," Sandor said. She saw how it hurt him to say what was truthful as far as it went. She looked back toward Elisabeth Bridge. "Haven't you?" But Sandor was already leading her into the darkness ahead. Cars skimmed the oil mixed with rain, pigeons queued on the slim parapets. "I can't say," Sandor said.

She sighed for the effort he made, for his scrupulous cruel reticence. "That's just it, there are only your acts," Margit said. They were all she would get, except that he pulled her to him where they stopped and her face and her mouth and

her forehead were suddenly wet. She touched the hot damp
on his eyes. "That's just rain, isn't it?"

He was trying not to shake. "No, it's not."

. . .

The boats all lined up on the bank, like worn metaphors
for some useless landlocked escape. The clock struck twelve
times and then once. She pushed a boat from the shore, she
rowed out. The boat had splinters in the oars, a bad leak
in its hull. Margit bailed uselessly with both hands while
Sandor battered his knuckles and scoured his palms on the
press. The light too high up and too dim, the paper too
rough to hold ink. He ran a candle under it, while soaked
to the waist, laughing and witless, she rowed with a calm
recklessness. The basilica lights and tall lamps winding
up Gellért Hill, all the lights everywhere faded out, flared
too bright then went black. In any direction was land she
would find when she bumped against it. Sandor blew on
the paper to dry the black ink, the blue engraved government stamp. Margit let the oars slip, she fumbled ashore on
her knees. Her yellow valise tipped from the humped awkward boat when it rolled and she splashed for a while, felt
around, the tips of her hair in the lake. He rolled her forged
residence permit once more through the platen until it was
smooth as her skin. He'd given her Erzsébet's name for her
new maiden name, Pista's last, he considered the irony of
this. Not far away Margit spilled the pond from her shoes,
wrung the hem of her muddy blue dress. He hid the paper
in his sleeve. She didn't know which side of the small city

pond she was on. Even if he found the boats in the dark he would not find her there. The wind blew against them. Fingers outstretched, they felt the pitched moonless night in their grasp. A forest, he thought, he was lost. She saw all the candles light up in the windows and thought of her mother's graveyard, Budapest as the church where she wed.

Her dress pasted flat, she carried roast chestnuts that leaked through their sack. A clutch of daisies, though there was no one to give them to now. She pulled its petals apart, left a trail for Sandor in her wake, broken stems, pollen dust.

Loves me not.

She pictured herself in a country where she couldn't understand what anyone said. With Pista and how it would be with his stiff uniform on the bed, medals on his shirt, a paycheck, but she couldn't love him for that.

She should never have gone to her Angel Street house just in case Sandor came back. Her chair, her blue vase, she already missed him so much. She searched in the vase for loose change, found an old cigarette. She smoked it. She floundered across the worn sheet. She lay down. She stood up.

She found underpants she'd forgotten to pack, she waited for her dress to dry. She turned toward the wall where shadows of bars shuffled light. Her hair hurt. A dog barked.

What now? So now what?

A car by the curb in the dawn, footsteps in the street that weren't his, then no knock. She was hardly surprised.

"If I knew you were coming I would have swept," Margit said.

One of the men slapped her face, knocked the sack from her grasp. She forgot she had been holding it. Chestnuts rolled under the bed with a flat hollow sound. She felt her half-smile with both hands, said, "It's not me you want."

The taller man combed his hair with his palms, his face florid yet tired. "Who, then, Mrs.?"

Margit shook her head. She thought he couldn't care if or what she replied.

"He jumped in the river, swam west," Margit said.

The man almost laughed. "He can't swim."

Somehow she wasn't surprised they'd know that.

They turned her mattress upside down, the porcelain bowl, Sandor's spare pants on the chair with its unmended cuffs. They searched its pockets: her barrette. They gathered stray papers from under her bed. They carried Pista's radio, one holding its box, the other the cord like the tail of some small dangerous animal between them.

"What's going to happen to me?" Margit asked. The words came out choked and too thin, she could not swallow right.

The taller man shrugged. "You'll live or you'll die."

Margit nodded. Of course she knew that.

Out in the street, obituaries blew under a flat common sky. Smoke-bitten wind ached her throat, burned her eyes. Womby clouds swam in puddles across the wet ground. Pigeons rose through the dense collapsed air toward the factory's red-starred facade.

Margit touched her hair, felt an absence in it. Her tin comb left behind, her door left ajar while standers-around in the street turned their backs.

Six o'clock by the driver's scratched watch, by the factory clock in cold light. The car smelled like pálinka, beatings, and mercy denied. Angel Street went by so fast, lamppost, other cars. She longed for a glimpse of her husband's old coat where citizens switched battered trams. The sky seemed to slide into light, the car drifted past Rákóczi Square where she'd fought with Sandor, about what, she forgot. By the library's lions they'd argued about enough money for rent.

Margit realized she wouldn't be saved by his glasses fogged up and his torn epaulet. She wanted some talisman now, a choker of gray metal type from the press. If they hadn't caught him, maybe he'd find her barrette. She had nothing of his.

The rain stopped but it started again, flat wide drops that obscured passersby in cheap hats and tight scarves. Margit envied them now.

Dizzy, she said, "I've never before ridden in a car."

The windshield wiper's metronome smeared wet leaves and dirt on the glass. The driver lit a damp cigarette, held it up to her mouth. "Enjoy it," he said. She wasn't sure if he meant the smoke or the drive, the small blue Trabant slipping under the Chain Bridge's necklace of extinguished lights.

He fished out her yellow valise, a square moon on the small city lake. Her footsteps led away from the bank. The case grew lighter as he walked and the water leaked out. Daisies littered his path. The river curved left, his shoes chafed, trucks blew fumes over him. He couldn't help but think of his wife with her hand in her coat, never gloves, the other hand holding her cigarette. Smoke rose in her hair the same gray as the clouds, her skirt blew on her legs.

Pista's bicycle stopped beside him.

"If she went to your house," Pista said.

Wind creaked the hanging stoplights. "Then it would have been better if she drowned herself," Sandor said.

They climbed on the blue bike with the yellow valise between them. He could tell they were both thinking about Margit riding the wet handlebars, how the leaves in her skirt were the same yellow gold as the colors she tried on her hair, how they anticipated her hair would soon change like the leaves, that they'd get to see this.

The rain stopped, left its pale fading ghosts on the broken sidewalk. In the dull scattered light the Angel Street house had the look of her absence on it. They pushed past the door left ajar as if anyone could come in and they had, took the porcelain bowl, stripped the bed. Boot scuffs on the floor among chestnuts, a note in her script:

ciggies
soap
bread

The sadness of its meagerness. "Ah, Pista, what have we done?"

"I thought they'd take you and not her," Pista said.

Sandor pulled out the forged document, its blue ink had run as if someone had wept over it. He took Margit's blouse from the yellow valise, wrung it out and he put it on wet. "I never believed what I did really meant anything," Sandor said. His small guilty joy of walking around in his body that came back from war was only because of her untended nails through his hair, her fingers spread over his brow, joints yellowed from stale cigarettes.

"It doesn't, it's just the attempt they can't stand," Pista said.

Sandor folded the paper he'd made for Margit, sailed it into the street. He peered through the bars at the regular day with its pigeons and trams, at Budapest's poor metaphor for his wife's body no longer hers, it belonged to the state. He could have betrayed everyone until now that his acts had her value to them. He touched Pista's sleeve. "I always loved best what was taken from me, what I couldn't possess."

Pista closed Margit's case, held it tight to his chest. "Now that she's gone, we can both love her," he said.

She'd finished her last cigarette. Between the blue car and her fate she lifted her face to the rain. She felt a raw tender love for the pigeon-swept light, for this country she hated and feared. Under its gray proletarian sky, how women alighted from trams in cheap wrinkled dresses she'd mended for them. The way cold rain fell on the prison's gray stones seized her breath, made an ache down her arms to her wrists.

All night she paced her cell's radius of two steps. The blood on the floor was still wet. She covered her ears, chewed her hair against echoes of insults inflicted on flesh. Margit wet herself. A daughter, a wife, what difference did all that make now? In the morning they gave her a paper to sign and she signed it, whatever it said.

She missed her yellow valise with its scissors and needle and thimble and thread. It was all she had left, two dozen women and her on a truck waving toilet paper farewells. They blew kisses, tossed wishes from over Elisabeth Bridge. She felt dizzy with stale bitter sweat and the sour smell of women who'd also peed in their pants.

What she desired was 'presso with sugar, a sewing machine, West German cigarettes. A bolt of shepherd's check cloth or batiste. Sandor home from a job he couldn't be shot for or hung, the tilt of his glasses her yearning to lie across sheets mussed with twilight erased through cool hands. His unshaven cheek on her thigh and limbs easing afternoon light into bells. The river's reflection of lamps. The Danube's slow curved esplanade littered with walnut shells. Almost Christmas, her mother is kind and not dead and the three of them walk to the square through a forgiving snow toward a band playing all the old lieder from war once again.

But the truck had pulled up to the train and the seats on the train were torn out so they all had to stand, just like dirty Jews, someone said.

Outside the train's window, wind parted wheat over low rolling hills. Metal blades of mechanical scythes swiped iron through the earth's yellow hair. It seemed pointless to cry, so she held her face to the glass, let the rain weep instead.

He'd been wandering the pebbled easement by the banks. Intending to weigh down his pockets with rocks, prove he still couldn't swim.

He knew where she'd be. Not in the abandoned freight car, these days, even those unmoored coaches were watched. Sometimes she stayed in the tunnel connecting the river's concourse with Vörösmarty and Petőfi Square.

If a soldier was sleeping with her, he would kill him, he thought. He thought: *I could do this easily now.*

The tiles in the tunnel were cracked, water trickling in. Piss. A caged bulb cast a stuttering green, like a radiogram. Geometrical shadows plunged at sudden sharp angles, disappeared in concrete.

She lay curled in her coat where water had run down the wall, stained it the shade of dried blood. The light jittered like an old film. Trickles and drops echoing. Sandor leaned close, checked for breath. Her hair a nest of newspaper scraps, pigeon fluff. Her fur coat smelled like a wet dog. Her eyelids twitched. On her side, her knees pulled to her chest, her calves looked cold, her bare ankles blue-veined.

For a while, he let her pretend to sleep. Overhead, the rain started and stopped, he didn't care what the rain did. He crouched by her side until she sat up, rubbed her face. She said, "I heard." White paste cracked the edge of her lips. "She's been taken away, now you're here." She leaned into the wall, her coat opened up, panties, a soldier's uniform shirt underneath. In the light, her long legs and the space where her belly showed were sea-green.

Sandor took his hand from his coat. A hundred forints crumpled in his palm like a soiled crushed green dove. "I can buy you a bottle," he said.

Erzsébet smiled up at him. "Now that she's gone, you'll get me drunk, sleep with me, finally, is that it?"

He scraped a shoe on concrete. He hadn't known this was his possible plan until then. "I might not want to," he said.

She pushed on his shoulder to help herself stand, wavering over him. "Hiding behind your scratched glasses. The cheap mystery of yourself." Their voices seemed flung from the walls.

She pulled him to his feet, held his elbow for balance as they stepped across broken glass. The outer dark pressed on the ceiling, compressing the odor of urine, a trashed pigeon's nest of wet twigs.

"Where's tonight's soldier?" he asked. They did not surface into the air.

She stopped. Erzsi touched her mouth as if feeling for lipstick. "Same place as your wife. Abandoned. Betrayed." Vertiginous shadows bisected her face. "Aren't you going to hit me for that?"

Sandor pushed her along with his fist in the small of her back. They went to the place in the tunnel where whores paid their pimps. Streetcars racketed overhead. Men sold laudanum, cheap booze in this place. Sometimes Sandor traded fake venereal health certificates here.

Erzsébet uncorked the bottle even as Sandor paid. He saw her hands shake, watched her drink, hold her breath so it wouldn't come up, drink again. A fine line of sweat broke out on her pale wide forehead. "Phoo," she said. The bottle already three fingers gone by the time they climbed up to the street.

No moon, the sky ran right down to the dirty river like a curse. Erzsébet held his sleeve. She thrust the bottle at him, but then she pulled it away. "I forgot, you don't sully your body like this. You probably want to stay pure for the sake of your wife's memory." Her laugh turned into a cough she tried to shake from herself.

They walked by a one-legged vet selling broken briquettes. Erzsébet opened her coat to him. Sandor gave him his change. Erzsébet took half of it back. "Have you ratted out your friends yet?"

Sandor looked back toward the Ministry steps. "The building was closed. Anyway, these days you need an appointment," he said. A thin simulacrum of dawn, the lights from the Óbuda Gas Factory smeared the sky.

She stumbled against him. "I like you much better this way, when you're wrecked."

Sandor kicked a loose paving stone. Pigeons rose before them. "I've finally caught the Hungarian disease."

A police car passed, its windows fogged with dawn mist. A palm wiped it clear. "You thought you were immune," Erzsi said.

Vendors were tearing down stalls in the dark along Kossuth Lajos Street, though its name too had been changed. They didn't talk about where they were headed but Sandor could guess. They both wanted the danger of it. Erzsébet paid for the tram.

"Holding out," Sandor said.

"Of course," she replied. "A girl has to take care of herself."

Sandor looked down at his shoes. "Unless she's got a husband, of course."

"Yes, I can see how that helps," Erzsi said.

Fissures of shadows bisected the walls of the Angel Street house. Erzsébet threw herself on the bed, bottle clutched to her chest. Sandor righted the tipped-over chair. A draft from the open window had blown refinery dust across everything. The radio gone that used to play Scriabin, that soft sentiment. He crossed the distance to the bed. He averted his eyes so Erzsi wouldn't notice the sour, bitter clench of his jaws, the way he was holding his breath. I won't mean to hurt you, he'd said to his wife their first time in this bed. Intentions were dust, he must have already known then. Erzsébet's hair fell over her face as she drank. She pulled him down, held his wrist to keep him away, bring him close, Sandor couldn't tell which. "Jesus, what it takes to get you under your marriage sheets," Erzsi said. She lay on her back with her coat opened out, mushroom smell rising up. Sandor touched the trough of her ribs through her uniform shirt, she touched the bottle to his cheek. The cold glass made him flinch. She tugged his clenched fist to her chest.

"We were happiest when we were supposed to be dead," Sandor said. She leaned against him. She smelled like the whole night he'd had.

"Nothing was expected of us except that," Erzsi said.

The odor of fire and blood when they crawled, swallowed mud. Erzsébet on her belly in rain.

"A room and a bed, we're out of our element," Sandor said. The high grassy field where they lay, her skin the color of lye dusting corpses nearby. Clay in her hair, snow for light, his fingertips tapping her wrist: *You alive?*

"Not like old times," Erzsi said.

The city had burned under ten thousand kilos of bombs but they'd made it across, watched the Vígszínház Theater in flames, crouched in the heat of the Serbian Church by timbers that fell near their heads. She'd licked ash from his palm, cocksure even then.

"I was afraid of you then," Sandor said, kept his eyes on the dust on the floor, away from her limbs in the light of the yellow streetlamp. Felt in his empty pockets. Looked up at Erzsébet's sarcastic mouth.

"But not now," she said. She finished the bottle, threw it on the floor where it rolled. "You just want me drunk so you can fuck me," she said. She opened his coat, found Margit's blouse bunched up under his arms and stuck damp to his chest. "That's pitiful, Sandor," she said.

Sandor blushed. "I saved it for you but it's not your size."

"That's right, I'm too large for it," she replied. His pants pressed against her pale thighs. Sandor studied her cold dirty eyes in the light from the yellow streetlamp. He touched his brow to her head.

Erzsébet turned. "I'm not just flesh you can use for forgetting," she said. She seemed perfectly lucid, lifting her face to the streetlight outside through the bars, a denial of him, of herself.

"I thought that's what you liked," Sandor said.

She struck his mouth with the back of her hand. A dog barked. He rubbed the bridge of his nose where his glasses had been. He saw his own face in the long startling look she gave him.

Sandor pushed her down on the dusty mattress. "That's the first time I've been hit by a woman," he said.

"Careful, you'll grow to like it," she said. She rolled over on him.

"We could have done this when I carried you back from the camp," Sandor said.

She held herself up by her arms, she looked down in his face. "I was dry in the legs."

"You're not now," Sandor said, his voice drunk, his hand there.

She twisted beneath him, as if she was fighting him or herself. She rolled off of him, really drunk after all, pressed his hand from her legs. "If you slept with me now, I'd just be letting you punish yourself for Margit," Erzsi said.

"That's you, you're my punishment," Sandor said. Margit gone so what difference did it make now, what he did. He looked at his hands, filth under his nails, palms scored with blue ink. He'd meant to do good with these hands. Carry. Feed. Help. He looked toward the door, but no one would be coming through there anytime, he'd made sure about that. He unbuttoned Erzsébet's soldier's green shirt, put his mouth in the cleft of her breasts. His lips burned with her salt, alcohol through her pores. He lifted his head from her chest so he could see in her eyes his own reckless regret. Slowly, she pulled him away by his hair. "We should have died when we had the chance, like you said," Erzsi said. She'd removed her panties, but it was mere habit, he thought. She lay by his side but she didn't move against him. He shook, Erzsi covered her eyes with her arms, bit her lips. Someone played a violin in the street. A cop walked past the window's iron bars, he could tell by the shoes, his own were still on in the bed.

"It's you who doesn't want this," Sandor said. He thought he sounded relieved, oddly glad.

"Sure I do," Erzsi said, but she wasn't trying very hard to convince either of them. She buttoned their blouses, her coat. "It was too soon, then too late for us, Sandor," she said. She smoothed down her patched ragged coat with both hands, then she laughed. "Now we get to stay innocent."

What's the use writing these letters to you in my head? Ah, Sandor my lover, my husband, my death. Look at this clabbered gray sky, peaked breasts of silage, sag-bellied, dangle-belled cows. We've known skies like this our whole lives. The quality of the light, one more insignificant town with its statue of Stalin still holding its own and the graves that he made.

Two more towns, this train comes to an end, we'll be walking the rest of the way after that, they've quit plowing the tracks up ahead. The newspapers aren't getting through, no more news I can already guess from the impassive faces that search my own features for clues. But I have my cheap black and white polka-dot scarf for the snow falling onto my head. It isn't so bad, I got used to that in the camp.

I shouldn't, I know, but I still always think about it: the barracks, the yard, the woodpile. The greenhouse, the place we assembled and where we assembled loose chairs, the stove where we burned half of them. The crapper six holes in the ground. Tarnya Camp's guardhouse, its blue clinging smoke, the tower, the light, the barbed-wire fence. My shadow that ran before me under it like my last innocence. It was all you'd expect from a camp, what you might become familiar with.

When we disembarked, a lone boy threw indolent rocks at our train. Boys do that. Our guard raised his gun. I couldn't tell if he meant to miss or if his aim was poor but the boy didn't fall, the rocks stopped. For a moment I'd wanted him shot.

Cold rain numbed my face and also the wish I'd just had. At the foot of the tower, guards huddled around cigarettes, rain draped their shoulders, the same pelt that ran down our backs. Wind tugged my inadequate dress. I lamented my thin city shoes and the whole rest of it.

Sixteen women and me, we were already learning to march in an orderly line. Soon we were holding our clothes in the rain, trying to fold ourselves in our own arms. I'd never seen whole naked women before, the various ways that cold flesh could assemble itself. I forced my gaze toward the factory girls' sullen mouths, the peasant girls' startled cow eyes. The long metal wand of a delousing can sprayed my hair and my chest, my behind. When it bruised the insides of my thighs, I stopped thinking about you right then.

I stepped nervous and quick past the guards, the one spigot leaking red rust. I walked fast, as if squeezed through the vise of the air, pressed between earth and sky, out of breath.

What can I tell you that wouldn't be trite, obvious? That I pissed and shat over a hole in the ground? My legs splayed, stubborn flies, newspapers crushed soft to wipe, while outside women called, *hey, new girl, quit diddling yourself.*

I could make you a list of the things I had taken for granted, but instead let me say what was there: that the barracks were wood, pieces of wall torn away for the stove. We had our first lesson on Lenin and Marx, standing two hours on the moisture-warped wood. How rumor had it there weren't enough bullets to shoot everyone if we ran. They must have exported them, too, along with Hungary's wheat, corn, and wine. And it wouldn't have been any use, the village had even less food than we did. We crouched to eat our lumpy soup, women guarding their bowls with their eyes and their hands. All of this might be familiar to you: how you think if you're scared all the time, that after a while it will stop but it just doesn't.

And my dress was already a rag and my socks a drenched mess, so I made myself try to forget Budapest in the rain, the same rain that falls anyplace, on wrought-iron lamp-posts, the benches along the Danube, on lions that guarded the opera house steps. On trams and sweet cakes that we licked from those frilly napkins in our palms in the rain in the park by our room with the swings.

Because that was no help.

In Tarnya Camp's barracks, the windows were set so high up in the wall, to see the whole sky you had to stand on a dangerous chair. Later a girl hung herself just like that from the window's iron latch with her dress knotted tight on her neck. Her crime was she'd been related to some prince. The guards cut her down, made a joke at her royal lineage, at her body's expense. Annoyed, they made us march in the snow all night long in bare feet. But that came later, Sandor, when our feet were already innured and some women said, almost casually, she's escaped. By then we shared thirteen coats among fifty-two girls. How we divvied them up is by towns where we'd lived. Some of the women who came from the farms between towns tried to claim two towns' coats. Canny, those peasants, the veterans said. Behind the outhouse, they beat those girls' faces with legs from the chairs that we made.

But that's just another camp story, you must have heard plenty yourself. Or maybe soon you'll live them.

For the moment, back then, light darkened in time through the barracks' high glass as it will. It would soon fracture, I thought, days I yearned to end that would not, moments I'd want to hold on to would be swept aside. I smoked a cigarette butt so far down I was smoking my nails. Women picked fleas on their cots, their dish-shaped faces lantern carved. I could see the round mark on the wall where there once was a clock. I could hear the guards stumbling around in the dark, they were drunk. I tried to take a deep breath but there was no such breath to be had, not for twenty-nine months.

Take it easy, new girl, this isn't Auschwitz, someone said.

But what good was that, when I hadn't been there to compare?

Where I was, though, we groped for our bunks stacked three high along three of four walls. My hand for a pillow tucked under my head. My knuckles were cold, I rubbed snot on my cheek, I was twenty-six then. Underarm sweat, a sour smell in my crotch, the damp air was teeth-rattling wet. The mattress was straw, the blanket a dreaming of warmth. Some of the women were lovers, I heard them, not really surprised. *Lenin, sweetheart, oh my Marx.* The dark ticked, someone laughed.

His hands in his coat, feeling about for loose change for the tram. He'd left Margit's blouse on the bed, found an old shirt of his, ink stains on its sleeves. He felt like composing the document of his loss from Budapest's clear-eyed despair, the city resigned to its rustle of fast-falling leaves. Or maybe it was just him. A rusty Trabant passed him once and then twice. Soon he'd be facing phony civilian clothes, those elbow-shined secret police uniforms. He was ready for it.

He watched the car belch its blue smoke at the end of the block, its own forlorn mist. Not police but his comrades climbed out, waved at him with a hesitant purpose, an unsteady casualness. Angled and awkward, they covered the distance too quick. Their faces were stupid beneath some flushed rigor of expectation and dread. He recognized shame and submission, but also resolve in the set of their shoulders, a feverish self-righteous stance. Before he could put words to it, he knew what was happening to him. Sandor shielded his eyes, suddenly prescient. He didn't bother to run, he smiled down at his feet. Their hands firm on his arms and his back, he smelled pálinka, fear on their skin. The three of them muscled him forward wedged in their short hasty steps.

"Et tu, Brutuses," Sandor said.

"Watch your head," Laci said as they shoved him in the back seat.

No one spoke in the small blue Trabant, Laci and Csaba and Gyuri harsh-breathed as the car crossed Elisabeth Bridge.

"Fellas," he said.

They passed a bottle around but Sandor wouldn't drink. Gyuri sat squeezed beside him as if he might leap. "You smell like a woman," he said.

"That's just Erzsébet," Sandor said.

The boys laughed, then grew contemplative.

"It's not what you think," Sandor said.

"You're the one thinking it," Csaba said. The car passed a convoy of green army trucks. "Now that they captured your wife, you'll have to betray us," he said.

"I promise I won't," Sandor said. He heard how this must have sounded to them. He said, "Who put you up to this?"

Csaba hid in a cough, Gyuri turned red. "Try to guess," Laci said.

"He must have done it for love," Sandor said. Outside the car, rain dripped from pedestrians' shoulders and hats.

"If they don't already know who you are, Margit will tell them," he said.

"We can't be logical now, we're desperate men," Csaba said. Rain gathered in potholes and ruts, earth and sky wore the dull brown and white of a torn cigarette. Cool, and they hadn't brought coats, so whatever happened would have to be fast, Sandor thought.

"I'll forge a paper that says I'm deceased," he told them.

"No more papers, that's what started all this," Gyuri said.

The car rocked to a stop. Sandor wondered about not the what, but the why of such a dumb fate. Perhaps it was just punishment. Because of his unblinking gaze at his brother's smashed death. But this was mere disingenuousness. Careless pride got him into all this.

Leftover rain beaded the hood of the small blue Trabant. They strolled with false casualness up a path of gray mud. The woods were bucolic, rainwater ran in a ditch.

They had some old gun.

"I suppose you have bullets in that," Sandor said. He could not wipe the smile from his mouth as they walked him around aimlessly in the woods for a while, guided him tenderly over pinecones and rotten tree trunks. Laci was crying, Csaba was stoic, Gyuri would not look at him. Their voices were taut, hissing under their breaths. "What if we make him promise to run for the border?" Csaba asked.

"Cross my heart," Sandor said.

"Shut up, you're the prisoner here," Gyuri said.

Sandor recalled he'd played this game with his brother before, tied his eyes with a rag, walked him into a tree on purpose. He couldn't help thinking that first ruination of trust led to this. A bush in the woods they had backed him against. Gyuri held his arm at arm's length, Laci pointed the pistol at him. His eyes red and wet, he couldn't have aimed very well. "Wait, don't shoot yet, let me get out of the way," Gyuri said.

Sandor looked at his firing squad, a dappled confusion in shadows, threadbare as he was. "No blindfold?" he asked. "No secret trial like Kádár? Not even a tree to lean on." He turned toward the woods, to run, when somehow the pistol went off.

"Jesus God," Gyuri said.

It didn't hurt, much. Sandor lay on his back, wondering if he'd see a white light. If all those he hadn't loved, much, would forgive him and hold out their arms. The boys bent over him. "We're sorry," Laci said. Csaba was trying to unbolt the gun, which had jammed.

"If we were each other I might have tried this myself," Sandor said. The bullet had passed through his side, he felt full of largesse, a calm benevolence. He looked up at birds flung on the sky, tried to memorize swoop and arc, the whole history of flight. He turned his head, laughed at the farce of his own pinkish blood, but he almost passed out. He watched the boys' feet move about beside him in the scrub. His shirttail rode up, he liked how the grass itched his back. Grass along Lake Tisza's banks in the spring when he'd wed: That was hope, that was then.

"What will we say happened to him?" Gyuri asked.

"A hunting accident," Csaba said.

"Hunting reactionaries," Gyuri said.

Sandor felt like laughing again but thought better of it. He said, "Hunting real communists."

"Another Trotsky," Laci said.

His father liked Trotsky the best. Combing his hair in the yard, the sad understatement of him. *Don't marry a sad girl*, he'd said. *Don't do what I did.* Cleaned his press. His mother canned apples and plums. Didn't care for her much, maybe that's what he'd confess.

"I'm bleeding to death," Sandor said.

They were touching his face and his hair, relieved, as if now that they'd made the attempt, they could call it an accomplishment.

"Don't shut my eyes," Sandor said. He wondered if Margit would want him to live. Maybe it was a sign that he would that he couldn't pray yet.

"You did it for money, you're really a capitalist," Csaba said.

Sandor thought of the papers he forged: scrip for food and for clothes, for housing and passes to go from the city and live in the country, a permit for work or for school. If you were a Jew, a paper that said you were not. The year you enlisted, even if you never had. If you wanted to wed or pretend that you had or had not. He said, "Got to buy Margit ciggies, soap, bread."

"He's delirious," Laci said.

Sandor felt his shirt soak with blood. "I offered the glorious future," he said.

"Just like Stalin," Laci said. They lifted him up in their arms. Sandor laughed, he said, "Jesus removed from the cross."

They carried him toward the car. "Don't blaspheme," Laci said.

"My life is supposed to be passing in front of my eyes," Sandor said. He tried counting the times he had slept with Margit, what he'd never done, what he had. "Pista will love her," he said.

"He's raving now," Csaba said.

He tried not to bleed on the seat of the rusting Trabant that careened over ruts, bottles rolling around. Gyuri said, "If it hurts, moaning helps." Sandor covered his face with his hands. A great loneliness came over him. Nothingness. He kept coming to, arms tied to a hospital bed, and his legs. Three dark men beating him, their shiny blue suits shifted the light from outside. Somewhere in there he was telling them he loved his wife. A chair and a bucket and mop, a window revealing the tops of some trees, the dark undersides of gray clouds.

"Where am I?"

"It's our little joke. The hospital where your friends carried you."

He wished there was any picture on the wall, Stalin or Lenin, his wife.

"Before the war, which side were you on?" someone asked.

"Communist, then," Sandor said. He had no photograph of Margit.

"I was never that," someone said. Someone said, "Lovely teeth your wife had."

He wept for her teeth while they left him to shadows and piss and his blood in the bed. They took time from him, an unknown quantity of it passed. After a while he wished they'd come beat him again, end his dread, and they did. They seemed playful and cheerful to him. Maybe they didn't care if he told or whatever he said. "My wife draped her bra on a line from the door of our room to the sill. My glasses would catch in the straps, fly right off," Sandor said.

"That's not a confession, it's merely nostalgia," the man bending over him said. He couldn't make out their faces too well.

"Where's my glasses?" he asked.

The man said, "You don't want to look."

Anyway, he couldn't have, blood filled his eyes because they beat his head with the mop. "My best friend fell in love with my wife," Sandor said. He pictured the boys' snowy breaths as they flipped dog-eared cards toward where Margit had tented the sheet, her knees drawn to her chest. The men in the room filled up the bucket with water and drowned him in it. They left him the shame of his body's beshat bloody mess. They came back with a hammer and beer, cigarettes.

"Which handed are you?"

Sandor pitied himself. "Left," he lied.

"We'll spare that one, then. They unfastened him from the bed, dragged him down to the ground. Someone sat on his chest, held his wrist. He couldn't remember it now, but he'd learned in school how many bones in a hand. It wouldn't take much to save it: *Laci hid the press. Csaba swiped tips at the Galamb Cafe to pay for the ink. I printed the fake documents, Gyuri carried them under his hat.*

"You broke my father's hands, too," Sandor said.

"It must be hereditary," the man with the hammer said. His eyes, Sandor thought, weren't unkind. The hammer was already bloody from somebody else.

They worked, and their work was his hand.

He wished he'd pass out, but they kept throwing water on him. "Don't be brave," someone said. If he hadn't yelled himself mute, he'd have replied he was not. They lifted him back on the bed, gave him a cigarette. "Don't set yourself on fire," they said.

"I couldn't, I'm all soaking wet. They laughed high in their throats, giddy with violence. "You can get names from any of them," Sandor said.

"Sure, this is gratuitous." The man who spoke retied his wrists. "The whole city's made up of stories like yours." Tied his legs.

"So it's not personal, then," Sandor said.

No one replied, it mattered so little to them and not so much even to him. He wanted nothing to do with this body that lay in the bed. They unwrapped his side where the bullet went in, took the lit cigarette from his mouth, stuck it there. Sandor thought he had already made all the sounds they could make come from him. They pulled the soaked sheet from his belly down over his knees. He felt lucid about what they might do to him next. A relief to be finished with that. If he lived, he'd be pure, clean, unblinded by lust; maybe wisdom would come.

Pista came in the room wearing an officer's hat. "Fellas," he said.

The men seemed relieved they could stop.

"Small country," Sandor said.

"Smaller man," Pista said. He took off his cap, folded it. "Are you pretty much finished with him?" The hammer lay on the sheet, messed up with fresh blood. He picked it up, tapped it gently against Sandor's thigh.

"Where's Margit?" Sandor asked.

"Tarnya Camp," Pista said.

"Is that all you have to say about it?"

"Everyone just wants to get through the night without having to carry you out of here dead," Pista said.

"It's still daytime out," Sandor said.

The men laughed, they seemed pleased to have been made to laugh. "You won't be so lucky twice," Pista said.

"Of course you already know about that."

Pista stood over him, clinically studying his hand. "Look what you did to yourself."

"You did this," Sandor said.

Pista tried calming a twitch in his cheek. The men drank their beer. Outside the door, nurses passed, careful not to look in. "Better confess or they'll cut off your dick," Pista said. He winked, or perhaps it was only the twitch.

"You'll tell Margit for me," Sandor said.

Pista sighed. "Maybe they'll kill you from kindness instead."

Sandor smiled. A quick death made sudden good sense. He said, "You know so much about them."

Pista rubbed the new Party pin on his uniform's ironed lapel. "I *am* them," he said.

Outside in the dull bluish light, leftover rain pearled the shivery leaves of the trees. Sandor tried thinking of water that ran in the woods, a fresh stream. If he could have laughed he would have; he wouldn't care for the forest again. Pista wrapped his hand in a rag. "I'm saving you, idiot," he said under his breath.

"No matter what anyone does, everyone dies slow or fast," Sandor said.

"Don't be morbid," Pista said. He sat gingerly on the bed.

"Don't get me all over your crisp uniform," Sandor said.

Pista wiped Sandor's hair from his face. "They won't really kill you, they want to see what you'll do next." He looked down at Sandor's manhood. "But they'll kill Erzsébet."

Sandor thought it would not be unseemly to pray or to beg, but he couldn't kneel or sit up, or support himself on one arm, or place his palms one to the next. "You're lying," he said.

Pista narrowed his eyes. "Go ahead, take that chance."

She'd wrapped her legs around him as he carried her from the camp. *I'm not a small woman*, she'd said. Then, he was not a small man. He looked at his friend, the soiled sheets, his wrecked hand. He could not carry Erzsi again, or even reach down to his side that had bled on the cigarette stuck to him there like a gag. He would learn all about himself now. A pity that this must be love, and what he'd do for it: He gave them the names and the rest.

She counted the barbs on the fence hedging Tarn-ya's south side, sixty-nine barbs between posts. She used them to count up the days she'd been sidling up to that wire, one side to the other, and then she'd start over again. It had been several times.

The fence was not electrified.

Afternoon snow in her hair, on her shoulders and back. Tuesday laundry day, Wednesdays they hauled stones from a pit, one pile to the next in the yard. Harder to carry each day with the turnip and coal rations cut.

Hey, seamstress girl, but she didn't care to be called or called that.

A mouthful of pins, buttons in her chapped palms. Her shoulders were damp with wet snow or provisional sun.

Always some dress like a slippery doll, a dead doll in her arms.

Cold and hungry, she thought: on Thursday, the man who brought coal, how she wouldn't have to say much, just brush by his legs, brush his legs, let her wrist graze that boy's coal-blacked arm. She told herself it was all right because she was frozen and starved, he'd bring her some food or warm clothes from outside, that they'd find some small darkened place with just enough room to lie down. From the war Margit knew about tight wedgy darkness like that.

Wednesday she took off her ring, slipped it under her tongue.

Thursday came, she brushed his arm.

He said, "So, seamstress girl," so her name was of use after all, it set her apart to remember her by.

"Excuse me," she said, then, scared, she brushed past him and ran to the yard, biting her palm by the place where her dresses froze on the clothesline. She gathered them all, the faithful familiar squirm of each one, shouting "Safe," like the child's game she'd played in the space between buildings when she was a child.

Next week he followed her out in the yard, threw her down on the ground.

Not here, not now!

But if not here, where? If not now, when? This was camp, everything was right now, his cold hand up underneath on the pants she wore under her dress, on her thigh.

Guards watched from the tower in the field with its brown wizened range weed and rocks. Fifty-two girls took their turns on tiptoes on the chair until the barrack's windows fogged up.

They hurried behind the outhouse. She let him lead her by the hand, as if they were off to a dance. He pressed against her, covered her face with both palms.

"Goddamn it," she said. "How many shovels of coal is this worth to you now?"

Was she talking to him or herself?

His pants down, her face dark from his hands, all those clothes that were still not enough against cold to be wrestled aside, their coats and his knees tangled up, her fists on his shoulders, she wanted to cry but the wind would have carried it off.

"Ah, seamstress girl," the man said, breathless, done, while she crouched on her heels in the snow by the planks of the leaning shack.

She struggled up on her knees, he wiped snow from her ass.

"So, next week, then?"

"Coal man," she said. "Bring more coal." Then she laughed.

Pista got a prescription for him, Sandor slept for a week or a month in his bed. He awoke into leaves like the color of Margit's valise. Dawn flickered, a grainy newsreel. A phonograph played Russian records, the only kind you could buy. Fragile, the disks broke from their own sentiment. He lined up Pista's empty bottles by the couch to watch over him when he left.

Dizzy, he lay on his sheetless mattress. Rain, leaves or snow, he couldn't see what fell outside the window very well. Pista brought him new glasses, cracked the same place as the last. He could almost see clearly except for blind spots in his head. Pant cuffs flapped by the bars of the Angel Street house like countryless flags in the wind. He straightened his trousers' damp crease with his awkward left hand. Now he would not have to plan anymore, even think. He'd be the same as the rest, unabsolved under statues and flags.

Thököly út, Kiraj út, Szent István Kert, the names of the streets held no meaning for him. The static of rain in the puddles distorted his steps. A girl at a crossing looked just like Margit in 1946. *How it would be: I never told you differently*. He passed the sidewalk where he'd sold documents. He leaned over a puddle of rain, his features felt bare and ashamed, his eyes burned.

Erzsi found him at the zoo, making faces at the smaller apes. She laughed at him through her teeth, in his face. "Did they ask about me?"

"Not exactly," he said.

Erzsébet shrugged. "I wouldn't have cared what you said."

He leaned up against a lamppost and showed her his hand. A statue of Stalin leaned under the trees as if he, too, was looking at it.

"Jesus Mary," she said. She recovered herself. "Can I touch it?" she asked.

He eased it into his coat. Margit had rubbed it when he'd mashed it up in the press, she'd used toothpaste once as a salve.

Erzsi bought peanuts she tossed in his mouth one by one. "Now that you gave up the boys you're a whore for the state just like everyone else."

The rain stopped, sun nearly broke through the haze. The cages smelled rancid and sweet, drying animal fur, Erzsébet's cheap rabbit coat and dead meat. She held out a government paper from Szentes: His father was dead. Smoke from a fire burned the sky, it left ash on his shirt, on her sleeves. He sat on a bench, lifted the document up to the light, "It's not counterfeit," Sandor said. One hand shook and the other one ached. *He took me fishing, we dangled cheese balls for bait.* Minuscule fish had glittered the shore then turned milky, opaque. His father had fallen asleep, cheese and string by his feet: *the old man.*

"He used to say we're all dead men on leave," Sandor said.

"That's Lenin's line," Erzsi said.

On the train, he leaned into the glass, cold and wet, his forehead feverish. Peasants drove carts through the fields, as they always had. *His father's cheek puffed for a kiss; he'd backed away, then, without knowing the reason for it. Schoolboy arms crossed on his chest, guarding a secret contempt that he couldn't name, yet.*

"My silence killed him," Sandor said.

Erzsébet's cigarette smoke coiled dull white like train steam in her hair's manic red. She looked coolly at him. "Sometimes the things we don't say are what save us," she said.

He thought of himself in the hospital bed. "Or they kill," Sandor said. Some of the towns had changed names but not his, it still meant sainted. Rain swamped the yard where his father had tucked the hundred forints in his shirt. The old man lay under the blanket from his childhood bed, head lolled to the side like he was abashed to be dead.

"You left him to die in this house by himself," Erzsi said.

"He sent me to war," Sandor said.

No one had shut his eyes, it seemed he was turning away on purpose.

"He gave you a reason to come back from it," Erzsi said. She pulled up the blanket, exposing hard toenails curved over, uncut.

"You did that," Sandor said.

She pretended she hadn't heard. "Didn't even invite him to your wedding," she said.

He followed his dead father's gaze toward his pencil-marked height on the wall. "He wouldn't have come," Sandor said.

She looked up, her face pale. "You didn't want him there."

He shivered. He only felt bad for himself. Then he couldn't stay in the room with Erzsébet's eyes upon him, near her body and the one in the bed. He searched the whole house for money to pay for a hole in the ground and a stone for the name and the date. Empty jars on the pantry's top shelf. They used to give him nightmares, the plums in their purple compost like shrunken heads. His father had labeled the homunculi with the names of Hungarian kings. *No escape from our history*, he'd said.

Sandor leaned in the door where Erzsébet sat on the bed, bent over his father's mute form like sharing secrets. "We'll have to burn him," he said.

His father's hair stuck up in tufts, she patted it down with both hands. "You don't expect me to be a party to that," Erzsi said.

They stood in the rain while his father's smoke rose from the kiln where the peasants baked bricks. Across the horizon, bent figures seemed to grow out of the dirt to glean weeds from from the earth. Useless, mud from mud, Sandor thought. The people cost him and his father their hands, blood-love for this land. His father had underlined words for the Magyar travail in the pages of books flagged with torn paper slips for his son's benefit. He could not easily place them there with those mangled fists, mark the record for him, set the cold metal teeth of blunt type into names in the *Hódmezővásárhelyi Hírlap*. Betrothals, feast days, obituaries in small print. It seemed right that now his father's son could hardly remove those small paper scraps, turn the pages with his left hand.

Erzsébet studied his face as he stepped foot to foot by the kiln. In her eyes he could see his own guilt. Overhead, a crow flapped through the haze of his father's burned flesh.

"There goes your conscience," Erzsi said.

He carried the boxful of ash gingerly, as if he was wary of it. He set the old man in his cheap scrap-wood box on the counter beside his chipped cup. Mouse droppings in the sink, a spoon and a rifled mousetrap. Outside the window, his father's stained underpants floated like ghosts from tree limbs. Wind blew through the house like after his brother lay under his mother's escaping footsteps.

They lay in his father's deathbed. *His books were the smell of his skin, pages turned with pained water-soaked fingertips, watermarks across history's parchment like lost continents.* Wind stripped the tree where his boyhood swing used to hang, its ropes frayed and slack. The hoe leaned against the woodshed, among the more innocent farm implements. Erzsébet lay beside him, her long body under his hand. She laughed. "Look at us. What would your father say about this?"

"He'd remind me that I was conceived in this bed," Sandor said.

She blew impatient smoke in his hair. "Lucky I can't have a child, it might have to repeat everything." She pressed herself into his back, a petition of need. "Well?" she said. "Well?" She touched him, he removed her hand. She moved toward the wall. "If you were a man, you would have died for your boys," Erzsi said.

He scratched Erzsi's neck. "You just about did."

Erzsébet turned to face him. "I talked to Pista. I know what happened in that hospital bed." She smoothed the sheet between them with a quick nervous hand. "You shouldn't have saved me again. You ought to have let me be done with what started in the camp."

Sandor sat up and slapped Erzsi's face. She smiled at him through her tears from the slap's suddeness. "So we're even," she said. She pulled him on top, wrapped her legs on his waist, tore at his sweat-soaked white shirt. "Now, do it now," Erzsi said.

He couldn't lift himself over her gracefully with one hand. "You told me we'd stay innocent," Sandor said. His elbow and knees struck her cheek and her hips, but she didn't flinch, didn't help, said, "We never have been." They kept their clothes on as they met because death had got in the mattress. "Fuck you. I hate that I love you," she said.

Their train left at six. Bouquets of scooped peasant fires capped the rain-shellacked hills. Behind him his abandoned home at the field's edge where real country began. Before him his Angel Street house just this side of where Budapest ends. Margit wasn't waiting for him. In the city they carried his father across the Chain Bridge. He held the box awkwardly, Erzsébet opened it, stuck her thumb in the ash and bone chips. "You should try some kind of prayer, just in case," Erzsi said.

Sandor gripped the box in his good hand. *His father asleep. Black hairs on his father's pale wrists he had rubbed until they'd stood on end.* He said, "God is malevolent."

Betrayed and betrayers crossed the span between Buda and Pest. He leaned over the side, tipped the box in a gust of wet wind. His father blew all over him.

Dear Sandor, I hear you're not dead.

Her cold hands, paper spread on her yellow valise. The train has been stopped by the state, by snowdrifts. She's made up her mind this will be her last letter to him: *November 8, 1956. They're sending another engine to pull the cars backward through towns.* History's wounds she's just passed. *Perhaps there'll be no need to write after this or I won't or I can't.*

She scrapes her knee when she jumps, touches it, lifts her hand to her mouth, a red laugh. She's never been sentimental about spilled Hungarian blood.

A woman alone, she meets men. This man in this town, he makes shoes, he says she could stay here with him. "A girl needs an advantage," he says.

She doesn't want to go to his house, she just wants to

go, but a girl has to eat. Leave a trail of bread crumbs for Sandor to follow at least.

Did he want something mended, perhaps?

"I stitch shoes, I can sew my own clothes," the man says.

She studies his wrists, she wonders about the utility of his puffy fingers for this.

Six o'clock and the new locomotive has come. A light wind from the west stirs the branches of trees without leaves. "Where's you husband?" he asks, though she isn't wearing her ring. Margit shakes her head as they walk from the tracks, already angling toward his house. She doesn't want him to tell her his life but she thinks that he will. "I was a radioman in the war. I wasn't fat then," the man says.

Was there a sergeant, a cook? A baby pulled from a blue cow? She looks anywhere except toward questions she doesn't dare ask. At crows on the wires, leaves on snow tramped by horseshoes to mud. His house is a little bit falling down but all right.

"If you can sew, you can learn to fix shoes," the man says, "It's done with a big needle press."

That last word startles her, then she smiles. They stand on his steps, wind blowing her coat. This town: a granary, quaint thatched roofs. Storks from the old poetry still alight from the chimneys at dusk. A typical cart hauls damp wood, the usual crone sweeps the slush uselessly at the side of the road. "It's all so goddamned familiar to me," Margit says with despair on her breath.

He says, "What do you know about anyplace else?"

She's never been with a fat man. His long guileless eyes and no charm, she likes that. "I'm tired of it," Margit says.

But time has run out for the consideration of likes or her long weariness. There's only this moment, the one where the train blows its typical whistle and goes.

The man turns up his palms toward the train that just blew its whistle and went. They could cover her face, easily half her back. She wonders what it would be like to be so largely held. Her slight discreet body, her calm and implacable mind, it was Sandor who once put it like that. Sandor's wrecked hand on her brow, he was right, it's all been a political act. Like fucking to eat, or eating to live, if only to find out whatever comes next.

The man's front door is wide, but she won't go farther than that. He's handing her food on a plate, she's eating as fast as she can, it might be a while till next time. Stuffing whatever it is in her mouth, too fast: trying to keep it down.

The checked napkin he holds at arm's length is a flag to entice her inside. She longs to be kind, wipes her mouth. "If I slept with you I'd have to forgive myself after," she says.

They both stand there startled by this.

"You could just carry your guilt," the man says. Behind him a picture of him in his radioman uniform. She likes a uniform, still.

"I want to travel light," Margit says.

Inside his house she can make out wax grapes on a shelf, porcelain statuettes and his floor has been swept. "I think it's already too late for that," the man says.

Margit picks up her valise. Sometimes she hardly feels any regret, sometimes she feels all of it.

"I'll lead you toward the border," he says. He also wants to be kind but she won't owe him for that. She has to decide by herself if she'll cross, or if not she might like to lie down in the snow on the ground. But she couldn't do that, Alma already used up that act. Margit hands him the letter she wrote. "You could mail this for me if the post is still working," she says.

A scrap, some smudged lines.

"You think it'll get there like this?"

The paper greasy from her palm. Margit says, "I'll write down the address of the Interior Ministry, Budapest."

He raises his brows: *It's like that*. Let's use mine so he can write back, the man says. Margit laughs. Crows crowd the man's yard for the crumbs she has spilled on the ground. He's folded the letter into his shirt but now she wants it back. "You'll read it," she says. Perhaps that's her intent.

"Sure I will," the man says.

Margit shrugs. "Then add I was faithful to him."

He moves his hand toward hers. "I'd like to have to lie about that."

She steps into the road, "There's been enough lying," she says, though what would it hurt if she did or did not, if she had her betrayal with this man?

Leaves on the ground, the sky's windblown graveyard of clouds. She's already moving from him, the warmth of his house on her chest. His broad back and that big leather press. Resistance is her form of faith. If she were to sleep with him now it means Sandor is dead.

"You have convictions," the man says from his door.

Margit tucks her hands in her coat. "The Russians have convictions, too." *Belief doesn't make a thing true*, Sandor said. Nonetheless, one has to act. She holds tight to herself for a walk toward the border, a fence.

October it rained all the time. He was born in this month thirty-one years ago in 1921. Short dark days. When it rained, Sandor thought of Margit. His hand ached.

Late afternoons, on the floor or leaned over the creak of the chair, Erzsébet didn't care what he did or she did. They were not necessarilly gentle or kind. He liked that. She brought him a glove because Margit would have, furry brown, with a finger chewed off. He wore it like some ersatz count while they lay everywhere he and his wife never did, then they moved to the bed. "I always wanted to sleep with a big skinny woman," he said. Tangled up in her long arms and legs, he grew quiet as they rolled over Margit's hairpins. Erzsébet shifted from him. "Suddenly there's a crowd here," she said.

He pulled Erzsi's wrist, said, "Maybe it's one of your soldiers from under the street." He covered her body with his until there was no way to stop and no possible thought. After, he liked feeling guilt.

Taller, long-hipped, she knelt behind him with no clothes, pressed herself to his back. She rested a hand on his shoulder, the top of his head. "It's not going to last," Erzsi said. Sandor wasn't sure if she meant the Rákosi government or the new five-year plan or this.

Sometimes they went to the zoo, the animals humbled by rain. The cages seemed empty, no people but him, Erzsébet, a few monkeys, the birds. Wet, they ate peanuts, suddenly they were *us*, then she left for the men he'd carelessly mentioned in bed.

Time: shadows on buildings restored since the war, though most held their old bullet holes. Sandor poked his fingers in them. Mostly rain, and when he had enough he went to the library's warmth, read Schopenhauer, cheered himself with sublime German pessimism. When he walked out he tried to distill what he read, as if one day he'd insert the dark difficult words in some forged document. He held on to their mood: Budapest.

The Danube, its wet yellow trams ridden aimlessly between Kispest and Pest. He thought about his father's hands. His father liked Hegel and Kant. Pages underlined and dog-eared, the old man mourned certainty, blew nostalgia into a wide handkerchief. Birds filched his long pencil shavings for nests. Not a little proud of his hands as Sandor was of his, *because now I've suffered, too*, but this was a common Hungarian trait.

Wind blew across Vörösmarty Square, the trees sighed for it. To order his mind, Sandor tried to think discrete thoughts:

If he had a job it would take seventy hours to earn enough forints for one pair of shoes. His head full of bullet holes, print. People turned discreetly from his hand. Erzsi waved from a tram, he ran to catch up, she jumped off, she kissed him openly in the street. Well, this happened once. They sat on the paws of the lion by the opera house steps, didn't say anything for an hour while she smoked and philosophy dissipated with her smoky blue breath, his hand warm on her slightly damp blouse underneath her fur coat. Choked with heartachy rain and soon, snow, he felt filled to the throat.

Long nights, while she stayed in the city, the tiled underground where rain dripped, he gathered her clothes from the floor and tossed out the candies and earrings she'd brought home from men. Pista shuffled a deck of torn cards but Sandor felt too distracted for games. He said, "Read my fortune instead," as he knelt by the low window bars, watched for Erzsébet's steps.

"That won't do any good," Pista said, but Sandor didn't want to do good. "Knowing my fortune or waiting for it?" Sandor asked. Clouds passed over the moon as he thought about how he used to make Margit wait just like this. Two o'clock, four, shadows moved time from the floor to the ceiling and bed.

"They're going to take her away," Pista said.

"They already did."

"I mean Erzsébet."

Sandor forced himself slowly to walk to the porcelain bowl. "I paid dearly for that not to happen," he said.

"She's charged with moral corruption. It's not politics," Pista said.

"Aren't they one and the same?" Sandor asked. He felt Pista watching his back as he rinsed out his cup with one hand.

"Your wit's still intact," Pista said. Out in the alley, someone banged trash cans around. "I've fixed it to send her to Tarnya, look after Margit."

Sandor wondered if Erzsi and Pista discussed his wife's future in bed, at the zoo, or the dim passageways as he laid out the cards with her fate. He smashed the cup in the sink. "I thought 'looking after' was what the camp did."

"It's the best of worst camps," Pista said. "At least Tarnya is run by us Magyars," he said. They looked at each other a while. Sandor would have laughed, but his hand hurt him more when he did.

"It'll be for the best. You don't want adultery tagged to the list of your crimes," Pista said.

Sandor picked out the shards from the bowl, he dropped them like coins one by one into Pista's cupped palms. "Who's keeping your list?"

Pista fed jagged chips to the vase Margit used to save change for the tram. "You are, your hand is my conscience," he said.

Sandor squeezed his fist, the pain worse when you talked about it. "My conscience sickened and died from neglect," Sandor said. He put on his coat, the brown glove.

"Sure, that's why we're going to see Erzsébet," Pista said.

They pulled up their collars, stepped into the street. Daylight didn't rise, it had simply become manifest, Sandor white as the sky as they drove through the dawn through the outskirts of Kispest toward Pest. "Erzsi says women make love to women in camp," Pista said.

Though it was cold, Sandor had soaked through his shirt. "So you're saving my marriage," he said.

"It's for Margit's sake," Pista said. He didn't slow for red lights, puddles streaked stoplight red. It had started to rain. The car crossed the nameless industrial span between Buda and Pest.

"That's two women you've taken from me," Sandor said. Remnants of some Stalin parade, banners and streamers turned mush still littered the Ministry's steps.

"Good thing you still have a best friend," Pista said.

Erzsi seemed neither surprised nor resigned as she waited for them. Laughing, her makeup had run. A government man held her arm. Bedraggled, she'd fought. "My twin Judases," Erzsi said. Pista led the government man to the idling Trabant. Sandor fooled with the hem of his coat beside Erzsébet on the bench.

"Judas loved Christ the best," Sandor said.

Erzsébet narrowed her eyes. "Just another false god." Sandor looked at his shoes. He wouldn't dice theology with a woman whom God had personally tried to wreck. "At least ours murders us honestly, without pretense of justice or love," Erzsi said. Her breath smudged the air, the car exhaled acrid blue smoke. "Love enrages me, Sandor," she said. She tried lighting a damp cigarette, the camp he had rescued her from and the camp yet to come in her trembly hands. They looked at the street, at the rain, at the car steamed with breath. "How many times can you save my life, anyway?" Erzsi asked.

Sandor considered the futility of all acts. "Twice so far," he said.

She stood over him, dropped ash in the cuffs of his pants. "So you kept me alive for this little vacation to Tarnya," she said.

He held her cool fingers inside his good hand. "It was worth it," he said.

"For you or for me?" Erzsi asked.

"I'd do it again," Sandor said.

Erzsébet pulled away. "For who's sake?" The rain stopped, then it fell, the windshield wipers on the car stopped and started again. "I won't miss you," she said, took his wrist, made him look at her face so he'd know what she meant: her lank bony spine as she rode over him, her hair like a bright collapsed fire on his chest. She squeezed his wrecked hand so he would remember her pained narrow smile of runny mascara and rain as she turned, walked away, the halo of cigarette smoke risen over her head. She looked back before climbing the steps. "But the zoo, that was nice, wasn't it?"

Like autumn turns leaves, leaves fall and the rain becomes snow, it covers my shoulders, the train I have left far behind and my hair, my face numb like my feet were in camp.

In Tarnya snow fell like regret. My monthlies dried up, another woman hung herself. When weariness bludgeoned me dreamless at last, someone stole my socks while I slept. I could have laughed, except for I wouldn't be able to live through the winter or work without them. I roamed up and down the whole camp staring at women's ankles and wept.

Always a colorless, hourless sky, the blurred field unfettered by trees. Past the fence, new girls trudged toward the wire, fear and a little hope, still, in their gun-prodded steps.

Erzsébet wore the same scruffy fur and cheap boots but her head had been shaved. I wanted to laugh or to cry or cry out, it did not matter which. Like meeting a lover in snow by a train our eyes met, our eyes held. Could we have, we would not have embraced, I was glad circumstance held me back. Fate passed with hardly a shrug, a near smile between us. There was nothing to do but take hold of the stone that was handed to me, pass it on.

Time was rocks. Women like large forlorn crows shook afternoon light from black skirts, beat their palms on their thighs for some warmth. Erzsi and I, we swayed by the wire in an orgy of weed cigarettes. "I slept with your husband," she said.

I sighed, I was hardly surprised, this was just one more fact I could do nothing about. I said, "He enjoyed you so much that he turned you in, is that it?"

Erzsébet's eyes reflected the blinded-eyed sky. They gave almost nothing away. She said, "Anybody could have."

I ran my palm over her scalp, a petty revenge and I took little comfort from it. I said, "You've returned to the place you belong." The scars among angry red scruff made me jerk back my hand.

"So we're going to fight over him while all this is his fault," Erzsi said.

Whatever forbearance I had passed from me like the light from the seven-hectometer yard. "I choose to blame you," I replied.

Erzsébet flicked hair from her brow but her hair wasn't there. "His father died is why I slept with him, I did it from pity," she said.

I narrowed my eyes. I'd already set aside whole human categories of despair, longing, grace. "I'm happy they shaved you," I said.

Erzsi opened her palms. She studied the women digging for edible roots on their knees with bare nails in the dirt. She said, "I can't go through this camp shit again."

I looked at my shoes, snow skittered across my ankles like a threat. "At least there's some justice," I said.

Erzsébet laughed. "Then how come you're walking around with no socks and you're freezing to death?"

That evening I dreamt of my feet being amputated. The saw was a strand of the wire from the fence. Sandor held the wire in both hands. "You slept with the coal man," he said. The rasp of the saw was the women outside scraping dawn from their tins.

In the yard Erzsi knelt on the girl who had stolen my socks, she'd stuffed them inside the girl's mouth. "You have to break her fingers," Erzsi said.

Break them! Break them! A shrill madness seized everyone. Snow fell on us all, on the women who watched, on the casual guard brushing slow-falling snow from his gun. "I won't do it," I said.

"I didn't tell you the best part," Erzsi said. "They caught Sandor and smashed up his hand." I didn't believe her until I looked into her eyes. I lay down on the girl tenderly as if she was a bed. Erzsi's body felt rangy and hot. A collision of bones, we breathed into each other's faces while women beat spoons over us. We bounced on the girl as if she was a carnival ride. Snow fell across her jerky legs, her hair fanning out behind her on the snow-covered scrub. I held her

fingers in mine as if I might have comforted her: a big girl
but still soft, we hadn't even learned her name yet. Erzsébet
yanked her hair like she needed that tangle all caught in her
fist. "Aren't you going to have pity on her?" Erzsi asked.

The girl moaned beneath us, pressed up with her belly
and chest on our thighs and the backs of our legs. I bent
back her fingers, they cracked.

The letter from her in his coat. The dirty sidewalk, dog-eared cards.

"Who's wife was she, anyway?" Sandor asked.

Crouched on their heels, weightless coins, some matchsticks in the pot.

"*Is* she," Pista said.

The deck two queens short, their knuckles were stiff from wind.

"I'll see you, raise you her barrette."

"You can't bet stakes you don't have."

The sky hung from clotheslines. His palms dirty from two days outside. "Why? She's good for it." He swept coins from the ground.

"Show your hand, you haven't won yet," Pista said.

Sandor thought he should husband what words he had

left for his wife. He said, "You've seen my hand." He turned from his friend, he would have turned in his friend. They knew that. He left Pista chasing down cards through a cold sudden gust.

Nothing encumbered his hands but the Tarnya post-mark's smudged blue ink, the thin paper pale as the ghostly indent of his gone wedding band. His aspect in windows he passed suggested transience. He paused in the wind, surprised that the steady hand holding the letter from Tarnya was his:

> *It's Christmas, we get to write one letter home,* she wrote him.

If he could, he'd have turned his shoulders on himself. Under the statue of winged victory in the plaza of black pulled-down hats, a woman blew wisps of stray hair from her brow like his wife.

What kind of a girl I've become, Sandor, you couldn't guess, Sandor read. Wednesday's newspaper blew by sopped with gutter-soaked lies. Her handwriting spiky, abrupt: *Snow and wind blows all day and all night, but you don't need a weather report, so I'll get to the point: I clutch your treachery to my chest like a newly-torn dress.*

Her hair seven years in his grasp, stiff yellow weeds by the bright yellow chair where mornings she'd waited for him, so nervous she couldn't keep anything down. *Christ, Sandor, I thought you'd been caught.* They'd jumped up and down to get warm, pins in her teeth, soon all tangled up among strangers' clothes she had sewn in their bed.

A pity we only get one piece of paper for this, Margit wrote. *So I have to know: What we had, was that love? Does love last?*

Two crows in the crab-apple sun, the light gray like the blunt-penciled letter she sent: *I hope you are well and I don't want to miss you, sometimes.*

At the Galamb Cafe, to honor his wife, he ordered water and bread. His face felt afflicted, the woman beside him kept looking at him.

"I recognize you, I bought some papers from you," she told him. He touched his fingertips to his lips. Pushing her palms through her hair, she was trying not to look so much older than him. Sadly, he thought, she'd feel compelled to tell him her name, she'd insist. He bought her a torte, watched the slight sheen of sweat on her brow as she ate. "Too sweet," she said. "Are you sweet? Like this cake?"

He didn't want to care for this woman at all and he liked her for this. He took off his glasses so he wouldn't be able to make out her face. "I'm like bitter chocolate," he said. "I leave a bad aftertaste."

She shrugged as if this didn't matter, she moved to his table and rested her chin on her fist. "You're afraid now," she said, "though you weren't before, I can tell."

Sandor rolled his eyes. Tarnya pulled like a falling-down fence.

She shivered, her eyelids were damp. "Me, too, but I like it," she said.

He thought he should wipe the glazed torte from her mouth but thought better of it. "I used to think fear was the proof I was doing a thing that was worth it," he said.

She touched his sleeve like it was a casual gesture, unplanned. "Then you did something bad that made you more frightened than you'd ever been," she told him.

Greedy, her hand, Sandor thought. "Like what you're contemplating with me," Sandor said.

She lifted her head, pressed her thumb to the pulse in her flushed, exposed neck. "I haven't been blameless in years and I'm fifty," she said.

He put on his glasses, glad that the lenses were fogged so he couldn't see her so well. "I won't sleep with you just to make you feel younger," he said.

Sleeplessness etched her eyes. "Do you practice to say things like that?" She ran her fingers on the edge of her glass, a gesture that unbalanced him.

"I'm already rehearsing the past tense for us," Sandor said.

She pushed back her chair and swayed in the salt-colored light over him. "Don't think I'm lonely, it's only my body that's lonely," she said.

He wanted to reach out to her, steady her, but he didn't do this. "I can't afford anymore bitter nostalgia," he said.

Casually, she leaned down, grazed his face with the back of her hand. "Don't kid yourself, friend. Hungarian man. Sure you can."

She sat with the coal man at dawn in his truck, her feet propped on the dash. The cab wasn't warm, not their regular place to lie down. She said, "You could drive me right out." Coal everywhere, so she was a little bit smudged.

"But I won't," he replied.

"Sure. You prefer it this way." She rubbed coal from her dress.

He didn't reply for a while, then he said, "Listen, Margit."

She looked over at him. "Oh, boy," she said. "That 'listen, Margit,' I know that."

He played with the ends of his shirt. "That new redhead," he said.

Erzsébet's hair had grown in, a soft brush, it was even more red. Margit moved close to the door. "Well, I don't care. So give me a cigarette, then."

He lit it for her; it, too, was coal-blacked. She blew smoke on the glass. "Jesus, it's freezing outside." Her body felt already cold and alone. She looked toward the fence. "I didn't not like you," she said.

In Kispest, rain fell across snow that had not melted yet. Sandor went to the station, watched trains headed toward the camp. He could not make himself go. Starting to go but not gone. Time, the trains passed, one hundred arguments with himself.

"Make up your mind, or do I have to carry you there?" Pista said.

Almost gone but not yet. Rain like the sadness he'd have to endure banged the tin overhang. But he liked the rain, how it offered a mood for regret. "What could I say that wouldn't seem useless to her?" Sandor asked. He'd say what he must to allow her a way to stay married to him. About how he loved not the dark but the woman who stood before him. She would accept it, expect it, even, because that's how it was between them.

"Tell her that when she gets out, you'll make a new five-year plan," Pista said.

Sandor looked at his hands, the good and the bad. Soon they'd both be numb as his hair as he reached through the fence. He thought of his shame as just cheap sentiment toward every small thing, small birds on old snow, lamp-posts topped with snow hats. Communists.

"She won't forgive me," he said. His words sounded false with that terrible pride he so quickly forgave in himself. He felt almost buoyant with knowing how bad it could get.

"No, but you'll have to forgive her for that," Pista said.

Sandor could see them both clear by the camp's spike-sharp fence. His marriage's winter, his breath like the thought it would end. *I know you're not sorry*, she'd say, *but I never cared about that.* He wondered if he could still make her believe he believed what she said, if he'd even make the attempt.

"You're just afraid she won't take you back," Pista said.

Sandor laughed. The train waited for him. In the cold future he'd reach past the wire and comb down his wife's windblown hair with one hand. The wind would keep messing it up but he'd keep combing it.

"No, I'm afraid that she will," Sandor said.

Late afternoon. The weight of wet snow on the roof of the slant planting shed. Sunk to their knees, looking for smokable weeds, scrawny fruit for the wine Erzsi brewed. Curled pill bugs under the boards, soft-spined creeping insects for the soup. The shed far enough so you could pretend there weren't barracks nearby.

"You fucked him, too," Margit said.

Erzsi regarded Margit with a sly ignorance. "Who do you mean?"

Months of sour apple wine strained through rags. A clear narrow view of the fence so you wouldn't forget where you are, the days shortest now, rashes, lice.

"The coal man, in his truck." Margit wanted to get off her knees, rub their small-stoned indents. Outside, women who could sang *who's lonely for men?*

"Only because it was warm." Side by side on the floor of the shed, coats buttoned up to their necks. Erzsébet telling so many lies who could tell when she lied? "Now I'm what you have left." She raised herself up on her arms, put her mouth against Margit's mouth. Not a kiss but a fact. Margit did not close her eyes. Swallowing, dry, she tugged loose wet hairs from their lips. Later she thought, *you didn't even try to draw back.*

Elbows, long bones in cold rags, Erzsi's pants at her shins. Erzsi's hair, everywhere stoplight red. Margit rolled away on her face in the dirt. She had heard about this. She'd heard this. Spittle cooled on her chin, pigeons walked on the loose metal roof of the shed. Erzsébet climbed her hips, plowed her back like a field with her belly and chest. Sprawled apart, breathing hard, Erzsi pulled Margit's dress, Margit helped. What she didn't know she could guess: She pushed Erzsi's head down the length of her coat with both hands.

Shame: her own smell. Eyes rolling up in her head. *Oh, God*, glad that Alma was dead.

Then she was amazed it was still daylight out, that there was an outside out there, at her salt across Erzsébet's lips.

"Now you me," Erzsi said, greed, loneliness in her body and arms, the V where her muddy legs met, guiding Margit down there.

Don't laugh now: wet coal dust, like old wine. Margit surprised how Erzsébet's ribs rippled under her hands reaching up.

Hoarfrost at the edge of the glass. Margit shaky but laughing a little and wiping her face with both palms. Erzsébet held a cigarette against Margit's lips. "You're more impressed with your feelings than you are with me," Erzsi said.

Margit smoked, happy she'd somehow had her revenge. Later she thought, *whose revenge?* Later she realized how quickly she'd need her again. Searching to see where she was, but Erzsébet cool, with nothing but time to haul stones, the patience to wait out the rocks till they moved by themselves.

Not snowing now, shadows of underpants patterned across the cold ground. Erzsébet looked toward Tarnya beyond the camp fence. "It wouldn't be hard to see anyone who sneaked up."

They studied the footsteps of women and guards, cart tracks on the opposite side. Margit touched Erzsi's thigh. "You'll tell him, I bet."

Someone had knocked out a tooth: Erzsébet's knocked-out smile. "No, you will."

He jumped from the train, tore his pants. A brown shape by the side of a road, who goes there? Winter engulfed his thin shoes. Familiar, the wind through his knees, winter woods and the wrong clothes for it. Borsova, Doboka, in villages buried since Szent István's time, he collected flat tooth-colored stones to throw over the Tarnya Camp fence. Threw them at dogs, instead. Melted ice on his tongue, made a fire to dry out his socks.

He got a ride in a cart with twined hay in the back. "Going to Tarnya to visit my wife," Sandor said. The man whipped his horse in the eyes.

"There's no wives there, friend."

Sandor didn't need to ask what he meant. "And my lover," he said.

In the salt-colored light, Sandor navigated by breath. What he owned were his small vanities: how he parted his hair, how he tightened his belt. He felt nostalgia for himself: *I came this way, once.* He had only just come back from war, he had yet to assemble his press. *I was a real Communist, then.* He'd become older, but when?

. . .

The nervous wind rattling the slats made her jumpy, asweat. Still shaky from Erzsébet pressing her skin, she put on her charcoal and beets, camp makeup that had to be damp to adhere to her chapped bitten lips.

Erzsébet steadied her wrist. "Look out the window," she said.

A distant commotion of brown on white snow, a fade, a slipped hunch, the motion that caught in her throat where the field met the fence. A rock flung.

She told herself bird, sparrow, crow, but she knew Sandor's aim: stones tossed on a crop of old rain. She turned from the glass. "I go first."

Erzsi shrugged. "You're the wife."

Dawn rose windy, violet. She walked to the wire as if she could steady the image of him with her brief, cautious steps.

"You're alive," Margit said. *But not quite.* Her coat flapped in the wind.

Sandor stretched his good hand through the wire. "I brought cigarettes."

Margit grabbed them as quickly as any camp peasant would have. "You forgot to bring matches," she said, searched her pockets for them. Wind pasted his pants to his thighs, Margit's coat to her legs, the flame cupped in her unsteady hand. A brief, cautious triumph to the toss of her hair, "Smoking now with my husband," she said. Her eyes teared from the smoke and the cold.

"I haven't been able to take a deep breath without thinking about you," Sandor said.

Kind, how he didn't mention her coat looser now, its deep rends. "You've been practicing that," Margit said.

Wind rattled the barracks' wood slats. He could not meet her gaze, scraped his shoes, dug his heels in the dirt. She suddenly thought of herself on her knees in the shed. She exhaled a blue cloud, her pulse a flung rock, a missed stitch. She leaned back, she felt narrow with him. "What happens next, Sandor?" she asked, grateful for the wire between them.

"You're going to finish the rest of those smokes," Sandor said.

"I'm already queasy from this one," she said, though she wanted the next cigarette and the one after that. Beside them, two crows pecked at stones, they seemed to be counting the meager alottment of moments they had. Morning chill in her bones, she stood far enough that he'd have to reach past his grasp if he wanted to touch. "You smell like you've been in a fire," Margit said.

"Had to burn leaves, dry my socks."

Margit looked down. His shadow was already gone. "But you're not wearing socks."

"It didn't work out," Sandor said, flapped his singed trouser cuffs.

Margit laughed. Flustered, she plucked at her dress through her coat where a button was lost. "I've worn this same dress all along just for you," Margit said. She was testing how good she could lie, but it wasn't exactly a lie.

He stepped foot to foot, rubbed his knee through the hole in his pants. "Things get wrecked, you mend them," he said, as if this was some feat only she could perform he'd forgotten about.

"I guess you suppose I'll just mend them again," Margit said.

Sandor shook his head. "They're my only pair, I can't take them off."

She put out the last cigarette, saved it for Erzsébet. "Steal some then."

"If I do that, there'll be no need to fix these," Sandor said.

She remembered this logic of his. A near smile tugged her mouth. "You haven't changed," Margit guessed.

Sandor spread his left hand, hid the disfigured one. "And you," Sandor said with a question in it. She watched him peer over her shoulder for clues to what he shouldn't know that she could decide not to tell. She leaned into the fence, her sleeves catching on it. Its wire bit her palms, but she couldn't seem to move them. She lowered her head to the barbs, felt scratches bloom on her cheeks. They didn't hurt, much, her face hot, frozen, numb all at once. "Erzsébet's waiting her turn," Margit said.

He reached through the wire, combed her hair with his fingertips. It felt to Margit like he'd been rehearsing for this. "I'm glad you came first." Sandor lowered his head. "I'll steal you a brand new barrette."

She blushed. Cursed herself. She would never forgive him for this. "Idiot. Just bring food," Margit said, "Your dumb pants." She opened her coat, pulled his bad wrists toward her ribs, not sad for the bruises on them. She looked down and let out her breath. It was worse than she'd imagined it. "Does that hurt?"

"It's the hand I used to set type."

Margit nearly smiled. "Oh, that's good, Sandor," she said.

Sandor looked away fast. The sun rose on the field with its crows and the barracks' worn slats. "I'm sorry," she said. She meant for having made the remark, not the content of it. They stood there a while, Margit holding his wrist gingerly, Sandor wiping his eyes. "Another year, Sandor," she said, pressed her palms to his chest.

"I'm not good at waiting," he said.

Hands already accustomed to hands through a fence. Behind them the flat scrape of pans.

"I could never hold out, myself," Margit said.

He's standing before Erzsébet. Her hair is a wild russet thatch, it has not grown in yet.

"What are you going to do, hold visiting hours?" she asks. Light snow falls over their coats, obscures their shapes by the fence. So far, he's spoken her name, nothing else. Her smell—smoke, dried sweat, sweet perfume splashed over her unchanged skirts, daubed on her unwashed neck.

"Why have you come?" Erzsi asks.

He doesn't say it's from duty, desire all mixed up in it. A guilty need to see the results of his deeds. For them to take pity on him, though already he sees there's scant pity to spare around here: blinding white snow, women carrying stones under it.

"I arranged something, Sandor, I'm getting out soon," Erzsi says.

Three o'clock, in an hour it's dark. Wind blows over their eyes.

"I suppose soldiers can be bribed the same way everywhere," Sandor says.

"You're not hurting my feelings," she says. The women have finished hauling cold stones from one place to the next.

"I won't carry you this time around," Sandor says.

She steps closer to him, her lips split from cold, peeling red. "You'll always be carrying me," Erzsi says. Whatever she uses for lipstick is vivid against her gray skin.

"I'm going to live differently," Sandor says, though he doesn't know how he might accomplish this.

She looks down at his knuckles all smashed. "Living's a talent, she says. "Like some people are naturally good with their hands." She pulls his wrists toward her belly and legs. "Feel me up. Use your bad hand," she says.

All these clothes in the way. Fumbling her skirts, Sandor laughs, she won't help, she leans into his fist. Her pale forehead presses the wire as she moves against him.

After, he wipes a thin streak of bright blood from her brow. Snow has soaked through her dresses, dried and got wet again. Stiff layers the shade of the woodpile and wood, of the villagers' shoes the same brown as turned earth.

"We can't do this again," Sandor says.

Erzsébet smiles. "That's just something you need to say now."

They watch the snow cover their tracks, obscuring the barracks, the guardhouse, the camp whited out.

"We can't bring the city to Tarnya," he says.

Erzsi straightens her dress. "We don't have to," she says. "Even here, we're ourselves."

He tramples a path back and forth across black frozen mud from his shed to the camp. Bare strangled trees behind him, brown carts on the road's scabby soil through the snow. Men straggle home from the meatpacking plant, dark rusty blood on their jackets and pants. Ruts gouge the wagon-churned road, horses the same dirty brown, dirty white as all that.

Margit studies herself in a pounded-out-flat sardine tin, pushes Sandor's barrette through her hair for a bouffant effect. She walks through the yard where she stands with clothespins in her chattering teeth, reaching up to the frayed rope clothesline, one knee bent.

He crouches behind a snowbank as he has yesterday and the day before that, pretending to hide just to watch her do this.

Who has time to be lonely? the women all sing. They know he's her husband out there, Erzsébet is her husband inside, in camp nothing's missed. Everyone sees how the seamstress girl can't decide between them, kicking ice or the coal truck's black tires, exhausted from searching the fence and her camp lover's flesh. Her ambivalent gaze toward the road, then the shed, whistling for Erzsébet.

Nightfall, when the guards are half drunk, women watch Margit's flats scuffing up frozen mud, her slight shape on the day's white collapse. Count her steps to the barbs where he passes her weedy bouquets, cigarettes. They wipe steam from the glass to watch him unbutton her coat and her dress awkwardly under it. They imitate her nervous laugh.

Sometimes it's a game, how she leaves her dress dissarayed just for Erzsébet's glance. She pats the black eye Erzsi gave her for this as she sews Sandor's torn skinny pants.

On Erzsébet's cot, in the dark, Margit peels off her dress pasted wet to her back. "Have you told him about us?" she asks. The lice-picked blanket in her fist might be her Angel Street sheet, her scraped half-moon knees tenting it.

Erzsébet smiles as she only does in the night. "Don't worry, I'm saving the news for an auspicious moment," she says. She pinches Margit's breast, hard, that pull like the rushing of blood inside Margit's head as she lies across Erzsébet's chest.

. . .

Dusk and he's stood so long in white snow he's snow-blind, it has scored his eyes pink. He's grown used to what wire allows, the almost enough of a touch, the barbed gap a kind of carress.

This time it's Erzsi who comes to the fence, smokes a weed cigarette. "Soon I'll be sprung and then what?"

"I won't sleep with you when you get out," Sandor says.

She blows smoke in his eyes. "Only each time you lie down with your wife."

Sandor tilts his head, tries his best interrogative smile. Erzsébet mimics him. "Go ahead, ask Margit," Erzsi says.

. . .

Sandor walks to the place where Tarnya and Tarnya's paved road run to abandonment. The shack is mere loose wooden slats for the rearrangement of wind. Sleep is like being awake except that it's colder and dark, no church bells. In the morning he makes a small fire in a pan, shivers into himself.

Margit paces the fence as she watches for Sandor's quick steps. At the edge of the field, two crows, the milk cow, the goat named Stalin.

Sandor's glasses reflect the white sky as he hands her another barrette.

"I only have one head of hair," Margit says.

"Give it to Erzsi, she likes pretty things," Sandor says.

Margit doesn't blush, though she thinks Sandor's waiting for it. She puts the barrette in her hair as a way of not looking at him. "We have to decide about us," Margit says. She scratches the bites the wire has dug in her arms. Florid, they itch when she thinks about how it will be when there's no more barbed wire between them.

Sandor scrapes his heels on the ice. "Are you scared about what happens next?"

Her dress buttons snag with the necessity of reaching for him through the fence. "Should I be?" Margit asks. Small rusty holes on her dress, burns on the pants she keeps mending for him.

"Maybe we should ask Erzsébet," Sandor says. The wind opens a gap between them, their shapes close to the wire as they dare without cutting themselves.

Nobody asked anything. One night the fire in his pan got too large, Sandor burned down his shack. He was finally warm enough, clothes and hair singed by flames. Margit's yellow valise he had brought all that way was the one thing he had he could save.

He wandered into the town, toward its single light from the engineer hutch by the tracks. He played cards with the engineer girl. She kept looking down at his hand as she talked about Marx.

"I'm in the resistance," he said.

The girl frowned. "It's the perfect state, so how there be such a thing?" He couldn't tell if she might be joking or not. She wore her hair in long braids down her back.

"You're almost charming, in a socialist way," Sandor said.

"Charm is a bourgeois conception," she said, her face flushed.

Sandor thought of himself at her age. He would have been in the war, whatever he'd learned in his father's old books blown apart. Truth now belonged to the engineer girl. Her ideals that caused everything bad might even save him, he thought. He said, "I used to make bombs."

She undid her braids. She made him aware of himself in a way he'd not noticed in a while. He wondered if he'd told his lies to get her to perform this act. She reminded him of the way Margit watched him set type.

"What happened?" she asked.

He'd never have time to tell her, he thought, and he lifted his hand. "They worked," he replied.

She got him a job, one hand good enough for a flagman who flagged the freight cars. He hastened the trains toward the border where guns disabused optimists. He slept on the floor of the engineer hutch while the depot clock froze overhead. Mornings, he watched as the engineer girl shunted locomotives around.

She came in from coupling and uncoupling cars. "My big choo-choo set," she told him, the day white as her breath. He ran water over his hand, sometimes he could almost flex it. When she pushed herself to his back, it wasn't just to get warm.

"I thought Marxism didn't allow for such close dialectics," he said.

She did not move from him. She said, "Take me away from this place."

He turned, pulled the hair from her face. "My wife's in

the camp, over there," Sandor said, like they didn't both know where it was, or it might be a lie like the stuff about bombs.

She said, "I'm too smart to stay here." She undid her engineer coveralls' top, three snaps on each side. Sandor fumbled them shut. Soon he would have to return to the fence, ask Margit what Erzsébet said he should ask her about. He wondered if others also regretted the future as well as the past.

He looked at the posters, a tractor, a combine and threshing machine on the wall. He said, "Perhaps you can think your way out." Maybe she could; he could not. He looked at his hand as if he'd done the damage himself and he had. He hadn't picked the wrong side, but the other side won. *Won hands down.* Sandor smiled at the dialectics of where the blame lay and whose fault.

The engineer girl tried to look fierce in the dim rising light. She said, "I'm not kidding about what I want." She must have thought he'd been smiling at her because she was only eighteen, she'd grown up in a house made of sod.

"No, Marxists aren't known for their sense of humor," he said.

"Marx's humor was swell," the girl said.

Sandor picked up the cards but could not shuffle them with one hand. "Then tell a Marx joke," he said.

The engineer girl touched the side of his face. "You're living in one," she replied.

Margit thought they might all freeze to death. Lucky the coal man brought coal, luckier still that Erzsi and Margit knew him. They loved him, perforce, in half-hour shifts, each in turn and eventually all three of them in the coal truck's cramped cab. "A lesson in physics, a new way to make heat from coals," Erzsi said. Margit drew tapered hearts, Erzsi drew oval skulls, love and death's pictograms on the glass.

Sometimes when Sandor was late meeting her at the wire, Margit wept all over the yard. Sometimes it was all she could muster to drag her footsteps to the fence, her duty to visit with him.

"The women aren't singing," he said. He'd brought hard candies, a fish, and another barrette.

"They're praying for relief from the cold," Margit said.

Behind her coals tumbled like dull Christmas bells in the bin.

"Too bad we traded the old weather gods for the son of a new one who just dies and dies," Sandor said.

Margit pinned the clasp in her hair. "Anyone can do that."

In the barracks, the women hung Margit's barrettes from the holiday tree, then Christmas was burned for the heat. By New Year's two women had walked in the snow and lain down and they didn't get up. They were her mother's age if she'd lived.

By almost March, a few skunk cabbages, saxifrage broke through ice. "I've cut my deal," Erzsi said. She'd gathered what she owned in her coat, what she stole in her sleeve, camp makeup, cigarettes.

"It's just more whorishness," Margit said. They were saying farewell in the shed.

Erzsi laughed. "Kiss my ass."

"I already did that," Margit said.

Erzsébet held her there with both hands, face to face in half light. "A new physics lesson, how bodies attract and abandon each other," she said.

"That's not new," Margit said. She grasped Erzsi's waist, her hair in her hair as she shifted her hips.

Erzsi kissed her on the mouth and walked out to the yard while Margit got down on her knees and smashed crockery shards.

A few drops of rain. In the camp the women have nothing to cover their heads but the rocks, if they could hold them aloft.

Twelve women stand by the fence, the rest behind barracks' windows where it's almost warm. The women outside are hoping to see the bad-handed husband and lover up close, but he's nowhere around.

The seamstress girl won't leave the shed, the tall redhead has no bag. A car waits for Erzsébet by the gate, she won't have to walk from the camp to the town. She turns on her heels in what's left of the ice. Maybe she's trying to make herself dizzy like drunk. The women are waiting to see if she'll laugh or cry or fall down, she's done that. Instead, she says, "Shit," says, "Margit, you idiot," and climbs in on the passenger side.

The coal truck's wipers swipe finger-smeared traces of damp hearts and skulls on the glass. The coal man keeps his windows rolled up, his truck follows the car.

Pigs in the road: the car and the truck have to wait while they cross. The major from camp is blowing his horn while Erzsébet smokes, she does not turn around. She reaches into the major's crisp uniform pants. He slaps her face, backhanded, hard. They all look at a horse carcass by the side of the road slashed by peasants with axes and knives.

Tarnya is a small town. Everyone knows when somebody leaves on the train and what time. The engineer hutch's windows are fogged up. Sandor has picked up his flag and walked purposely to the side of the rails where trains arrive, away from where they depart.

The coal man watches Erzsébet cross from the car to the tracks. He keeps his window rolled up as she boards, the major's hand on her ass. He watches the coaches but he doesn't see her inside. Maybe she's already lying down like she did on the seat of his truck, so she doesn't see Sandor running across to her side of the tracks, shoelaces undone, shirt untucked.

The hard ground started its early spring thaw just as Stalin died. Tarnya held a mordantly joyful parade, Sandor didn't sing the old songs from the war. Rákosi, Hungary's Jewish king, was deposed. Nagy claimed he'd let all the prisoners out any time. Spring was mud, the weeds were too feeble to pluck. Margit played cards with the woman whose fingers she cracked. A vain, silly girl, she'd become beautiful in the camp. She brought Margit homemade gifts, an unironical doll made of socks, one of twigs. Margit was as touched as she'd let herself get. "I was in the resistance," she said.

The girl filed her nails with a stone. "What happened, they catch you?" she asked.

Margit sighed. "I saved my husband by getting arrested," she said.

"That man with the hand," the girl said.

Margit held her palm to her brow as if trying to remember far back. She needed to fashion the past from what she could invent. "Before the war, he took me to glittering dances in old Budapest," Margit said. Though she would have been twelve. Though what she recalls about him had come after the bombs: Sandor's shoelaces undone, that she'd found this charming then: Sandor running toward her, almost tripping on them across snow and ice.

The beautiful girl held her wrist. She said, "I could take Erzsi's place," let her hair fall across Margit's lap. She looked even lovelier in the dim setting light. Margit didn't laugh, she appreciated the attempt.

"Your gesture is superfluous," Margit said, "now that we're getting out." She hadn't noticed what real beauty was before now. If she ever cared about it, it should have been at the age of the beautiful woman who stared at her eyes. Young girls all blood and rush, how she should have been at that age, but Margit could only guess.

At the fence, she lit her next cigarette. Sandor bought them for her with the flag-waving money he earned.

"The new regime's commuting sentences," Sandor said. Margit looked at the ground. Sandor took off his glasses, wiped them on the tail of his shirt. "Isn't that what you want?"

"What I want," Margit said. It seemed to her lately the closer they got the farther they moved away from their bodies and thoughts and their eyes hardly met. She didn't say anything else, she did not mention Erzsébet. They were saved by the guard-tower light over them, relieved at what neither would have to explain, if they even could have.

A white day, the vague shape of the sun through the morning's high clouds. April first, she'd be the third woman out. In the barracks the women can see their white breaths, the stove has gone cold in the night.

"I'm glad we didn't do anything," Margit says to the girl whose beauty is marred by the hand she bent back.

"You would be, you've already done way too much," the girl says.

Margit doesn't say she feels like she's been all alone in her head all this time. Maybe she shouldn't think. She's wearing the dress she wore when she arrived, pressed for her husband between the slats of her cot. Her coat is haphazardly patched. She carries no sudden departure mementos, no scarf. She wants to leave as she came, not a single barrette, no makeup, though her hair isn't blond, and it hasn't been cut in six months. Her sturdy shoes have held up, but her underwear's so thin it perverts modesty just to wear it at all.

She sits for a while on her bed while women come whisper good-bye. She hangs her head, because why would she cry? She picks up the brown bag by her side, her sewing things and the sock doll inside. She looks at the wall where the portrait of Stalin is gone. A forbidden crucifix there. A film star. She squashes the butt of an old cigarette, it has traces of Erzsi's red lipstick on it, tucks it into her dress.

The women hang back, a few follow her to the door, fewer follow her into the yard.

In the metal shed where the officers drink is a paper to sign. It says she'll be good from now on. A guard searches her bag. "What do you think I might be trying to smuggle out?" Margit asks.

He rattles her needles and laughs. "Coal," he says. "You paid for enough of it."

Margit can't be bothered to blush.

The women are carrying rocks, as she passes, they put their rocks down. She looks at the large pile grown smaller, the smaller pile growing large. She thinks, *soon I'll be glad.*

Seventeen steps from the heart of the yard to the wire. The beautiful woman's been following two steps behind. She slips her address inside Margit's palm. "Will you write?" Margit folds the note in her sleeve. "I won't, but I'll think about you," she replies.

She nods to the guard by the gate where the coal truck might come anytime. Sandor guards the outside. In the space between wire and road, he's holding her yellow valise and white flowers.

"I expected a different weather," she says on the opposite side. Still, the air and the sky and the ground seem so wide. She won't meet Sandor's eyes. She turns toward camp but the women have already turned to their rocks.

She takes the valise, not the flowers. If he took her hand, she'd accept them, she thinks, but Sandor walks slightly ahead, she walks slightly behind. Margit smells the scentless white blooms. Hothouse flowers, they must have cost a lot, must have been hard to find.

Low scrub alongside the road, old snow heaped by a plow. Margit runs toward a copse of thin ice-burned trunks. She hasn't been close to a tree in six months. She presses her brow to the bark as a truck not a coal truck goes by.

She barely remembers the crude potholed street or the mercantile shop. Women carry fishnet bags, someone sweeps market day from the ground. Men look up from tables along the sidewalk. She watches Sandor's barely perceptible nod while men study her calves. He should be carrying her yellow valise but she won't give it up. A few women pass, Margit glances from them to her husband who studies the mud.

"Haven't you made any friends?" Margit asks. "Aren't they coming to say their good-byes?"

Sandor looks at his shoes. "They play cards this time of day," he replies. He keeps checking the train station clock but it shows the wrong time.

"What else do they do here for fun?" Margit asks.

"They watch trains," he replies.

The two of them sit on a bench farthest from the engineer's hutch. Margit keeps an eye out for coal trucks, on her husband who tries not to look like he's looking around.

Side by side in their raggedy clothes, she lights her first free cigarette. "Here I am smoking freely," she says.

"And I'm waving your cigarette smoke from my face once again," Sandor says.

She laughs. She thinks, *Christ, this is hard.* "Listen," she says, shakes her head, touches Sandor's bad hand instead. "Does it hurt very much?"

They both look at his fist like it's not what they're talking about, some unpleasant suprise. "Not when your hand's over it," Sandor says.

Margit squeezes her knees against her valise, puts her face in the flowers. *Don't be foolish, don't cry.*

Across the platform, a woman in coveralls waves until she's obscured by a truck. The train comes.

Dear Erzsébet: Who else can I write to but you? My dead mother, perhaps?

Here I am, free, scared, and sad, writing letters to you in my head.

The sky is so wide, a hard icy blue. The wind seems to want to come right through the panes of this roadside cafe, stirring the red and white checked tablecloth, the white napkins, our hair.

We've ordered a beer, but we don't drink beer, and roast meat, pushing it around with our forks. Food sickens me. Erzsi, you know what this means.

Sandor eats with one hand, he puts down his fork, he strokes the inside of my wrist. It means only, *here we are, us.* He's looking at me but his wandering eye is on Saint Stephen's portrait on the wall, though I know he's not really seeing it. I wonder what that gaze observes when it doesn't see me. You, perhaps? The blank nothing? Our fate? I would not really want to ask him. Would you, Erzsébet?

. . .

Dear Erzsébet: I bet you never got a letter before, not from Nyírbátor, headed west. I'm just nervous, that's all. Here, too, the free air is open and sharp, like a brisk stinging slap.

You'll probably leave this brief note somewhere careless until it grows thin as the light in our old basement room, pale as the Tarnya Camp wall, its days and months tallied in coal. What I wish to write is porous as thought on such a bright windy day it takes your breath away, your eyes tearing up. I'm sentimental, you see, and I'm scared yet I'm hoping it's love.

. . .

Erzsébet: We'll be on our way toward Debrecen in a minute, he says. We'll be sneaking trains east to west. He says, "We'll have to walk some, maybe hide in the woods," and I know he's thinking of you, of the plural *you two*. Before you even get this, I think, we'll be home.

This must be the season for burning the dregs of last season's harvests too wizened and sour, too crabby or wormy to bother about. I have a new fountain pen I won't use Sandor stole, though he left behind two polished stones, three pressed leaves in exchange. You know how he is.

. . .

To Erzsi, far from Tarnya now, in Karcag, halfway through the Great Plains. I don't want to despoil this one piece of paper I have is why I'm writing on snow, across tablecloth dust, in dirt with the heel of my shoe.

April fourth and I'm wearing cheap Emke perfume I found here in a store. I've spilled it on our coats. "We smell like a whorehouse," I said. I'm afraid Tarnya's made me a little bit coarse, or perhaps it was you. We have three hundred forints that Pista has wired us and our smelly clothes. We have foamy mustaches from beer Sandor bought we've smeared across each other's mouths with our mouths. This will make you jealous, I hope, but I know you better than that, and of whom?

Sorry, I'm a little bit drunk. I'm thinking about my narrow thighs under your palm. Jesus, God.

. . .

Erzsi, I'm thinking of you. Waking from sleep, your ungenerous lips, your remorseless face. I see you've left the window open, letting what will come in come in. I see you there now, you don't take off your coat for the cold, looking up at the fishy-skinned sky and ignoring this note. Dawn makes the page indistinct, that low white unforgiving light, and you blowing cigarette smoke on the pane until you grow dizzy, you hear your own blood in your ears. Or maybe that's me.

Down in the street where we lived, where Sandor says you're encamped in our Angel Street room, a dog barks, the ice truck comes and goes. You look at the wall, its continent shapes that by now might have merged into a single contiguous stain. The one Communist world, its plaster swollen when it rains. You're brooding in fine sneezy dust, not sweeping the room to prepare it for us. I see you turn from the glass, touching your hair all grown out. The tick of the pipes, the radio news leaking in from next door. It claims there are going to be some reforms any time. You're still keeping enemy lists in your head like you did in the camp, gathering evidence. Sandor told me you never don't think of the war, his palm on my sleeve, and I said don't mention her name unless there's a funeral involved. Your fingers close to mine on our cot. I wonder how much you'll say about us, my slight feet and hands, yours so large. You wiped my face once, and one time you lifted me over your head as if I was your child, but you would never have put it like that.

The weather has turned into almost pleasant at last. In front of this Szolnok cafe, birds are waiting to carry messages. Sandor studies his hand all day long, fascinated by it. The white tablecloths here are filmed with fine patches of soot like the walls of our Angel Street house. I'm just happy to pick up my yellow valise, Sandor's diffident touch as close as he dares to the flare of my dress in the wind. I haven't told him anything, although he must certainly guess. About the coal baby inside my womb: Erzsi, maybe it's yours. Here's a good joke, why don't we tell Pista it's his? Excuse me, I'm more drunk than I thought. This letter crimped tight in my fist, there's not a lie in it, it says simply, "We're on our way, Love, Margit." I'm walking toward a train, ankle deep in rough weeds. I'm putting one foot in front of the next, no one's carrying me, I'm afraid to come home, Erzsébet.

No one greeted them. No Pista and no Erzsébet, they weren't really surprised. The Angel Street room seemed so tiny to him, mean and cramped. The bulb overhead cast a pale lurid glow on the floor's unswept dust and the bed. He stood by the window: the spindly tree, loose chain and legs of the swing. Why would this have changed? He looked at the street, nothing passing that he hadn't seen. "I hate this place more than my hand," Sandor said, he held up his curved fist.

"Well, you can't cut it off," Margit said. She undressed with her back turned to him. She seemed more full in the thighs and the hips, though that couldn't be, she had starved, so he'd seen, so she said. Her gestures were quick, they seemed aggressive and hostile to him. At the base of her spine, a fine blush, a dull sweat.

She wrapped her arms on her knees on the dirty mattress. Lit a cigarette, pinched it between her forefinger and thumb, a new gesture to him. Ashes fell in the bed.

He said, "You smoke like you're still in the camp."

Past the window's iron bars, the streetlamp left stains on the street, on the failed yellow grass. She squinted at him. "Now I'm in the big camp," she said.

No one had touched anyone yet. They hadn't talked about what had happened or what might happen next. Sandor took off his clothes, felt her curious negligent gaze on the government bruises that left permanent marks on his neck and his chest. He lay next to her on his back. The bed tight, hardly room. Margit climbed, a tight bony sprawl over him. She ran her hands down his sides, nervous, efficiently brisk, as if willing herself to define who it was she lay with.

She thrust him inside, they began. Her body seemed ruthlessly wanton to him. He tried slowing her down, to shift her around, arrange her in forms they'd assumed before camp, but she wouldn't have it. She rocked back and forth, her hands pushing down on his shoulders, his face. Carelessly bold how she moved over him: Sandor recognized it. Jealousy made him giddy and grieved, made him pull on her hips.

"God good Jesus," she said.

He knocked her wrists out from his sides, she fell forward, hit her head on his head. Her hair in his mouth she moved faster now, turned her face.

"Look at me," Sandor said.

She showed him the whites of her eyes, smoky tallow,

bloodshot, older now. A passing headlight cut her features in half: resistance and lust, a blurred struggle toward relief. She tore herself back and forth over him, her fingernails raking his arm, his forehead. They were grappling, he thought, with the redheaded woman in bed between them. She knew this, too, she cried out, she rolled off, wiped her thighs with her palms. A hurried negation of pleasure, he thought, how bodies attract or repel one another: a new kind of pleasure, perhaps.

She sat up, lit a fresh cigarette. She said, "We were cold in that camp." She would not look at him.

He sifted her voice for regret but he heard none of it. "You needed some warmth," Sandor said.

She blew smoke over him. "We made some, we bought some," she said. She studied his face to make sure he figured it out. It was about the possible uses of love, a mere fact. She got up and walked to the wall. Tottering. Dangerous. She turned off the light. His white arm off the edge of the bed, streetlamp on her belly and sex. Trunks of spindly trees in the dark, in the park, the swing's legs, her quick bruised footsteps. She leaned down, cigarette in her lips, her hand on his shoulder to steady herself. Ashes fell on his chest. She curled next to him but he turned on his side so she pushed herself into his back, maybe only for warmth, though it wasn't cold in the room. He thought, from now on, he'd never be certain of Margit's intent, and also that she must have never been able to believe in his. He felt nearly chastened. Through the windowsill's gap, sulfur from the tungsten refinery plant burned his throat. The springs creaked. "This is terrible, Sandor," she said.

After a while, she folded her arms on his chest and he turned into them. In the weight of her eight-year embrace a reply would have seemed an offense. Margit put her hands over him. Slowly and calmly they began again.

The month passed, and the next. The hot morning pasted his shirt to his back, his hair stuck to his head. He stood on the river-walk stones with a dress in a sack he was delivering for Margit. By the boats mired in dark oily pools, fishermen gutted fish on the steps, Erzsébet in men's pants helping them. Somehow he wasn't surprised, it was only a matter of time until he found her by accident on purpose.

She stood before him. "You've been avoiding me," Erzsi said.

"Yes," he said.

She looked him up and down, the package under his arm. She said, "Messenger boy."

He wasn't hurt because that's what he was. They crossed the narrow street. She tilted her head toward the fishmonger's shop. "I live upstairs. That major who drove me from camp moved me in."

He smiled. "Should I be surprised?"

She shrugged, took the package from him, walked fast through the door so he'd have to follow her up if he wanted it back. As if he wouldn't have. Not for the first time or last, he thought a mistake was about to be made as he watched her ascend.

In the room right away she stripped off her pants, her man's shirt. She did not seem to mind the open window, anyone could see in.

"We shouldn't," he said, though he didn't say what, or as if that ever stopped anything. He'd not tried to find her because he was afraid it would be exactly something like this.

She stood half a meter from him, touched his hair with both hands. "For my scent," Erzsi said.

But he had just come from Margit, the twined sack with the dress she'd just sewn on the floor between them. "Let's do it so not having done it won't be the excuse for why we can't do this," she said.

Sandor looked at the curtainless room with a fan and no bed. In the fish shop downstairs someone recited the prices of mullet and cod.

"What about your major?" he asked.

Erzsébet turned out her palms. The fan blew her hair everywhere. "Oh, I'm marrying him."

Sandor backed away. "Ah," he said. He noticed the polished men's shoes by the door, a man's tie on the sill.

"It won't change anything," Erzsi said.

Sandor studied his own dirty shoes. "No," he said. "Of course not."

She walked around him, her thin body whiter than pale in the afternoon light. She said, "It's not bad, a roof over my head." She stood on the coat she used for a bed. She bent, untied his package's string, fanned the dress, slipped it over her head. "It's swell having things," Erzsi said.

Sandor thought she was only repeating something her major had tried to convince her about. The dress was too tight, she ripped out the seam Margit had carefully sewn, a light, delicate stitch. Sandor winced.

"He treats me badly," Erzsi said.

"And you like that," Sandor said.

Erzsébet stepped close to him. "All this time and you don't understand. The point is I hate it," she said. She reached down and undid his pants. She held him and laughed, a small comedy as she pulled him like that toward the wallpaper patterned with sun.

He told himself: just this once, if only to pay Erzsi back for having slept with Margit. Or maybe the opposite. It hardly made sense, yet there was a sexual logic to it.

She hiked the dress past her hips, rubbed him against herself, her slight smile mocking him. He'd made love like this, once, in the war. The soldier's bed, it was called: any wall. Her shrewd body helped, his hands on her shoulders to steady himself.

"Is this how your major likes it?" he asked.

She leaned back enough for the space of a fist between them. He looked down at the buttery light on the place where they met.

"Your wife slept with me," Erzsi said. "And also with the man who brought coal to the camp," Erzsi whispered to him.

Sandor made a fishbone sound in his throat, his legs shook. "I already guessed about you and Margit," he said.

Erzsébet moved into him. "So this is revenge, then," she said. He felt the teeth of her smile on his neck. "What will you tell Margit?"

"You're kidding," he said.

"But she'll know, she always knows," Erzsi said.

He thought he'd do what he always had. He'd blame her but that wouldn't work, so he'd implicate history next and the nature of man. At the last he'd pretend he meant well. He said, "I'll tell her I always lie." He felt useless and sad thinking this.

Erzsébet didn't laugh like he thought she would have. "And you'll think yourself clever," she said. They moved for a while in the sun with a mute competent cleverness. Despite Erzsi's grip, the awkwardness of standing up, he felt alone with his economies of untruth in this room blown about by the wind from the fan. The fishmonger calls in the streets, his movements on her seemed like spurious lies moving through windblown air with the sun coming in. He thought, *it was always like this*, his perjury, his squandered intent that left him desperate.

He wanted Margit. "Let's stop now," he said.

Erzsébet pulled the back of his hair, her eyes dense. "She's pregnant but she isn't planning to tell you she'll get rid of it," Erzsi said.

He pushed her away, she slid down the wall before him.

Her sweat left a dark silhouette. She half lay, half sat, smiling up, the dress rucked around her long waist. He had the thought, if he stayed in this room long enough, his wife would have time to dispose of her consequences and he wouldn't have to forgive her for it. Mercy leaves the forgiven one guilty, forever in debt, it was something his father had said.

"Why did you tell me?" he asked.

Erzsébet lay supine on the coat, shadows crossed on her belly, the yellow fabric of the dress. "Because you want to love your wife," Erzsi said.

Sandor looked out the window, down at the city bleeding its big famous river, the gray boulevards bleeding out. "It's because you want to love her," he said.

Erzsébet shook her head, she rose, crossed the room quick, as if motion would obliterate what he'd said. She reached around him from behind, the dress damp on his shirt. "To punish you, then, for her sake," Erzsi said.

He turned in her arms, the parquet's blond dust blown about by the fan. Dirt stuck to his clothes, Erzsi's brow and her neck as she moved against him. "Let's finish, Sandor," she said, but he steadied himself on the sill, his bad hand in the small of her back. He grasped the seam of the dress and pulled out the rest of the thread, Erzsébet's side suddenly bared to him, a white stripe from under her arms to her waist. He ran his good hand along there with a spent tenderness. "There, it's finished," he said.

I said I wouldn't write anymore but I can't help myself. Just so I don't skip anything, since the border is where it is and the rest. I'm tired of hearing about it myself. Maybe there's no such a place, and this is a dream and I'll walk and keep writing these letters to you in my head until I wake up or I'm dead. That could happen. We're not supposed to escape and there's soldiers hunting us and it's freezing and dark, and since we're near the border we've heard there are mines. So it helps to write this in my head. How I had forgotten the city back then when I got home from camp.

As you know I was pregnant by then. I didn't want my guts butchered inside by some government quack and the one thing of value I had for a black market scrape, what we called it in camp, was right there on my hand.

In the time I was gone, what happened to all the small shops? You couldn't keep count when I left and now there seemed to be none, or replaced by these stores where the purpose seemed merely to stand in a queue for an hour and half, then leave with empty palms. It made me think about what happened to all those leaders we'd had. Zoltán Tildy, Ferenc Nagy, that shyster lawyer Dinyes. Which year plan were we on? And of course the old flag was retired. So I went to a Jew in the quarter where Erzsi had lived before she was in the first camp. The one everybody's forgotten.

"This is pretty cheap gold," that man said.

"It's an heirloom," I said, but of course it was somebody else's not ours.

"If I was you I wouldn't appeal to my memory," he said.

I said, "But it's all you've got left."

"Rather, don't have," he said.

I looked at his palms spread on the counter, so clean and precise. I was thinking I hadn't seen fingers so clean in a very long time, if I ever had. Not yours, Sandor, you have street hands, and Pista's are stained with the army and Party on them.

"You're not a secret doctor, are you?" I asked. Because I'd had the thought, since Stalin had cooked up the Jewish doctors plot, and I forgot for a moment that Stalin was dead and that's why I got out, that I could make a clean trade then and there. No cash would have had to change hands. Then I thought, *but this ring business was a trifle after all.*

I wasn't thinking so clear, being secretly pregnant and thinking about how you traded your ring for ink, hardly gave it a thought, and the child I was going to get rid of inside. The analogy there. I recall thinking the ring had been mine for eight years and this thing inside me a few months. I was just being realistic, I'd thought. Truth is, I had no sentiment: A child is just nausea and cramps until it comes out, then it cries. Then sixteen more years of the same, that's what Alma once said. Truth is I have little sentiment now, but after the camp, I had a desire to own what I could, but the ring had been close to me longer, Sandor, can you understand that?

I've been meditating on value, you see, I've had plenty of time. You know what we hear: the place where we'll run to has washing machines, styles of dresses I've never heard of before, back-bloused loose tops, jackets with flared narrow skirts, pillbox hats. Philco radios and jazz.

At the pawnshop disguised as a grocer I counted the bills in my hand. I almost fainted from greed and the baby inside. Though I said, "Is that all?" It would be nice to be able to tell you that man relented and gave me more money for sentiment's sake, because I was lovely and told him where I'd been, why and how I'd got knocked up. That he took pity on me, took me back to the small room upstairs and he gave me some black-market coffee and we talked about the old days when Budapest was a sort of Vienna but its pedigree was worth more than a hundred dead Krauts. After all, didn't Hunyadi drive back the Turks in 1456? Of course less than a century later they sacked Budapest but we wouldn't have talked about that. My mother said Jews sold us out, their fault because everything was. That, too, we would not have discussed. And they got theirs, after all.

But that didn't happen, Sandor, just taking the ring was a favor, he said with crossed arms. I watched him open a drawer, toss it in with too many similar rings like the rings that you bought in 1946 when we wed. Maybe you bought it from him. When I walked outside I almost forgot where I was, like I said it had been a long while, the whole stinking city of sewage and old bullet holes in the walls, and new walls and those ugly concrete Soviet blocks. I walked by the small city pond, now there were plenty of ducks, the new economical plan must be working, I thought. I thought I'd take my money and run for Vienna right then. I laughed out loud in the street: enough bills to bribe one shoe out. And then I felt dizzy and threw up behind a newspaper vendor's kiosk: ten years of Rákosi's bloody toadying reign, he'd been finally sacked, the *Szabad Nép* actually printed that.

I felt guilty about that damned ring, so I bought us what fruit I could find, tinned Chinese orange and pineapple slices in some kind of glutinous sludge, it made you sick, too, later on, splurged on Bulgarian cigarettes of which I smoked six right away on the tram to the Angel Street house under the "no smoking" sign. Ah, Sandor, I miss them already, our good old good times, and I'm not being sarcastic at all.

On a hot muggy day with low clouds, in the dirty bathroom down the hall, Margit lost the child. She stood shivery legged, wiping blood and relief from herself with the hem of some strange woman's dress. She'd mended and washed it but now it was ruined and balled in her fist.

She wanted to call out for Sandor but Margit could guess where he was. She felt faint, put her forehead to the glass, the pane cool, six a.m. The small bathroom window looked out on the alley where dogs picked through trash.

She couldn't afford not to get paid for her work so she washed out the dress, threw her underwear under the sink. She waited for cramps and they came and they passed and she washed off her legs. The water was cold, she stood barefoot in the puddle she'd made, wondering how to think about this. Getting rid of the child would have been a political act, but this choice had been taken from her, the one freedom she had. *Feed the child, dress the child, wipe chestnut puree from its mouth*, what her mother had said. She made up her mind she would not sentimentalize this. Calmly, she sat on the toilet and sobbed in her hands, choked and gasped, wiped snot and tears on the dress. *This poor dress.* She laughed, bit her fingers to make herself stop, catch her breath.

The dress had been white, she rubbed at the small yellow flowers on its hem. She folded it under her arm, stepped into the hall, let her hand on the wall guide her steps to her room where she lay on the floor, pulled the blanket down over herself. *Thank God Sandor was out*, he'd left some loose bills on the bed. Once her mother had bought her an ice cream, and Margit had been so eager for it, the cone fell on her stairwell's dark steps. "That cost your father a lot," Alma said. She had been inconsolable, then, she had wanted to die. Only a word when you're six, before war and the rest. She felt cold, pulled apart, hardly dared close her eyes. Sleep took her violently and she dreamt she gave birth to a coal baby with a bad hand.

He needed to empty his mind of all thought so he could think what to do next. If she got rid of the child: if he would have left her, then. He rode the tram to the Museum of Banknotes and Coins, a lecture on Hegel and Marx. This is how it would have been all the time if he left Margit. The absolute sternness of thinking alone and no one to think back. He would not even have to go out of whatever small place he lived with a hot plate and plate, cup, spoon, knife, and the sound of the tram over railway ties.

The room was all men and he despised them out of hand, but he wanted masculine words, not their content but sound. Women's voices were tactile as skin, they made him a shabby fabulist. There was nothing he wanted from men. The child wasn't his, but it could be a brother to him, or if a girl, his great love. He wouldn't have minded a child, he'd have taught it the press.

In his dirty white shirt and no socks, in the high-ceilinged room with brown lamps, he remembered his father who'd read Schopenhauer out loud, all that willing and rapaciousness.

Outside, through a gap in the thick brocade drapes, plane trees leaned. The sky had turned high-clouded, white as the face of a child. He realized he'd been describing this room to her or to him in his head, the drapes and the context of Marx and the tree and the white narrow view of the sky. Maybe it was safer having a child as a thought and a silence, a form of address. But if he wanted safety he could have been Pista, he thought, pushed his palms on his knees. *Let's go check on your mother*, he said.

She awoke from her merciless dream, she looked at her legs and the floor but no blood so she put on the very best dress she'd been sewing for somebody else.

She picked her way over cracked cobblestones past the hunched and the pregnant and lame sprawled across every bench. She took the tram past the Pantheon of the Working Class, the sky blanched as her face and as hot. Someone offered his seat so she must have looked sick. The car rattled over the Danube, people fished from the banks. *Little fish.* In the district where Margit got off, women held parasols. The sidewalks were washed. She was glad she had dressed carefully, she watched her own self-posessed steps, her finger's quick jab on the bell she heard ringing inside Pista's flat.

His hair had been badly cut or he'd just woken up.

"I'd like you to buy me an ice cream," she said, never mind the months passed. She hadn't spoken out loud in a while, her voice rough. He said her name once, his eyes doggy, soft. She shouldn't have come.

A decadent recamier, a landscape on the wall, framed, not torn from a book. A glass-fronted armoire with plates in which she saw herself, hair sleep-wild and wild from pulling at it as she'd walked. "I got pregnant in camp and I lost the baby," she said.

She caught the quick jealousy in his eyes he could not will to pass fast enough. He said, "Have you told Sandor yet?"

She saw his hope to know first so she nodded, it could have meant yes but was not and she knew he knew this. "Erzsi will tell him," she said. This came to her suddenly, and that Sandor had gone to find out, though he wouldn't have known his own motive, she thought.

"Camp's made you prescient," Pista said. He motioned for Margit to sit but she stayed where she was, her feet shifting a small precious rug. "I see you've acquired good taste."

"Why did you come here?" he asked. His boldness, her possible answer was making him shake. She smiled kindly like it was the very last kindness she had. She'd come to ask him to take her away. Sleep with him. She wouldn't be able to go through with any of it.

Pista guessed by the way he turned slightly from her; she felt badly for him.

"Do you still have your blue bicycle?" Margit asked.

He lied. Yes. "You're soaked like it's raining outside. You remember," he said.

She'd sweated through the soft dress, a dark pelt down

her back, under her arms to her waist. Between want and need was only a step from the rug, she'd not even have to touch him anywhere to begin. "If wishes were horses," she said, almost sure what that old saying meant. She paused because she was certain this moment would end and she'd be the one finishing it. If wishes were bicycles she would have pedalled through showers with him. She moved closer, her hands by her sides. She felt like a beggar just outside the gates of her own happiness. "Poor Pista," she said. "You tortured my husband and now you are torturing me," she told him. She laughed. "And me, you. Fair enough." She couldn't hide the hysterical edge in her voice. She walked around him and looked out the glass at the clean boulevard. "They must make you guilty a lot to give you an apartment this nice."

He moved to her side. "You get used to it."

"But the two of us, Pista, we're not guilty yet." Margit spoke to the window, her face felt obliterated by light. "I need to keep it like that, one pure thing."

"Unsullied," Pista said. It wasn't assent; she was glad there was still a question in it. "But what about me?" he asked.

Margit swept her palm toward the view from the hills. "You have your consolations," she said. The words sounded petty and false even as she spoke them.

"This means nothing to me," Pista said.

She faced him, so close their clothes touched. "Truth is, it does, or you wouldn't be living like this."

He was going to speak but next he would tell her he'd give it up all for her sake, and she didn't want him to lie, or worse, to be telling the truth, so she covered his mouth with her hand. The heat in her palm: She should not have done that. She stepped back, he held on to her wrist.

"Everybody's slept with you except me," Pista said.

Margit had to smile, she liked his childish petulance, that he didn't know the half of it. She thought about Sandor returning from Erzsi wherever they'd lain, where she might lie down with her next. "Love survives humiliation," she said.

They stood by the swing in the mean little park. He wanted to ask if she still had the child but he didn't know how, and she wanted to weep and confess, but exactly to what?

She said, "You've been to see Erzsébet."

"And where have you been?" Sandor asked. He wanted to see Margit's face, but she would not look at him. She didn't say it's too late, first she wanted Sandor to give her some argument.

He watched her pace back and forth, her forlorness of short rapid steps frightened him. He looked at her hand and she noticed he noticed no ring, but he didn't say anything. They looked toward the Angel Street house but they couldn't go in that closed space. She sat on the swing, his hand on the small of her back as her heels kicked his legs. "Is this safe now?" he asked.

Margit felt dizzy yet lucid as she gripped the chain. Half a million dead in the war, that's enough grist for the state, she'd rehearsed. "Push, Sandor, damn it," she said, but then she felt sorry for him, for herself, the half lie she was going to tell. "Not hard, it still hurts," Margit said. Sunset held light like bruised peaches on a blue plate. He looked at the the tilt of her neck and knew she did not have the child anymore.

"What would you have named it?" he asked. The swing blew a false autumn breeze through her dress.

"Not for my mother," she said. Sometimes she felt what she thought must be Alma's residual Tilt-A-Whirl spins, the urge to jump from any bed.

"Not our fathers', either," Sandor said. He remembered the old man's gray ash, the jars in the cellar, their fruit like plump drowned fetuses.

Eventually it got dark, their shadows grew long and involved. Margit climbed awkwardly from the swing. He pulled her dress loose where it stuck to her back like crushed wings. She searched her pockets for smokes, found one but didn't light it. "We have to change things or I'll have to leave you," she said.

Sandor looked up and down the dead street, there was only the light from the lamp. "Taxi," he said quietly to his shoes, hardly lifted his head.

Margit brought her cigarette to her mouth to keep from laughing out loud.

He said, "What could I say that would help?"

"Not *say*, but do, or not do," Margit said.

Nothing changed for a while but the sky, which grew speckled with clouds. It felt like a long time went by as he counted the stones and the leaves. One million heartbeats right now in this city, he thought, each new one replaces a death. "It's for the best, what you did," Sandor said. His voice to himself sounded just like the men who had talked about Marx or his father's explaining the press. He cleared his throat like a wishbone had stuck, said, "I could have taught it to work a press."

Margit stood with her back to him, the streetlight on her legs. "It's only because you say things like that that I killed it," she said.

He flushed as she moved beside him, he lit her cigarette. "I was being sarcastic," he said.

"Yes," she said.

She smoked while he stayed by her side, he tucked in his shirt for something to do with his hand. "You want me to believe you wanted the child," Sandor said.

Margit shook her head, it could have meant no or yes. "And you that you didn't," she said.

"Of course not," he said.

She didn't ask if of course that's not what he believed or of course that he didn't want it. An ambiguous moon slid between new dull clouds, then more clouds so low they felt them press down overhead. If they waited long enough, rain might clear the air, Margit thought. Eventually a taxi drove by and surprised both of them.

"I didn't go to the clinic," she said as they watched the

cab pass. She wanted to lie but she'd leave all the lying to him. "The child just bled out," Margit said.

Sandor remembered the woman who lay on the straw in the snow in the war, all that red blood on white. It would have been needlessly cruel to tell Margit he missed a boy who was already gone or a girl who they never quite had, but he saw that she guessed. "It's all right, your intention," he said.

Margit scraped her shoes on the ground. She didn't want to remind him what she'd always said, about how intent doesn't count, only acts. Useless to parse such distinctions, fate had resolved what their mismatched desires could not.

They watched the dark sky as they stood with their hands by their sides. If they waited it out maybe the clouds would release their cool gift. In an hour, but then who could tell, the first raindrops hit Margit's brow, Sandor's palm over it.

In what she plans as her very, very last letter, she writes, *To Sandor from me, somewhere outside Szombathely. Someone's made a small fire, we're burning love letters for heat.*

She wants to sum it all up, the causality of events that have led her to this. She could write, *I hate you because I love you and look what we did.*

That's one thing.

But he's had time to think about this. And what's he going to do about it where he is?

Instead Margit writes, *I could tell you what's here but who cares? You've seen a forest in snow: birds' feet, fleeing refugees' roped suitcases.* A few crows, always those with their cries that remind her of death.

She's been recalling the year after she got free from camp. After she lost the child. After time made a marriage of sorts of their marriage again: He attended those meetings on Marx which were really a front for the true communists. In the books he brought home she found Bakunin's arcane treatises, Bakhtin's translated typescripts.

You just can't keep out of it, Margit said but in truth she was glad he had something to do with his hand. Carbon paper coal black on his fingers across her damp chest. *I'd always hoped one day we'd laugh about all of this.*

She thought about faithfulness while she read his philosophy books in Erzsébet's room with its fan and no bed. She tried on Erzsi's clothes, pants too long, she laughed as she dragged them around in the dust, clomped loose-heeled in Erzsi's wide shoes, men's shirts drenched in Emke perfume to disguise their bad smell. She lay on the sunlit parquet reading *The Sickness Unto Death*. It cheered her to think of herself as tall and insufferable, coolly intelligent.

Only snowing a little so far while she's trying to decide what parts to leave out or write down. Titmice. Snow packed thigh-high, *we'll slide to the border on sleds made of twine-fastened bags.* Frozen hands. *Nature will kill you more surely than philosophy ever will.* But that wasn't right, she had thought, Marxism began as a book, after all. Those volumes she carried to Erzsi's and back were merely a torture of nature by language, bold explanations to stave off the end of our flesh.

In the fish-market room, Margit turned pages of *Either/ Or* dressed in Erzsi disguise as the real Erzsébet came back home with her fish-cleaning hands.

"Ah, you brought a prop to excite the love act," Erzsi said.

Dear Sandor: What you imagined we'd do, we did that. But no, that's too cruel, she won't write about her black hair down below, Erzsi's red. The opened book's pages riffled by autumn's cool open-paned wind. Or afterward, breathless, collapsed, Erzsi's elbows on the floor as she thumbs the thin paper and asks, *Does this make us more interesting?*

Sandor, Margit writes, *you alive?* She shivers and wipes the black soot from her eyes, then she writes, *In case I don't see you again, how it happened with us and the press, you don't know the half of it.*

What they both knew was that season's tense restless edge. The nervous, wary government now that Stalin was dead. Long days when they hardly knew how to act with each other, themselves. Shadows crossed the wall. Damp nights they lay centimeters apart and practiced useless wakefulness.

She needs to stop, now, warm her palms, think about consequence. Dusk, where she is, its blind eye. Not a building in sight, not like the city she's left, Castle Hill with cupolas and spires and she finds herself writing how philosophy was invented by men, women aren't built for it, *our thingless womaness,* everything all up inside, that dark vegetable sense.

But what do you care about this, or Erzsi and me in 1954 on the floor with our hands in our sex?

Because Sandor likes facts. How Erzsi was not in the room when the major came in. He surprised her afloat in Erzsébet's clothes, still swoony and hot from her touch, somewhat loose in the head.

"You're pretty but not quite so vivid," he said.

He's the one who suggested we set up the press.

"But you already ruined his hand," Margit said.

A big man with a tall manly voice: "We won't touch him," he said.

"No, you'll use a gun."

He paced off the room with a pompous retort of his boots, said, "He's had his turn, now we want to lure bigger fish," the cliche somehow true to its ominousness.

Margit leaned by the wall, Kierkegaard uselessly spread in her lap, and she thought *little fish*, though she'd rather not have.

"Why do men need to do things?" she asked.

Why do they? she writes. Only men could have invented the gulag, she'd told Sandor once.

The major spread his arms. "Because women demand it," he said.

I remember your brave uniform and my father's off-to-war pants and I think there was something to this. The major so solid before her in his crispy shirt, epaulets.

"Erzsébet might come back anytime," she told him.

He jiggled loose coins in his pants. "She's the one who told me you'd be here," he said. They leaned on the sill, studied fish and pushcarts, yellow trams.

"Think about being faithful," she said. They looked at each other a while with a wary complicitousness. He lit a cigarette, passed it to her, said, "All right, I've thought about it."

She had, too. *We were close in that room with its odor of fish, paper, sex, his cologne in the heat.*

Margit rubs her hands, sore and her rough palms are split in the fading blue light, hardly a line between sky and white ground. Pencil worn to a nub, she thinks about sharpening it with her teeth, sticking it in her chest.

It's hard to decipher her words in near dark: *I could have slept with him.*

She smoked so fast the major was already lighting the next cigarette. "We were as good as already lying in each other's arms when I came in the room," he said next. Held out money he took from his pants.

"Metaphorically," Margit said.

He laughed. "You've been reading too much."

She backed to the wall. "Here, for expenses," he said. "Go buy ink." She moved from the wall toward him. *I should have slept with him then.*

"If I do this," she said, she meant either/or, the sleeping, the press. She thought, *it never ends.*

I mean, it would have been smart, because she understood the philosophy of the exchange: If she opened her clothes, she'd not have to take the money from him. If she opened her legs, that would be the contract between them. If Margit refused, she'd have to accept the limp bills from his hand, start the press.

The major looked kindly at her. "One or the other," he said, made a fist over his head, tipped his neck. Margit was tempted to laugh but his smile held her still. *A choice that was not a real choice, but it was.*

"Ahh," Margit said, as if the air from her lungs had already seized up.

He waited her out patiently to accomplish her fate. *I could have lain down on the floor upon Erzsébet's coat. His eyes not unlike yours, a nice tender darkness to them.*

She needed to make her mistake, *and then we'll be even*, she thought. And her still in Erzsébet's reckless disguise, that philosophy cool in her head: She would be like a man, with Erzsi she'd even been one, so she took the money and put it inside Erzsi's shirt by her breast. A philosopher's choice, and she made the wrong one, on purpose.

Where else would they have reassembled the press but Szentes? Pista comissioned a government car, or a car had turned up, or he had to deliver a car, he was vague about it.

Two hundred kilometers of a low iron sky.

"How come you're doing this?" Sandor asked.

Margit sat behind them, touched the major's bills in her blouse.

"Because I feel guilt about you and your wife," Pista said.

Sandor watched Pista stare straight ahead. This was true just as far as it went. In Magyarország there was always a reason behind any reason, he thought.

Margit studied the backs of their heads as they traded the names of subversive groups the government planted or banned. Or lately, allowed. The Magyar Reformist Social

Democrats, names like that. Margit made up her own, the Patriotic Alliance of Hopefully Disposessed. Union of Socialist Ironists. She could have spoken the names out loud now. The breath of a tentative freedom was heady and scary at once, it frightened her almost as much as Stalin.

In Csongrád they left the Trabant, they carried the pieces of press to a wagon with hay in the back. Pista hoisted the heavier parts, covered them with a tarp.

"Erzsi's not marrying the major," he said.

The air smelled like manure, ripe plums.

"No doubt he went back to a wife he's kept quiet about," Sandor said. Chill wind blew their clothes, their hair into their eyes.

"Hung himself," Pista said. He looked at Margit. "I transferred his files. I've been promoted," he said.

Margit turned away fast. She faced Csongrád's marketplace stalls where they sold sides of beef, mangy sheep carcasses. No longer summer, no reason to sweat like she did.

The oxcart they hired blundered on sticking up wedges of war ordnance, past the factory that used to make soot but now strewed broken glass. Pista held down the tarp by sitting on it.

"Now my enemy is my friend," Sandor said.

"A good thing," Pista said. "Or you couldn't count them on the hand you have left."

Margit sat with the drover up front. He smelled like pálinka and soil, like the weather had become his clothes.

"Those guys your boyfriends?" he asked.

Margit kept her eyes on the horse's tail flicking at flies. She said, "What a big horse's ass."

The drover slapped the reins as he winked. "You never been up so close to a real one before, is that it?"

Margit thought about the coal man. She realized, if he'd driven her out of the camp, if she had quickened long enough, she might have borne his child instead of driving an illegal machine to Szentes.

In the room underneath the old house with the jars with their gone-to-muck fruit, Sandor taught her the press. She learned to space cool ingot teeth in the trough, how the platen came down and bit. He wouldn't have guessed how much she enjoyed doing this. She practiced on poems: *The newsworthy taste of desire.* How much she liked that! She fed the machine with an inevitable willingness.

"This is a mistake," Sandor said, but he bought her an iron-blue printer's smock with her name etched in script. She lowered her eyes, hiding her oil and ink smile.

"It's a necessity," she replied, bent over the roller, her hair held away from the dangerous parts with a finally useful barrette.

· · ·

What was necessary was standing around in the shadier districts of Buda and Pest, collecting sedition to set. She had to do this, Sandor could not show himself. He hid behind corners while she stood exposed in the shadows of iron and stone in a blue and white dress.

Sometimes she told him, *go home*, she wanted to be by herself.

Sometimes he left, took that chance.

. . .

Four a.m. she's still there, awaiting wild-haired anarchists. They bring manifestos on smudged slips of paper ready to chew and digest. Don't try to tell her your name, she won't want to hear about it. Believing that others believe is as close as she dares to approach a political faith. So she says. Though she might mend your pants in a pinch. Though she keeps the names they can't help divulge on a piece of paper just in case, unsure in case what, or if it's in her head.

Dawn drops its cool edge down her back. Who'll come next? The police? They roll by in their beaten Trabants, say things like: "Directing traffic?" But she has a pass to be out from the dangling major himself. She reads the note the policeman has passed to her in the street. The phone number on it.

"Hello, Pista," she says.

"Where are you calling from?" and she says where it is. "That phone's tapped."

"I won't say anything to incriminate anyone," Margit says.

"Not yet," Pista says. A staticky silence unspools between them, like the ghost of Stalin on the line, Margit thinks.

Still, she realizes why Sandor liked this time of night. No clocks, only angles of dark and streetlight. Dead leaves tick down. Every car that goes by reads her eyes. Wind comes while she waits. Rain tonight, rain tomorrow, she shakes off its transparent beads. Under the shadows, elongated by lamps, she's waiting for men she'll recognize by attempts at effacement, slight coughs. *Mrs.*, they call, or some whisper, *Dear*, as in, *Don't get killed, dear.* She thinks of a forest and some bow and arrow and her, quivering.

She carries no purse, because where could she put it?

Too far to walk to the Angel Street house after the evening's last tram. Her blouse holds the long folded-up diatribes, declamations tucked into the band of her white underpants. In the morning cafe she washes night from her eyes, hard and wary, like a man's. No lipstick or powder or grease to add or subtract from her face, no longer trapped behind that, looking caught, like some girl.

"Hello, Pista," she says, where she is.

"That phone's tapped, too," Pista says. The dead crowd the line with their staticky murmurs and pleas.

Margit says, "Maybe my mother is listening."

While sprawled on the Angel Street bed, Sandor is tired of waiting for Margit and trying to sleep: her old man. Her morning's hero chewing rye while she takes off whatever is wet.

He says, "Here's how you make up a code."

"Why would I need it?" she asks as she studies his face.

"Because I should have used one," he says.

She can't hardly read his handicapped alphabet. "What's this, German? Old Norse?"

Old conversations they've had push down over his mouth. *Somewhere this is somebody's happiest time.*

But now she believes this is hers because she'd never seen the attraction before: no handholds. A wire pulled tight in her gut but no net. Webs of consequence. A vocation become its own reason to do it again. Our task is to make possibility into necessity, that's what Kierkegaard said.

. . .

Four hours by train to Szentes. They sit apart just in case there's a search, the documents split between them. But only plain men walk the aisle, stop to talk to his wife, Sandor watches her flirt. Sometimes he thinks it's for him she does this, just to show him she can. Sometimes he's sure she could go off with any of them but he stays diffident. No one dares talk to him. He realizes he doesn't want anyone's words anymore except hers.

. . .

"I'm at the train station," she says.

Pista doesn't need to ask which one it is. "Bring me the names just in case."

"Just in case."

"Something happens," he says.

"To you or to me?"

The listeners in the basements and graves are all holding their breaths. "I'll keep them safe," Pista says.

Margit laughs and her echo comes back through the snow. "The names or the traitors?" she says, but the line has gone dead.

"Is it sad for you here in this house?" Margit asks.

"I've never had nothing to do except sweep," Sandor says.

Gypsies have come through, left behind gypsy dirt. Broken stolen things. Umbrellas, spoked wheels of a baby carriage. Sheep and goat shit in the yard he hoes into the ground. Unwieldy under his arm, this could be the same hoe, he thinks.

"What do you want to do now?" Margit asks. She stands over him in the upstairs bedroom with bare light on her legs.

"I want to undress you and not think about anything except this, and the memories of this," Sandor says.

But she undresses him in his father's bed by the cobwebby books of religious thinkers long dead. A late afternoon with rain damping down the dust smell. Mice in the walls and now she's the one leaving inky imprints on his ribs.

"It's like you're another wife now," Sandor says. First his war prize, then the state's shotgun bride, necessity's concubine in the camp, and now this woman with ink and graphite on her hands.

"Two wives and a lover, you can't handle it," Margit says.

But what he desires is to surrender the notion of ability.

The last time he was here, his father and then Erzsébet in this bed, he'd forgotten the shape of the house he was in. The cooking and pruning, planting and canning and cleaning and weeding and fixing it up of this place. Childhood games: When he lost the scissors in the weeds, his mother had said you can't come inside until you find them. This house made of round fitted stones fixed with mortar and mud. Chickens next door. His brother and him draped bedclothes across broken chairs, made a fort, a caravansary, his brother called it.

He'd almost forgot on purpose that he had a brother, back then.

In the white naked room, unasked questions elide Margit's face.

He thinks of his brother who must have looked down at the perfectly formed new male child that was him in the crib. "Now we can be normal again," is what his mother said. Truth was his brother had lived wounded-mouthed for nine years and gregariously innocent. The boy with the same patronymic whose cleft lip was cured by his mother wielding the hoe, that quick blow to the brain. The fact of his brother's arms, gap-faced breath, Sandor shaking him off; *family* shivered him. No one touched anyone in this house except his brother who nobody wanted to touch.

Sandor strokes Margit's hair. "I never loved anyone, even then."

Though only last month she might have asked, *Even now?*, now she doesn't even ask when, holds the front of his shirt carefully to protect herself against him. If he loved her as much as she thought she might want could she even stand it? If she lets herself, could she easily die for the cause of Sandor, of him? She might have, before she became her own man, Margit thinks.

• • •

In the room with their bed, the radio says Imre Nagy has been replaced. In the room with the jars, spare planes of dawn from the window float over her head. The astringent chemical smell isn't unlike her bleaches and dyes for blondness. Another window she has to look up at for light. Sometime she'd like to live in a room where she has some perspective of looking down at herself. She's glad there's no telephone in the house so she has to walk to the post in the rain or the sun and use up all her change. *Hello, Pista*, she'll say.

• • •

She never realized how delicate Sandor could be when he handled the press.

"You don't have to be so precise, we're not forging lies anymore," Margit said.

"Aren't we?" Sandor asked.

She removed her barrette. She said, "I'm abetting ideals my father died fighting against." She held back her hair as she leaned to pour ink in the well. "Yet my enemies are also the same ones he fought," Margit said.

He glanced at his surprising wife. "A Hegelian dialectic," he said.

She smiled coyly at him. "I hope you're not scared of me now that I'm smart." The tips her hair were blue-tinged. "I'm your resistance sweetheart," she said.

. . .

Rain, snow comes, the weather as stubborn as political arguments she typesets. Above her he sweeps the rooms and rereads all the books he has already read, but now through her eyes. Once more she has fallen asleep on the floor among trays of type and he carries her upstairs to bed.

He lays her across the mattress. He believes she doesn't like to be touched, that she's frightened she'll like it too much but she craves the results. Midday, midnight, the hour could be anytime, but it's just after noon, a slim sun in her hair, on her wrists. His desire is not for himself but how Margit lies on the sheet with her dress riding up, and then taking it off. For using his body in ways she'll allow so she blushes all down her bare front.

But Margit was hardly afraid of this part. She moved against Sandor unseen in the darkness behind her eyelids. Tuesday afternoon with her husband in bed in Szentes, she knew that she didn't have to be frightened of love anymore: Its equivalent context was work, and her task held their fate. She wished they'd been able to articulate it this way all their years: will and restraint, resistance and guilt and relief like proportionate sunlight and dusk and darkness on her breasts and bare legs. She opened her eyes and gripped Sandor's shoulders and back.

"So this is how adults fuck," Margit said. She shifted her hips under his. Happy now, sadness next. With a new sober grace she surrendered to citizenship.

Wet black leaves, peace in the land. Sandor brushed Erzsi's ratty old fur, straightened her tilty bouffant as they passed by the library steps. Pigeons and clouds reflected where Erzsi wrote *Pista and Erzsi* across storefront glass.

"He already loves someone else," Sandor said.

Erzsi shrugged. "He'll take two; he's a man."

Sandor searched her features for Pista's crisp neatness impressed on her flesh. From her odor of soap over snow, he knew she had cleaned herself up after being outside for a while. Dirt gone from her calves and her shins, though she had no place he knew where she lived.

"There's men all over," he said, "so why him?" Rain started to fall, they had to keep ducking umbrellas, wide hats.

"Because where have you been?" Erzsi asked. She opened

his coat and looked at the papers he'd tucked in his pants. Laughed at him openly in the street. "Working for Margit," she said.

Sandor pulled his coat closed. "Like you've been working for Pista," he said. "You must have coerced him by telling about you and Margit in camp."

She removed a pin from her hair. "And after the camp," Erzsi said. Her hair fell wet and red. Dark tired rain turned to snow, on his cuffs, her shoes already wet.

"So everyone gets their comeuppance," he said.

People walked by with wax paper parcels, pigs' feet, chicken necks, they waltzed Christmas trees onto trams.

"Pista says it's called justice," she said.

Sandor smiled to himself: Pista and Erzsi discussing ethics in bed.

"I like him now that he has Magyar blood on his hands," Erzsi said. She didn't have to bring up '44 and her reasons for this.

"Some of mine, too," Sandor said. He wouldn't show her his fingers again and his own blood-stained guilt. He brushed snow from her sleeves, wiped lipstick from her teeth, and she let him do this. He watched people climb and alight from the buses and trams, criminals in uniform, traitors in civilian dress. "So how is he to sleep with?" he asked.

She looked slanty-eyed. "His effort is earnest," she said.

"That counts, some," he said.

Erzsébet waved toward Petőfi Square where soldiers with pinecones slung over their guns guarded everyone from themselves. "You think so?" she asked. "You think good intentions might save us?" she said.

"I think we're like history," he said, "that it has conse-quence." He felt like his words were mere snow, without substance to them.

"I was there when history ended," she said. Her face seemed opaque in the yellow streetlamps.

"You've been trading on that for a while," Sandor said.

Four o'clock, already dark, holiday bells and Pista's cologne on her neck. "My losses might be to your profit," Erzsi said and he didn't miss the conditional future implied as she moved against him. "Aren't you jealous?" she asked.

He weighed the cost of her weightlessness under her clothes, held her bleakness to him. Still, if he found her once more by the road, he couldn't not lift her again.

"I don't care how I feel," Sandor said.

They stopped by the Galamb Cafe's rain-blurred steps, headlights on Erzsébet's legs.

"That's what's noble about you," she said.

Margit smoothed her ink-spattered dress, tugged her coat over it. Plows banked snow high in the street while she climbed a stairwell to a half-open door where the woman inside bathed a child and the husband told lies about why Margit couldn't come in. She took some loose nervous papers from him. Cabbage and diapers, close heat, she could not have lived like this.

She pulled her coat tight, a brown of no color at all, her heels tripping over a doll, a toy truck on the steps.

She swayed in a tram alongside fishnet sacks stuffed with beer, sausages. She pictured consequences. A knock on a door with the butt of a gun. The wife and child standing under pictures of saints, Jesus bloody over the sink. On the table, cheese rinds, a plate with a circus motif, sausage skins. She studied her trembling hand. She needed to look at a Christmas tree in a house and then baby Jesus would come, she'd eat *szaloncukor*, sing "Mennyből Az Angyal," about how the heavenly angel descends. Pista would have a tree, Margit thought, now that he was bourgeois enough.

Instead Erzsi stood in his uniform shirt opened up down the front.

"Cats dragging things in," Erzsi said.

Margit did not try to act unsurprised. *What are you doing here?* But she wouldn't be fool enough to ask that. She looked around but Pista was not in the flat, just Erzsi and too many rugs.

"Am I supposed to be jealous?" she asked. Her question was not insincere, sarcastic merely by default.

Erzsébet shrugged. "Of whom, exactly?" she asked.

Margit leaned on the wall. Dizzy, she'd forgotten to eat and resistance was poor nourishment. She said, "I didn't ask for his love." She sounded absurd to herself.

Erzsébet pinned up her hair, its blowsy bedded red. "Or mine, or your husband's," she said. "But you took what you needed," she said.

Margit went to the window, surprised she had taken offense. She looked into the night, the distance between her vision and snow a mere glare without depth. Erzsébet stood beside her, touched her arm, but Margit shook her head, felt her essence dispersed among too many bodies not hers.

In the Petőfi Club, in the room with brown curtains and low-hanging lights, no more talk about Hegel or Marx. He'd leave ethics and morality to his wife. In the book in his lap it said how in 8000 BC, the paleolithic cave dwellers of Bükk gathered fruit, hunted woolly mammoths. By the end of the Ice Age, clans herded sheep and milked goats, worshipped fertility goddesses. It must have been different then. Now he was glad both women he slept with had borne no future for him. Perhaps they were barren as tundra, the Ice Age declared by the state.

Outside, a flat snowbound sky, solitude's residue in the light. He read newspapers left behind. *Magyars rise, your country calls. Shall we be slaves? Choose, by God.* Of course, they wouldn't print that, but ever since Stalin was dead, the *Szabad Nép* seemed to be burning between narrow lines. He folded the paper to show Margit, what? A warning? A hope? She'd use the pages to wrap sausages for the train to Szentes.

"Get a job," Pista said.

Sandor heard his boots on the floor, didn't bother to turn. "I applied for some waiter positions," he said, barely lifting his fist.

"Hungarians think your bad hand is one-upmanship," Pista said.

"You'd know about that," Sandor said. He wiped his glasses on his sleeve. "If I worked thirty hours I'd earn enough for a shirt."

They parted the curtain, looked down. Pista touched Sandor's arm. "Erzsi says dirty things when we do it," he said. His clothes smelled like Erzsi's Bulgarian cigarettes.

"She does?" Sandor asked.

"She said your name, once."

Sandor looked toward the corner where he used to sell documents. "That's a dirty word, to some." In Pista's hair he smelled Erzsébet's damp Emke scent. "But that's not the name you wanted to hear in your moment of lust."

"She's wound tight like she's ticking, about to go off," Pista said.

"Stop lighting the fuse," Sandor said.

Snow blurred the streetlights. Pista said, "You've got your bombs all mixed up."

They stood for a while watching the spark of the overhead wires. Sandor said, "It's the damage that counts."

Snow turned to rain on the buses, pedestrians, trams.

"The government's been desecrating gravesites again," Pista said. He looked worn out from Erzsébet. "New heroes buried, dirt brushed off the formerly dead." He meant Rajk, who'd been murdered and thrown in a muddy stone lot. But quicklime was used and not slake. Unentombed, he had risen intact, rehabilitated.

"It must be the newest New Course I've been reading about," Sandor said.

Pista shook his head as if talking to himself. "They won't leave us alone after the East German strike, the riots in Poznań," he said. He paced back and forth in front of the glass streaked with wet. "Lucky for you, you were only a crook, and that I watched your back."

Sandor realized no one looked out for Pista but the state, how it could turn and bite like that turtle who ferried the snake across the Danube on its gullible shell.

"You'll have to make Margit stop," Pista said.

Down in the street, wind swept raindrops from hats. "But you put us up to all this," Sandor said.

Pista rubbed sleeplessness from his face. "The places she goes to aren't safe."

Sandor kept his eyes on the sidewalk, electrical lines. "How do you know where she goes?"

Pista waved his hand as if there was suddenly smoke everywhere. "Ask her about it," he said.

Sandor smiled. "That's what Erzebet said when I figured out about them."

Clouds lined up in the east to march and rain on Budapest. "She should have left you in '51, when you should have been killed," Pista said.

"I suppose you think she'd have gone over to you, then," Sandor said.

Pista sighed as if his words were like the water that rushed under all seven bridges at once. "She should have stuck to forging a few harmless passes, but you let her read these big books." He waved at the high shelves.

"She figured out how to turn the pages by herself," Sandor said.

Pista wiped his face with a handkerchief already damp. "You should have known she'd take all that nonsense to heart, not just think about it."

"Unlike me," Sandor said. The window fogged wet from their breaths. "You're making me tell her so I'll have to pay for her indiscretions," he said.

"Only because you don't care about them," Pista said, drew a heart with an arrow through it on the glass.

"And you care too much," Sandor said, wiped the pane with his palm.

"So have me tortured, send Erzsi to camp." Pista laughed.

Sandor drew the drapes against rain turned to snow and to dark. "Everyone wants to be punished," he said.

Pista shrugged. "It's a bad Magyar habit, like picking the wrong side in war and in peace."

"And in bed," Sandor said.

Headlights from Pista's blue car swept across Sandor's legs. "How come he didn't come in?" Margit asked.

They kept their coats on for the cold. "He's too shy to confess he's been sleeping with Erzsi," he said. He smiled as if he was embarassed for them.

She swiped her papers to the floor, said, "Why are you telling me, then?"

"Only because you'd find out." Sandor blotted the rain from his shoes.

"I think it's vengeance," she said from the edge of the bed, though she couldn't decide if it was Pista's or Sandor's or both.

"Sure, he knows about Erzsi and you," Sandor said.

She looked at her fingernails broken and cracked on the press. "I mean why you told me," she said.

"You want me jealous, too," Sandor said.

"Who else wants that?" Margit asked, but she knew who he meant.

He stood by the mattress and touched Margit's hair. "You wish you weren't but you are and you're mad that I'm not."

She shied from his hand. "Because you don't care who I sleep with," she said. It was more of a question than accusation or fact.

Outside the window cats whined in a loose creaky wind. Sandor wouldn't answer to that, he would not creep around in his house with his heart in his mouth. He said, "Pista cares enough, since he's having you watched."

She leaned on her elbows, considered the seemingly innocent tilt of his head. "He's not having me watched."

Sandor didn't look up. "But he knows where you've been."

She felt guilty but also relieved about what she'd say next. She said, "I must be telling him, then."

Sandor took off his glasses to wipe off the rain, hide his face. "Why would you do that?" he asked.

It would almost be boasting to tell him what happened, she thought. What didn't. Could have. "Ask him yourself, ask our new major," she said.

Sandor went to the window, looked out. "The only straight answers I get are from Erzsi," he said. They both laughed but the laughing was brittle, abrupt.

"Pista just wants to protect me," she actually said.

He studied his wife, her eyes with that half truth in them. "You're doing what I did," he said.

She wanted to say it's for love, like why he had done what

he had, except that it wasn't for her he betrayed everyone. "At least I do it for us," Margit said.

Sandor lit a cigarette, held it to Margit's trembling mouth. He considered what neither of them would give up, what they'd traded instead. That Margit was selfish like him and he liked her for this. "I believe you," he told her by way of absolving himself.

She opened her coat though her body felt frigid as his must have been. "More than I believe myself," Margit said. Bits of flamed paper from her cigarette fell onto her blue and white dress.

"I thought you're brave now," Sandor said.

"Don't mock me," she said.

"I married you for your courage," he said.

"No, because you just could," she replied.

"For the sake of the act," Sandor said.

No, Margit thought, it had been for his eyes that looked both at her and aside. There was no good reason, but reason was different from love. She brushed ash from her dress. "That couple who wed in 1946, they're not us."

"Who are we, then?" Sandor asked.

She dangled her hand by the bed. *Willful but weak, afraid of and wanting desire.* She said, "Ask me ten years from now."

He lifted her hand, tasted her fingertips. "But we'll never catch up."

She kissed Sandor's fist. "Maybe we're at our best when we're the history of ourselves," Margit said.

He laid her down on the bed. "I like to think of our glorious future," he said.

Margit didn't reply. The bunched sheet pressed a knot in her spine. She thought if the future was made from the now it would not be like that. She touched Sandor's side and tried to recall the things she had worried about when they wed, but they no longer seemed to apply. She kissed him on the mouth.

Horse droppings caked with green straw. Someone had seen the Virgin of Rákosi Square weeping blood. Some claimed it was merely industrial scum, though they might have hoped otherwise. Budapest swooned in a harsh interregnum of storms and cold fronts. The statue bled its metaphors into spring. Summer brief. In bed nothing was solved, nor by riding slow trains between Budapest and the press, between bouts of thin sleep, now that Nagy was no longer premier. Between new arrests, hope and despair, in the place where despair can breed hope, just like Kierkegaard said.

. . .

Four hours each way between her home and the press she would try to decipher the future in signs. Slow oil from a tug streaked indigo smears on the Danube's brown rush, held no message in it.

She worked in bad light. She tried to remember the names she'd given up, what could she have been thinking, doing that? she thought. She thought she was thinking too much. She copied out words from her books to typeset, about what it meant that time passed, or if, and the meaning of *meant*, or if there could be such a thing. Was there even a thing-in-itself? What Margit concluded was people did things, and that these acts, for a while, had effects. Imre Nagy replaced János Kádár, who was tortured, and Rajk had been long ago hung. She read between the illegible print, grease that turned the gray pages opaque.

. . .

In the room where she slept, a window blown open, the curtain had frozen, it dripped pools of stains on parquet. She looked for revelation in them and the pale ovals left on the drapes. She squeezed her eyes shut to see sea horse shapes under the milky-pink scrim of her lids. She could not hold them still, the specks hovered and darted like red in the yolk of an egg. *Zygote bone stone*: In the war, she'd kept repeating this rhyme to herself to feel safe.

She covered her face but even like this, light poured in. It was better downstairs, in the dark. She tossed her papers aside: freedom and justice and maybe a little revenge. Someone would read them, but she'd picked up those phones so there would be consequences. She covered the press and took the next train from Szentes.

. . .

No one had watered or pruned. Season-burned weeds and somebody had smoked, crushed cigarette butts on the grave. Margit crossed her legs under afternoon clouds. A twig in her fingers for scraping the dirt from her mother's chiseled name, but *to hell with that* is what Alma, too, would have said. Had said once she was glad her husband was buried nowhere. Told Margit how couples were stacked one on top of the other in plots to save space. *I can't imagine the dead much appreciate it*, she had said.

Margit remembered her mother and her but not once walking with her hand in hand. She didn't know if their hands fit. She recalled the expectancy of what it might be to dash right out into the street. She thought it was not unlike marriage to Sandor had been. And now there was some subtle sea change. It was all Stalin's fault, Margit said to her mother down there, though this seemed absurd. Yet who better to talk to about the absurd and the dead but the dead? Margit had the idea the release of Stalin's cold iron fist had made everyone loose in the brain. Gave everyone sloshy hearts awash in some kind of suspensory sentiment. And that this was too dangerous. No center, no hold, and she couldn't see six months ahead. Should she and her husband both die, she pictured herself inside Sandor's eternal embrace. No one should be that near. Nothing personal, Sandor, she thought, but she'd rather be thrown in a field and devoured by dogs. And she knew Magyar history enough to believe this was not an impossible fate.

She'd better talk to the living, she thought, even if it was no help. She picked up the phone at a corner kiosk.

"Hello, Pista," she said. She felt drunk from lying and love, the few varnished truths she refused to surrender to facts.

"Hello, Margit," Erzsi answered instead.

She was not going to walk down this street but the side street was blocked. In Petőfi Square, some official writers read manifestos out loud. There was Julia Rajk, returned from exile, slightly long in the tooth and gone gaunt. What Margit caught of her speech was, *men who had ruined the country, corrupted the Party, killed thousands and driven millions more,* then the crowd drowned her out.

This was an old story by now, but it hadn't been spoken out loud. Except Margit had set words like this on her press, such papers were on her right now. She should have been proud, but instead she was scared, her palms itched. Ever since Tarnya Camp, when the weather was going to change, her wrists ached.

Pushed to the heart of the throng roiling Radio Square, Margit, too, raised her fist. So this is how it begins, a speech and the sudden impossible lust of the crowd in the red-white-green slashes of paint on the wall. Sheets luffed from windows, hastily lipsticked and shoe-polish scrawled. *Oroszok haza*. Russians Go Home. Free Magyarország.

What was the chance of finding her husband among ten thousand scarves and slouched hats? Here he was, though, a small Magyar flag in his lapel, when had he gotten that? He took her sore uplifted wrist, his grip hard as if Margit might fall, but she'd been standing just fine. Later she'd find small bruised plums like he gave her in bed on her arm.

She counted the clops of police horses over the stones, a uniformed nervous phalanx. Lorries with canvases flapped. Streetlamps came on jittery in the cool moonless dark. Around them, the People in awe of itself, hoarse with *Isten áld meg a Magyart*. And why not have God bless the Magyar, or why? Sandor didn't sing, didn't shout. He scouted the possible ambush of cramped narrow streets, the width of the clogged boulevard. He jiggled his coins, a rattle that dried Margit's throat. He pulled on her sleeve, she said, "Isn't this what you want?"

"God save us from what we want," he replied.

Damp, her hand, hats knocked off, no place for her feet on the icy sidewalk. Someone trod on the heel of her shoe, it was gone. She stumbled over a banner's tramped shroud. The citizenry had the passion of bed, Margit thought, that same *no don't stop, can't stop now*.

"They're scaring the horses too much," Sandor said, he was trying to back out. A horse buckled and fell, rolled its eyes. A smashed bottle's pálinka fumes drifted over the crowd. Someone laughed, windows slammed, someone elbowed Margit in the jaw, a warm rust filled her mouth. She saw a hand on a rifle, fingers twitchy across the brown stock. She thought, *let it start.*

Maybe it was only glass underfoot, that sharp crack, then how quiet it got, as if everyone's breathing had stopped. Women clutched dizzy skirts, they couldn't run good on slick stones, couldn't run fast enough from a gun.

The woman who fell wore a fuzzy gray coat buttoned up to her neck. The side of her face was outside, her teeth worked pink foam in her mouth. Too old and heavy to suffer a beautiful death, Margit thought, then she felt ashamed of herself, her own meager trickle-toothed blood.

Sandor said, "Margit, come now," but she stayed where she was. She said, "I thought you believed in the cause."

"Because I thought you wanted me to," Sandor said.

Margit looked at the tilt of his head. "A ten-year misunderstanding," she said, then they ran until they couldn't run.

Their cheap shoes scattered October leaves, chestnut shells. Margit lit a shaky cigarette behind Sandor's cupped palms. Overhead, black jerky clouds, wind raked a tin sky. The number-two tram hardly slowed, faces pressed to the glass.

She gazed at a tattered red flag on a telephone wire. "What's going to become of our happy misery if we win?"

Sandor stroked her arm. "We'll invent new ones," he replied.

He knows where to find Erzsébet, in the alley behind where she used to live as a child. Sandor likes to think he knows more about her than anyone else.

She wears all the clothes that she owns, lets her cigarettes burn her forefinger and thumb. Sandor knows not to ask what she's thinking about.

"We had a piano," she says.

He sees a piano afloat down the Danube, its black and white keys' busted smile.

"I could play 'Edelweiss.'"

Sandor's all right, on his heels in the dark he knows not to reply. Her cigarette's tight red glow, her sleeves reaching over her knuckles, he knows, is what Erzsébet likes.

"We lived here in Jewtown. My mother had red hair like mine. My father had German pencils," she says. Staedtler.

Mars Lumograph. "You can't get eraser dust out of your teeth when you brush." How Erzsi describes his crisp sleeves: folded over just so, rolled exactly a third of the way up his arms.

A long silent hour goes by, the army trucks' jarring sweep of headlights. Half-tracks down the block, an industrial grind like eviscerated piano insides. He's brought her black bread, but she waves it away from her mouth.

"Each time I eat, I'm dying of hunger all over again."

Sandor chews the bread because what should he do, throw it into the street?

"I wasn't trying to survive, I was fending off death. Logic demanded its necessity," Erzsi says.

How good that the night is so dark, there's no eyes.

"I thought living would carry me not toward my end, but away from my death."

"You wanted to live in the future perfect," Sandor says.

Erzsébet flicks her cigarette ash. "I saw a dead woman, her dead newborn child frozen between her dead thighs."

He'd like to believe he doesn't want to know this but he does.

"So, Sandor, you wanted to help me," she says.

His old man should have seen this: Dózsa Street mobbed, Stalin's statue that refused to fall. Trucks pulled with ropes, the ropes broke. The welder from Csepel who fired his torch to the Great Father's knees. Stalin soft in the legs, Father pitched into the street. Finger shards, chips of nose, people grabbed souvenirs. Sandor helped winch the head on a truck, they dumped it in Parliament Square. The street sign festooned on its neck said *zsákutca*, Dead End.

Shadows on walls where Engels, Marx posters had been. Sandor on Rákóczi Street in the sun, his wife kissing his brow.

Radio Kossuth said, *We request our listeners place their radio sets on the sills.*

Sandor left his radio where it was, on the floor of the Angel Street house in plaster that fell when half-tracks and army trucks passed. He held on to his wife, her blue and white dress and her coat opened up to his touch.

We want to inform those who have been misled that if they sur-render by six they'll be exempt from punishment.

Six fifteen he was leading his wife through the center of Szabadság Square. Looking for Erzsébet. Someone shooting out lamps on the opposite end. Fires burned in trash cans.

Erzsi wore Pista's uniform shirt as a dress and his hat.

"Where's our new major?" Sandor asked.

"Left him tied to the bed," Erzsi said.

"You could be kidding or not," Margit said.

What would his father have said about the AVO guy who hung by his feet from a tree right in front of them? People beat him with sticks. Money fell from his pocket and lay unpicked up even by Erzsébet. Autumn leaves, twigs, debris, all lit up under him, Erzsi looking like trying to spit out the smell of burnt hair, burning flesh.

Wednesday at dawn Russian tanks crossed Elisabeth Bridge.

"What should I feel?" Margit asked.

A forest in snow. The cold wind. The slow German retreat.

He remembered the utility of turpentine and a rag. His hair smoked, and his clothes. Vivid again, to be dusted with cordite and spattered with somebody's blood while his wife and her lover shared quick cigarettes on Academy Street hung with flags red for blood, green for earth, and white must be the equality of death.

Sandor watched Margit holding a telephone to her ear in a booth with no glass.

Noontime, the crowd stood its ground, shy around Magyar tanks that hadn't yet turned their turrets on them. Soldiers rose from the hatches holding Hungarian flags, waving them harder even than the rest.

Order, the radio said. *Magyars, let's not lose our heads.*

People spit shyly on corpses that hung from lampposts.

"What kind of emotion's appropriate for this?" Margit said.

Sandor bent with a rag in his teeth. *The Russian forest at night. The joke about boiling your shoes.* "Emotion's not appropriate," Sandor said, struck a match to the matchbox he gripped in his legs. "Well, maybe glee," Sandor said, stuffed the rag underneath a stalled blue official Trabant.

"Jesus, Sandor," Margit said. She knelt beside him. Her hair and her dress, his revolution sweetheart heroine.

"There's no need to be desperate," she said.

The beer and the hammer and jokes, they had smoked cigarettes.

"There's a need," Sandor said.

She pulled him aside, the car scorched his brows as it flamed.

"You won't get rid of your past doing this," Margit said.

"You're right," Sandor said. He felt an odd and complete hopelessness: Only a great and good deed that seemed beyond him would have helped.

Radio Kossuth said, *We call on all janitors to keep the doors of the houses locked.* No coffee, nothing to eat, his wife down to three cigarettes.

"What are we going to do?" Margit said.

"You could try calling Pista again," Sandor said.

Margit blushed. "Not about cigarettes."

"I know," Sandor said.

Thursday, the only true fact in the newspaper was the date. In Parliament Square, tanks decked with flowers and flags fired their guns in the crowd. Two hundred people gunned down from the Construction Ministry's roof.

Radio Kossuth said, *We are sorry to say, the Children's Hour has been cancelled. Do not be angry, children, that you have to sleep without your bedtime tales.*

Stiff-bristled brooms in the night swept light snow tinged a resolute red. Sandor and Margit helped shut the dead's eyes, draped red-white-green flags over them.

Friday got fogged in, torn-up paving stones flew as they charged the Interior Ministry steps. His wife ran beside him to stop Sandor from foolishness. She had a gun of her own with her hair on the trigger she pulled in her blue and white dress. The kick knocked her back, bruised her shoulder and neck.

"Who gave you that thing?"

"Some debonair Ruski fellow in a truck. For a kiss." She was laughing at him.

"I could shoot you for that."

"I'm holding the gun," Margit said.

All the shooting made them deaf. Sandor thought Margit would not hear if anyone answered a phone or it rang and rang. He tried dialing the number himself.

Saturday clear as a high silent bell, shoes strewn across

wide boulevards where bodies wore fresh red cravats. Secret policemen burned in their Pobeda cars. They dangled from lampposts, their pay slips attached to their shirts.

"I love you," Sandor said to his wife.

"Say you love him," Erzsi said to Margit.

"He loves this," Margit said.

They lay down all three in the Angel Street house restless with can't sleep. He kissed his wife and she kissed Erzsébet. He said, "We'd better get out of this bed."

Wednesday they watched Soviet tanks leave across the Chain Bridge. Rolling field kitchens, their cooking fires stoked, white smoke dissolved in the wind.

People sobbed for the living and dead. Sandor and Margit reeled from corpse to corpse, drew back blood-soaked flags, faces sprinkled with lime and angelic, snow white. Sandor touched his mouth to his wife's weeping face, to her shoulder and neck. Free Radio Kossuth said, *It is our duty to admit, in the past, we've been giving a different interpretation of events.*

"I can't believe this," Margit said.

Sandor told her, "Just wait."

The newspaper printed a fact: No one looted the stores though all the store windows were smashed. People mobbed Imre Nagy on Alkotmany Street on his way to signing decrees. In Parliament Square, a cigány orchestra played.

In the Angel Street house Free Radio Kossuth declared, *The Minister of Education decrees the withdrawal of history textbooks.*

"You see?" Margit said.

Sandor shook his head. "History's not books, it waits for revenge." That's what his old man would have said.

Erzsébet smoothed the spark of nylons on her legs. "Nylons means the civilized world has been saved," Erzsi said.

"I thought the world doesn't get saved," Margit said.

Radio Kossuth said, *We would like not to fear death anymore. After order has been been restored, life will be more beautiful.*

Erzsébet laughed. "God only makes chaos," she said. "Order is the abyss."

Why did we go to Szentes? To bring back the press, to print our new freedom, you said. I didn't believe you because you also didn't believe it yourself. You never lied to me until then. Not told the truth, but that's not the same—why rub salt into wounds? Or maybe I'm wrong, perhaps you really did hope. We all did. We held hope to our hearts; no, we held hope like a gun to our heads.

. . .

They went slow, on laborious trains. They sat close, as if making a memory of this, or a myth. Slushed snow, gunfire from the woods. Fires burned, pigeons roasted on spits, peasants gave them lean looks.

"What's in Szentes except you get to hide from our victory?" she asked.

Sandor drank from a bottle of Barack though he didn't drink. She took it from him. "Stop that, you'll make yourself sick." Sandor smiled, then opened the window, threw up. Large metal armaments crashed through thick foliage and black trees, Sandor recognized them. He hoped they might be the cloy distillation of his guilt, but everyone else in the coach also stared.

The train rolled east, tanks rolled west toward Budapest. Margit stopped counting at one hundred seventy-six. They looked at each other and didn't dare speak while no one came out of their houses and passengers wept.

"We won't bring back the press after all," Sandor said. Maybe we'll bury it. A queer smile crossed his face. "We'll dig a large hole with a hoe," Sandor said.

"Hello, Pista," she said. She could hear bottles breaking behind him in the street.

"I was going to tear off my hash marks and stripes," Pista said.

"Don't gloat," Margit said. She looked up from the post office booth but there was no moon she could use. She thought of his good polished shoes and his uniform cleaned and pressed. She was glad they could not see each other like this.

"Where's Erzsi?" she asked.

"Drunk somewhere," Pista said. "Wearing nylons on her head."

Somehow Margit doubted it. "She's hardly ever really drunk, you know," Margit said.

"Better leave the country while you can," Pista said.

It was cold in the booth. Margit buttoned her coat. A few army jeeps drove listlessly up and down the dirt street.

"Maybe *you* should. Things have a way of changing," she said, not really believing this. Disappointed in him, in herself.

"If it comes down to it we can swim, like I taught you," he said. He sounded as far as if she had already left.

"What about Sandor? He can't even dog-paddle," she said.

"In a strong enough current he could," Pista said.

Margit was thinking about the deep pool where Pista had held her so she wouldn't sink. She knew she wouldn't do this for him.

"That's not swimming, that's just swept away," Margit said.

Sandor and Margit kept touching the cool metal parts of the press. "We could burn down the house around it, but it would still stand," Sandor said. They didn't have the heart to dissasemble it yet. "You want some time alone with it?" he asked.

Margit didn't laugh. "Do you, Sandor?" she said.

Soon they would take it apart, struggle the awkwardly bent armatures down the steps. Like pieces of herself, Margit thought, but Sandor was reading her mind. "Only metal," he said. He studied how she lit her damp cigarette. Ran her hands through her failed blond hair, that perpetual joke between them.

"Can't dig a hole in the dark," Margit said. She blew out cigarette smoke, her blue and white dress riding over her calves as she walked up the stairs and sat on the edge of their bed. Scars on her knees from the camp that felt good to be rubbed, so he did.

"It's the last chance for free Hungary," Sandor said. Stars came out, shoving clouds like raked mud.

"We could go back and fight," she replied.

"Sure, we'll hitch a ride on a tank," Sandor said.

Margit looked at the yellow half-moon. "We would have gone back, if this was the year when we met," she said, though she wasn't sure she meant this.

"I thought you don't go for nostalgia," he said, but she thought that was him.

"I'm going for it now," Margit said. She opened the window, looked down at the place Sandor cleared for the press, the air slightly hazy with dust from jeeps and tank treads. She lifted her eyes to the night, a protection that didn't protect. They moved without thinking about it to bed. They clasped what they could with the radio tuned to the static-choked voice of defeat imminent as their own crying out, that small death.

. . .

On the radio beacon transmitted through Miskolc and Várpolata to Szentes, at 0700, Free Radio Kossuth called, *Segítség, segítség, help*. It was repeated in German and Russian, then the broadcast went dead. The tick of the carrier wave could still be detected until 0943: *SOS*.

. . .

Crisp light singed the room, but they didn't get up from the bed. Margit covered her face with both hands.

"You're not coming back to Kispest," Sandor said.

"And you?" Margit said.

Sandor pointed toward the room with the press. Even down the dark steps, it still crowded them.

"*My* press," Margit said.

"It was mine first," he said.

Margit turned the radio up.

"I want you alive in the world," Sandor yelled over it.

"For your own sake," Margit said, his love dried on her belly and legs. "And haven't we had this conversation before?"

"We were young."

"We're still young."

Margit thought about Pista's small radio they had then. How Sandor wanted just news but she turned the dial to an opera instead. His hand merely bruised then from fixing the press. But now they both wanted the news, they both didn't want it.

"I was supposed to escape to Vienna," she said and he said, "It's still there."

She rolled into his arms. "Ten years, Sandor," she said.

"Three thousand six hundred fifty-odd days," he replied, then he held her close or she moved close to him by herself, their motions had long become equivalent. The radio blared martial music all over the place, a foregone undanceable dance. Sandor picked up his pants from the floor, emptied the pockets of papers and bills. "You take this."

Her a flurry of shaking her head. Mess of tears. Saying, "We have things to do yet." Touching his hair and his face.

Straightening his stupid glasses. "I won't leave you unless you come with me," she said.

He laughed, there was shooting outside, he looked down at his hand. "But I like it here," Sandor said.

Margit turned away. "You're staying for Erzsébet."

"I want to see what happens next," Sandor said.

And didn't he think she did too? "We're going together," she said.

"No," he said.

"Yes." She wrestled him down in the bed until it turned into something else. Another kind of a desperate fight that, if they tried, Margit thought, at least they could both win.

Not a dream, this defeat, so the radio said.

Margit still in Sandor's embrace, Erzsi standing over their bed.

"The people blindfolded the statues in Rákóczi Square," Erzsi said.

Margit spoke into Sandor's bare back. "You came all this way to say that."

"Because of Pista," Erzsi said.

Sandor had climbed from the bed. He wore the same shirt and pants he had worn since they boarded the train in Kispest. He said, "Why, did they execute him?"

"Not yet," Erzsi said.

But Sandor was already outside, digging the grave for the press.

Margit's blue and white dress lay bunched on the floor but she'd kept her coat on. They stood by the window, watched Sandor's undisciplined motions with shovel and pick.

"He'll need a large hole for his entire family to fit," Erzsi says.

"He's digging a route to the west," Margit said.

Erzsébet turned the radio dial but the time for the national anthem had passed. "I did a bad thing when I saw the Russians come back," Erzsi said.

Margit wondered what Erzsi might think of as bad. Her shoes were the ochre of mud like she hadn't ridden a train but decided to stumble and run.

"Everyone was informing so I had to try it myself," Erzsi said. She touched Margit's coat everywhere.

"So Pista talks in bed," Margit said.

"Everyone talks there eventually, it fills the time between sex," Erzsi said.

Gunshots from someplace not far scattered across the high wind.

"I found all those names you've been turning over to him," Erzsi said. "He shouldn't have kept them, so I turned them over myself."

They stood side by side by the glass. "He hid them inside of those books Sandor stole for your education," Erzsi said. She put her hand in Margit's coat, grazed her belly with cool fingertips. "Between your Schopenhauer. Your *Kant*." She touched Margit down there.

Margit couldn't help it, she leaned against Erzsébet's hand. "What did you say was your motive?" she asked.

Erzsi's breath smelled like she hadn't eaten in a while, dry, stale, cigarette-sour. "I said Pista threw me over for you." She scratched Margit's neck. "In a way that's the truth, isn't it?"

But you stole my husband, but I had him first, but neither one really said this.

"I told Pista what I did," Erzsi said, her hair fallen over her eyes, her abandoned attempt at a careless bouffant. Outside, the shovel and pick scraped against the hard ground. "Pista's excuse will be that Sandor and me cooked up the whole mess. Because I've been sleeping with him," Erzsi said.

Margit wanted to laugh. "With whom exactly?" she asked.

Erzsébet shrugged. "All of us with everyone." She let her coat fall.

"What's this really about?" Margit said.

"Pista should pay," Erzsi said.

"Like Sandor."

"Like you, too."

"But I love them both," Margit said. It had its own truth, she supposed.

"Your tragedy, Margit, your love. It exhausts everyone," Erzsi said.

Outside, Sandor stood by the hole in the ground, wiped his brow. "This finishes Pista you know," Margit said.

Erzsi's nylons had split, her skin gray through the hole by each heel. "If we lose or we win, he still would have won, do you see what I mean?"

"Just like the other major," Margit said.

"He killed himself."

"Exactly," Margit said.

Erzsébet held Margit's hair, weighing it. "Better leave while you can."

Margit tried parsing the angles of Erzsi's deceit. She said, "So I've been warned."

"You're waiting for official papers, I guess." Erzsi smiled.

"Sandor won't leave you behind."

"He owes you. Your turn to get carried across."

"Come with us," Margit said.

Erzsébet opened her vivid green dress. "But I have my new major to love," Erzsi said, then she kissed Margit's mouth.

What's to say about where I am now? Cold dark snow, cold dark light, and soldiers who would have us dead. Sandor, I think you're familiar with this.

I've been thinking, Sandor, about what everyone wants me to do and me, too. Such a forward momentum to this. Every footprint in snow, even the lean of the trees from the wind heading west.

Eclairs, there, lace. The Great Freedom, I hear. Dresses from patterns and stitching so clever I'll have to relearn how to sew. I can learn, I'm not dumb, it's just needle and thread, but what I'm trying to say is a few hundred meters from here it's the end or the start. Which is it?

Perhaps I've been reading too much but this dialectic is not mutually opposite.

A few brown hares and some squirrels that haven't been eaten yet. The forest is sparse, not easy to hide and people are noisy and large, they tend to thrash as they trudge. One by one, or small clusters, they trample all day toward the place where the wire's been cut. Bulky shapes stumbling over the pristine white ground like a cake or a white wedding gown.

This morning a suddenly very blue sky and here I am crouched between two spindly trees while the blue sky cracks ice. The fissure of footsteps ahead. I'm just trying to paint a clear picture for you of what this is like. I'm thinking this would be a good time and place for you to step from behind a bare tree in your thin shoes, your mangle-cuffed pants.

Because I'm also hungry and cold.

Suffered some.

Been in a camp!

I'm laughing a little, Sandor, because it's winter and there's been a sort of a war and the side that I'm on lost again. If I have to take sides. And one does. It's why you should be here to gather me up, sling me over your back, and just carry me out.

But you're not here, and you've used up your carrying strength, though I have some left, like you said, I'm still young, only thirty years old though I feel at least thirty-five. Sandor, that's a small joke.

Laughter here in the woods between the known and unknown. And me here in the temporal world and arrived at no truth.

No one mentioned Pista's gun.

Erzsi said, "Here's the rat from the ship he has sunk." She rose awkwardly from the floor where she'd been counting her change.

"Haven't we seen enough of this recently?" Margit asked.

Two soldiers leaned in the door but they didn't come in. Erzsi laughed. "His career's finished," she said. She offered her smile all around so they'd know who finished it. The basement smelled like the bomb cellar during the war, Margit thought, with that shit-your-pants dread. She and Sandor leaned awkwardly over the disemboweled press.

Pista tried to find words for a while. He said, "I'm bringing everyone in," then he almost smiled, too, as if he'd just heard what he said. He waved his hand with the gun, it took in the Szentes basement, the press, lingered on Erzsébet.

"Shoot yourself," Erzsi said, her features unbearably calm in the high window's afternoon light on her shoulders and arms.

Margit thought the piece of the press Sandor held could have been easily flung toward Pista's capped head. Then the soldiers could end this event. She thought Erzsébet brought everybody together for just this circumstance.

"Put that down," Pista said, his uniform soaked through the chest, wrinkled like he'd put it on very fast.

Sandor tossed the large metal hinge on the platen and roller he'd already stacked. It rang hollow and flat while they all seemed to wait for the sound to disperse or another loud sound.

"Should I raise my hands?" Sandor asked.

"Just the good one will do," Pista said. Behind him the two soldiers laughed.

Erzsébet leaned toward Pista who took a slight backward step. "So, lover," she said. She opened her coat, her dress still unbuttoned in front. "Pound of flesh."

Margit saw her own scratches on them, the furtive imprint of her hand. Sandor stood with his arms at his sides. "Whose revenge is this really?" he asked.

"It's just fate," Erzsi said.

Margit said, "No, it's farce."

"We're all speaking each others' parts," Sandor said.

But who was supposed to say what?

Pista, of course, who could say anything with his gun.

Erzsébet startled from motionlessness to all movement at once. Sandor reached out, he moved toward Erzsi but Margit held on to him with both hands. Later, if there'd been a chance, Margit might have said, Erzsi *lunged.* Said, the gun *just went off.* Later, she thought, Erzsi's life had a specific and nameable value at last.

The gun wasn't as loud as you'd think but also much louder than that.

What did she expect of herself? Margit put her hand to her mouth. They stood in the unheated room, dusty gunpowdered light through the high window slats. The two soldiers leaned like the ceiling pressed down on them all while the redheaded woman bled out. Sandor knelt by her side. Margit thought, I should be doing that. Sandor put his hand on her brow though the wound was all over her chest. Erzsébet spoke something fast. Sandor shook his head, but it wasn't denial or assent, it looked more like wonderment.

"I'm cold, Sandor," Erzsébet said. Her hair spread on the basement's cold stone was not the same red as her blood against her white skin and her knees, one leg bent underneath.

Later Margit would remember the vapor from everyone's mouth, Erzsébet's as she whispered to Sandor whatever she said. The harsh white of everyone's breath, except, suddenly, Erzsébet's.

He'll close her eyes, it's me who ought to do that, ashamed she was jealous of Erzsébet even in death. How Margit felt would take her the time it might take time to end.

"You saw everything, right?" Pista spoke to the soldiers who shrugged and lit up cigarettes. He used his unloaded finger to point. "Arrest this man," Pista said.

Sandor rolled his eyes. One of the soldiers smiled down at his shoes beside Erzsébet's legs, her rucked nylons slack like a loose second skin.

Dark red streaks left behind Margit tried to avoid as they dragged Erzsi outside.

The soldiers laid Erzsébet next to the hole for the press. They looked at the body, the wound in the ground, and the hole in her chest. "There's not enough room in the jeep," the taller soldier said.

The other one said, "Does she have relatives?"

"Up in smoke," Margit said.

Sandor shook and his glasses had slipped, he didn't straighten them. "Let's not be practical," Sandor said. A cool wind blew dry leaves and yesterday's snow from the boughs, high lovely clouds overhead. Margit looked at the house, the dirt track leading down the road to the train to the Angel Street park. Budapest and the tanks. She looked at Erzsébet. She thought Erzsi would fit in the hole *if we just bend her legs*, she could not stop the thought.

"At least put a sheet over her, for Christ's sake," Sandor said.

Margit went inside, pulled the sheet she had been fucking on, held it up to her face. The obvious irony was too obvious. She took off her coat and put on her blue and white dress, tugged it straight on her breasts and her hips. Combed her hair with both hands. Opened her yellow valise and looked at her needles and threads. Pinking shears. Her compact, its powder used up, but she had lipstick still. Objects the living could use, so she'd better use them. She put on lipstick, wiped it off, because what was she thinking about?

Because she herself wasn't dead. No tears yet.

The living stood awkwardly between the car and the jeep. Sandor tried taking the sheet but Margit clung to it. "You got to close her eyes," Margit said.

Sandor winced, he said, "All right, Margit."

She studied the body, she couldn't decide how to think around it.

"Should we say a prayer?" Pista asked.

Margit luffed the sheet as if she was making a bed. Now she could suddenly name what she'd seen in Pista's eyes as he fired and Erzsébet fell. Pity for himself. She tried not to judge but she judged. That's what defines how we love, a series of judgments, she thought.

"She wouldn't want that," Sandor said, his eyes wet.

"It hardly matters now," Margit said. She realized she hadn't touched Sandor since holding him back from following Erzsi to death. She wasn't sure she wanted to now, uncertain if she had a gesture to get or to give, a way to touch Sandor or be touched by him that would be appropriate. At least she was crying at last. But what was she crying about? For herself and a piece of geography, Erzsébet would have said.

"We could sing the 'Himnusz,'" Pista said.

"It has God in it, too," Sandor said.

Margit waited for Erzsi to say something smart from beyond. They waited for nothing without the distraction of rain, snow, or wind. Silence, the beautiful day, the first without terrible weather since Budapest fell. Crisp and clear, birds in the trees' brittle limbs.

"Now you go for the border or you'll be dead, too," Pista said to Margit. He pressed a passbook in her hand. "Don't worry, it's not counterfeit."

Sandor laughed, Margit almost did, too. Pista would have as well, Margit thought, if Sandor hadn't already stopped. She said, "Where's the papers for him?" She tucked her own document in her blouse, a familiar habit, she thought. "You could let him go, you could say he escaped," she said as if Sandor wasn't right there.

"I'm saving your life but I can't save your happiness, too," Pista said.

Was she supposed to be glad for the half she'd have left? "Won't, you mean," Margit said.

"He's allowed to save himself," Sandor said.

"Someone has to," Pista said, and Margit saw that it was Sandor who Pista loved best all along.

The tall soldier looked at his watch, at the sun.

What a dull story we make, Margit thought. The ideas we have of ourselves, everyone lives a grand life of the mind. Instead there's only this cartography of our landlocked desire. A body outside an inconsequent town. Necessity factored by time, while birds skimmed over earth emptied out from the hole in the ground.

The station is half a kilometer down the road. Margit rides between them. The soldiers follow in a jeep behind the Trabant, a tarp over the wreck of the press, the bedsheet over Erzsébet. Margit smokes, she keeps looking over at Sandor who keeps looking back. Thank God, after all, he's holding her arm.

Sandor, how will you live?
So you'll go, after all.

Who will you miss more?
Who will you, Margit?

No home and nobody home, and no one in the street.
Maybe there'll be a gap in a wall of the cell wide enough to see clouds passing under the sky.

Sandor, what have we done?
I wish I'd learned how to smoke, to remind me of you later on.

Next time, Sandor, let's pay more attention, all right?
There's no ahead coming up.

Who's to blame for all that?
We're all criminals in our hearts, Dostoevsky said that.

No more books.
Or a slice of Dobos torte in front of the opera house.

Scraping the paper cone with our teeth while there goes the city parade, black scarves and net sacks, the lit-up rooms of the trams.
We'll meet later on, over there.

Where, exactly? What day and precisely what time?
Lake Tisza in 1938. You told me about that.

But this is no picnic. Don't laugh.
The smell of our room and our bed.

And also Erzsébet.
I don't mind about that.

I don't mind you don't mind.
   If we don't forget everything will that help?

What we don't forget is what we will have learned.
   But it won't save us now.

. . .

Night and the station is mobbed by soldiers, police spies. Pista kisses Margit on the cheek. She kisses him despite herself on the mouth. "I can't forgive you," she says.

   "I can't forgive you, either," he replies.

   Sandor takes Margit's cigarette and he smokes and he winks. She wishes he hadn't done that, then they're all alone in the car, his face in her hair, hers in his. She can't look at him anymore, her hand on the door, her body aslant as she slides from the seat, bare knees turned toward the cold. There's always a moment, she'd said once. She wants to stay and to run. She wants his hands to drift to the back of her neck. To say, *we made promises*, but she doesn't dare say this now. She wants to cry for the ones that they broke and the ones that they kept. To cry and make everyone cry. A chance to touch the contour of his jaw, but she doesn't do this, or she might start believing in luck.

   The station clock says seven p.m. and she's out of the car, *don't look back*, but she looks. Sandor tries a smile, coughs and smokes. She sees Pista open the driver-side door for Sandor to get in, *please God, nobody wave*, Pista raising his hand but thinking the better of it. Just his hat as he climbs in the car, it could be any car in the long line of cars, police blowing whistles, the static announcement of trains as she walks toward the tracks.

. . .

Go Pista go Pista go, Sandor looking back, slamming the seat with his fist. The exhaust of their small blue car, one of many that blends with the rest of the cars and she's already gone.

Artillery, trucks choke the road.

"I never thought," Sandor says, but he doesn't say anything else. He's been thinking *jump*, he could run, but the jeep following would shoot him. If he escaped it would cost Pista's life. Sandor's hand on the door.

"They'll interrogate you again," Pista says.

They follow the radio signals repeating the government line. The word "free" has been liberated from the radio station names. Free Radio Csokonay, Free Radio Rákóczi, Free Radio Szombathely. Free Radio Pécs and Free Radio Győr, Kádár Free Government Radio and the Transdanubia Free Military Broadcast have signed off.

Sandor lowers his head to his chest, dirt on his trousers from digging the hole for the press. The pieces of it in the back of the car: evidence. This time he has no one to sell.

"Really, she killed herself," Pista says.

"Of course," Sandor says. "Though someone else held the gun."

The car has insignia on its side, the road swarmed with military, but they only salute Pista's car.

"There's fighting in Budapest, but it's almost finished," Pista says.

Sandor can't talk for a while. He's afraid for his wife. He's afraid about not missing Erzsébet yet. He tries hard not to make any pictures of anything. Not to feel his own skin, not to tell Pista what Erzsébet said when she died.

"Too bad about Stalin. If he hadn't croaked, none of this would have had to happen," Pista says.

"He was safer for us," Sandor says.

"They still might execute you," Pista says.

"You too," Sandor says.

"That's all right," Pista says.

"What will you tell them?" Sandor asks.

Pista taps his chest. "I put an end to the counterrevolution in Szentes," he says.

"Single-handed," Sandor says, catching the joke in it.

The drive is long, soon they'll have to stop to piss. The soldiers might drink, get drunk enough to shoot both of them. Who would know what really happened?

What really happened? The redhead took a shot in the gut, saved the blonde, is that it? That blonde was no blonde. In ten years he brought her ten barrettes. It took Erzsi that long to finish her long conversation with death. He hopes his wife won't wait for him on the opposite side.

The soldiers behind them are firing their rifles at anything that moves in the woods. Birds in trees. Clotheslines swayed by wind, white smoke from thatched roofs. Sandor closes his eyes, he's tired of looking at things.

It was finally dark as she walked with her yellow valise. She felt Sandor's hand on her neck but it was only the wind. She felt as if she'd been thrown from her very own door. She picked up a rust-colored leaf, the train platform running with them. She passed by a newspaper vendor's kiosk but the news couldn't matter to her where she went, the wind cold as cheap tin.

Nothing was nearly enough as she turned against it and counted her change and her bills. She unfolded the passbook from Pista, loose money tucked into the crease. She added it up in her head with Sandor's bills and spare change. She thought about throwing it all on the ground as some kind of sacrifice, punishment, but then she was no idiot.

Before her, cars coupled, that iron relief. *I've left him already*, she thought, their cold metal chill in her teeth. What woman would wish such a man? But she had.

The joke of those stupid barrettes.

Margit lights a fresh cigarette from the butt of her last, climbs her train's iron rungs.

Smoking's not allowed but everyone's puffing up storms, even the conductor gauzed in a private tiara of gray. He touches his cap. Now there is only her will and necessity's sudden demand. No one needs a ticket tonight.

She pulls down her window and leans out to look at where nothing begins. God save me from what I'm doing, she begs, but God must be off once again with his friend the east wind. Ahead is more snow and cold fields. I could leave you, she'd said to him once. She walks the length of the car for the hollow clang of her steps. She wants him to push through the door, jam it open with his fist, but all she has now is her hand on her face, and she must learn to like it. A newspaper blows down the aisle: Everything can break your heart.